Expatriates in Love

Stories of the Not-so-Innocent Americans Abroad

By Trina Mascott

Trina Mascott

PUBLISH AMERICA

PublishAmerica
Baltimore

First printing

At the specific preference of the author, PublishAmerica allowed this work to remain exactly as the author intended, verbatim, without editorial input.

This is a work of fiction set in a background of history. Public personages both living and dead may appear in the story under their right names. Scenes and dialogue involving them with fictitious characters are of course invented. Any other usage of real people's names is coincidental. Any resemblance of the imaginary characters to actual persons, living or dead, is entirely coincidental.

ISBN: 1-4241-3797-7
PUBLISHED BY PUBLISHAMERICA, LLLP
www.publishamerica.com
Baltimore

Printed in the United States of America

For my beloved Charlie,
who carries on the writing and traveling traditions

Newlyweds in Paris

Paulette swerved her taxi off the Peripherique and around the Place de la Porte Maillot whose bulky modern buildings she held in vast contempt. Her vexation lasted but two minutes and then she was on the broad Avenue de la Grand Armees with its genteel old mansions and—*viola!*—at the end of it stood the Arc, her favorite symbol of Paris. Even after twenty-five years of living in the French capitol, the sight of the Arc's solid, soaring grace took her breath away. Quickly, she glanced in the rear-view mirror at the American couple in the taxi's back seat: as Paulette had anticipated, the young woman gave an involuntary cry of joy.

"Kenny, look! *The Arc de Triomphe!*"

"Mmmmm," her companion responded, not raising his eyes, for he was busy kissing her neck.

Surreptitiously, Paulette had been observing the two young Americans all the way in from Charles de Gaulle Airport. That they were well educated she recognized from their vocabulary, since Paulette herself, thanks to her British grandmother, spoke excellent English. That her passengers were wealthy she surmised from their stack of Louis Vouton luggage and their chic travel clothes. That they were newlyweds Paulette knew from the way the girl—Laurel, the man called her—proudly kept regarding her gold and diamond wedding ring. That they were very much in love was evident from their ardent exchange of caresses. Even now, while this Laurel was staring raptly at the Arc de Triomphe, her Kenny was nibbling her ear and suggestively stroking her thigh.

5

In the twenty years that Paulette had been driving a taxi, she had developed the instincts of a detective when speculating about her passengers' lives. To each she gave a past and a present and, depending upon the size of the *pourboire,* she showered upon them silent blessings for the future. *Mais non!* She was being unfair to herself. A friendly smile could bring forth even more fervent benedictions than a large tip.

Every time Paulette brought passengers into the heart of the city from the airport or from one of the railway stations, she carefully watched their reactions to Paris. If they were excited and thrilled to be there, then she felt a cordial affection for them and drove to their hotels along the most scenic routes. But if they showed no admiration for *her* Paris, then she slammed down the quickest, least interesting streets and dumped the boors at their destinations like sacks of flour, no doubt sending them home with fresh stories about the rudeness of Parisian taxi drivers.

Sometimes, when she felt tired and her bones ached from sitting behind the steering wheel all day, she considered returning to Montpelier, in the South, where she had grown up. There she had her son and his wife, and two grand-daughters, and aunts and uncles and cousins and childhood friends whom she loved. But the thought of leaving Paris…no, it was impossible!

Paris.

What is the magic? she asked herself. Is it the buildings? The Belle Epoch, turn-of-the-century, massive, fanciful, ornate apartment houses proudly decked with intricate wrought-iron balconies? Or the rows of renovated 19th Century tall-windowed structures whose subdued facades hide delightful inner courtyards? Or the 17th and 18th Century mansions with grand sweeping wings and formal gardens and niches full of statues that have stood smiling down upon the passers-by for all these years? Or the hundreds of churches, each filled with hushed beauty, their stone steps worn to shiny hollows by generations of worshipers?

Or is it the multitude of trees? Of Parks? Or the winding, sparkling river? Or the squares, large and small, that one comes upon unexpectedly only to be overwhelmed with startled delight? Is it the most famous monuments soaring high into the air and crying, *Regardez-moi!* The Arc! Sacre Coeur! The Eiffel Tower! Notre Dame! Hey, look at me! they commanded.

Is it the ubiquitous sidewalk cafés in front of every bar and bistro and restaurant, some with seas of tables and chairs and colorful awnings and umbrellas and others with only one or two outdoor seats? Let it snow or rain or let a frigid wind blow and the squares and sidewalks become bare and bleak, but then let the sun shine for ten minutes and the entire city is magically blanketed with the chairs and tables and umbrellas that seem to have been waiting, in every café, bistro, bar and restaurant, just inside the door or in some hidden closet to spring out and suddenly be populated by hordes of people drinking espresso and eating *croque monieurs* and savoring elaborate ice cream concoctions, each with a Matterhorn of whipped cream.

Is it the sense of history that permeates the city like invisible soot? The legacy of art from the First Francois? The grandiose visions of Napoleon? The blood-and-hate and courage-and-love that created the Republic? The dreams and aspirations of painters and sculptors and writers from all over the world who think of Paris as their artistic Mecca and whose collective creativity infuses the very air we breathe?

Is it our flair for jaunty fashions and the skill of our hairdressers, even in tiny neighborhood salons, who turn plain women into beauties? Or is it the dapper men who flash warm-eyed glances at the passing women, glances that signal admiration and desire all in one brief moment of eye contact, giving both the man and the woman a surge of happiness to be alive?

Is it the food, so handsomely displayed in shops and at outdoor markets, each piece of fruit and vegetable grown and sold with passionate care and pride? Is it the astounding variety of cheeses, of pastries, of meats, of fowl and fish? And *mon dieu* the seafood!

What, what, what *is* it? Paulette asked herself, wild to know. It was all these things and more. It was discovering a street she never had seen before, or a fountain, or the lights at night glistening Utrillo-like on wet pavement. It was turning a corner and seeing a well-loved building caught in a burst of pink at sunset. It was *being* there, the daily thrill of simply being there. She could never leave. Never.

She slid her taxi into the madness of the Etoile where the Arc de Triomphe loomed above the seething traffic like a rock in a maelstrom. She maneuvered with utter ease through the jockeying vehicles for she could tell, just from the rev of the motors, exactly which driver she could cut in on and which would stubbornly refuse to give way.

Years ago, when she first began to drive a taxi, she'd had recurrent nightmares, dreaming that she was trapped on the inside lane of the Etoile, closest to the Arc. Round and round she went with rising panic, night after night, unable to break out. For months she had dreaded the round-about, detouring far out of her way to avoid it, until her developing skill had given her the confidence to pit herself and her vehicle against her bolder countrymen. And once she successfully negotiated the much-feared arena, her upsetting dreams had stopped. Now she went out of her way to swoop intrepidly through the Etoile's challenge.

Still, she had to admit that French drivers—herself included—displayed their worst traits in such circumstances: competitive, rank selfishness and an arrogance that evaporated, she hoped, the moment they stepped out of their vehicles. The men who, while driving, gunned their motors to cut her off were the very ones who hurried ahead to open the doors for her at restaurants.

She glanced in the mirror at the Americans in the back seat. Like most foreigners being driven around the Etoile for the first time, they looked as though they were plunging down a terrifying roller-coaster. The young man stopped fondling his bride and tightly gripped the seat. The girl grabbed her new husband's arm and stared with disbelief at the cars swerving around them.

"It is quite safe, *M'dame...M'sieur*" Paulette called out reassuringly as she guided the taxi out of the Etoile and joined the slow-moving traffic down the Champs Elysees.

Whenever she drove down this famous broad boulevard, Paulette liked to fancy that she was guest of honor in a parade. She imagined throwing kisses at the crowds on either side of the avenue while her eyes proudly swept the pretentious buildings lining the corridor as though she personally owned every one of them. It was a thoroughfare to saunter through, to observe the faces from all over the world, to window shop the overpriced garments and baubles, to sit at an outdoor café over a leisurely cappuccino, or better yet, to enjoy a quick hamburger or pizza. In all the rest of the city, Paulette was fiercely devoted to her country's cuisine, but here on the Champs she loved to indulge herself with American junk food. *Viva la Burger King!* she silently saluted the red sign.

She took personal pride in the chestnut trees lining both sides of the Champs. Now, in May, they were dense with crisp new leaves and long, sensuous pendants of white blossoms. *Oh, but you should see them at Christmas,* she wanted to tell the two young people behind her, *when they are strung with tiny white fairy lights that thrill you every time you see them.* But she refrained from speaking because Kenny was back to his eager carnal gropings while Laurel stared rapturously out of the taxi windows.

"It's the Champs Elysees, isn't it?" Laurel leaned forward to ask.

"Yes."

"I've dreamed of coming here," Laurel confided, "ever since I was little."

"Why is that?"

"Oh, I guess because my folks spent their honeymoon here, too. So did my older brother. It's becoming a family tradition."

Paulette nodded.

"I majored in French in college," Laurel went on, "and got my Master's degree in French history. I'm going to teach French at a junior college in Fall."

"Wonderful! Your knowledge of our history will make your visit so much more interesting." Paulette stopped for a red light. "And you, M'seiur, do you also speak French?"

"Heck no." Kenny shook his head. "That's Laurel's department. I'm a dentist."

"Where in the States do you live?"

"Spokane," Kenny answered. "That's out west, in the state of Washington." He beamed proudly. "It's the best darned city in the world."

"And you, *M'dame,*" Paulette addressed Laurel. "Do you agree?"

Laurel laughed. "I have to admit, I think Paris might have us beat."

Kenny grabbed her in a mock strangle-hold. "Ingrate!" he laughed, kissing her temple.

Paulette turned her attention to negotiating the Rond Pointe. She pointed out to her passengers the two great art museums, the Grand Palais and the Petite Palais, and the enormous car-clogged Place de Concorde. And all the while, she observed Laurel, admiring the girl with proprietary affection.

I know exactly how she feels, Paulette thought. Twenty-five years ago, when I first saw Paris, I also came here as a bride. I too stared with rapture at the city as the taxi took Alain and me from the Gare de Lyon to our hotel. Alain, like this Kenny, had been unable to keep his hands off of me. I was so young, only eighteen, younger than this Laurel who looks to be in her mid-twenties. Unlike Laurel, I had little education, but I loved to read, to the dismay of my parents, who considered it a waste of time, and to the annoyance of Alain, who thought that every minute of my time was his property. But that was the least of his faults.

There were, of course, many differences between herself and Laurel. She, Paulette, was petite while Laurel was tall with a strong, athletic-looking body. And Paulette suspected that Laurel had grown up in a prosperous household while Paulette had been raised, well, not exactly in poverty, but her merchant father had been obsessed with parsimony.

It pained Paulette to see that Laurel looked at Kenny with the same boundless, unqualified love that she herself had squandered on Alain. *Prenez-garde!* she longed to call out to the young woman. *It is dangerous to love so thoughtlessly, so recklessly.*

Paulette turned her taxi abruptly into a narrow street off the Rue de Rivoli and stopped at the entrance to her passengers' hotel. She thoroughly approved of their choice. The Hotel Louise, a renovated

19th Century Mansion, was small and elegant. Paulette knew it well for she sometimes recommended it to wealthy passengers who were disenchanted with the impersonal larger hotels. Here, each unit was an imaginatively furnished mini-suite.

Paulette got out of the taxi and, standing beside Laurel while Ken went into the hotel to find a porter, she looked into the younger woman's face. Seen this way, close up and not through the distortion of a rear-view mirror, Laurel was even more appealing than Paulette had realized. Health and high excitement gave the girl's skin a radiant glow. Her eyes were a warm honey-brown, full of humor and playfulness. But there was something in her smile, in her exuberant, open manner, that worried Paulette. Laurel was too trusting, too vulnerable, just as Paulette herself once had been. But would you have her be cynical and bitter at twenty-five? Paulette asked herself.

Her musings were interrupted when Ken came out of the hotel with a porter and the two men wrestled the luggage out of the taxi's trunk. Watching Ken, Paulette felt a twinge of anxiety for Laurel. Yes, Laurel was pretty, but this Ken was outrageously handsome. Of course Laurel must be flattered that such a gorgeous man was crazy about her. Paulette too had been infatuated with Alain's looks, forgetting to search beyond his appearance for the kindness that makes a man capable of love and deep affection.

"How long are you staying in Paris?" Paulette asked.

"A month," Laurel replied. "I want to see..."

"But we might not stay here the whole time," Ken interrupted, addressing Paulette while gazing sternly at Laurel. "I'm hoping we can do Paris in a week and go to Bermuda for the rest of the month."

Laurel gasped. "But Ken! *You promised!* A month in Paris now, and we'll go to Bermuda for our first anniversary!"

He shook his head. "I don't like it here."

"But you've hardly seen it!"

"I've seen enough. It's just a big old dirty city."

Laurel turned pale with dismay. "You're tired, Kenny," she coaxed. "You'll love it when we start going places..."

"Going where, Laurel? Churches and art museums? Crummy old palaces? No thanks!"

"All right." Her lips trembled. "I'll go see them by myself."

"And what the hell will I do while you're off traipsing around?" He gestured up at the hotel's facade. "Sit in our hotel room and watch TV? What kind of a honeymoon is that?"

"Kenny, please!" Laurel glanced with embarrassment at Paulette and the porter. "Let's talk about it later." Quickly, with troubled eyes, she turned to Paulette. "Thanks for a lovely ride. I enjoyed it."

"It was my pleasure." Paulette took a card from her pocket. "If you want a tour of Paris, or a trip to Fontainbleu or Versailles, or Giverny, or the Loire Valley...anywhere...call me. Here is my phone number and also my rates."

Laurel nodded and put the card in her suit pocket.

Ken took out his wallet and stared through the taxi window. He whistled when he saw the figure on the meter. "Tell me, lady, does that include service?"

Paulette shrugged. "M'sieur, is there a taxi driver anywhere in the world who does not expect a tip?"

Ken looked at Laurel. "Ten percent?" he whispered.

"Twenty," she whispered back.

"Ten!" He counted out the strange money, shoved it at Paulette without looking at her, then followed the porter into the hotel.

Laurel took a deep breath and smiled tremulously at Paulette. "Oh God, I can't believe I'm really here!" She patted the pocket where she had put Paulette's card. "I'll call you just as soon as we're settled. I want to see *everything*. By the way, my name is Laurel Morgan."

Paulette nodded. Words rushed into her mind but she held them back—words of warning, of benediction, of hard-won profundity. She so wanted to protect this lovely young woman from disappointment.

"Laurel," Paulette repeated, pronouncing it Laur-*elle* with a gargled rolling of the R. "Such a pretty name."

"Thank you," Laurel murmured. She hesitated, sensing that something crucial was being left unsaid. For a moment, the two women stared with misgivings into each other's eyes, then Laurel turned and followed her husband into the hotel.

An International Voyeur in Sicily

Jane never picked up hitch-hikers. Never. Not in the States and certainly not abroad. But it was raining and nearly ten miles to the next town and since she was driving slowly on the two-lane road and the man was staring intently at her, their eyes met. Abruptly, she stopped. It was purely a reflex action, because she had, just seconds before, decided *not* to stop. Even then she hesitated before pushing the button that unlocked the car doors.

"I was afraid you wouldn't stop," he said as he threw his faded green duffel bag into the back seat and got into the passenger seat. He slammed shut his door, brushed off the raindrops on his fraying khaki shirt and shorts, then smiled over at her. "Nice car." He pat her Jaguar's polished maroon dashboard as one would a "nice doggie's" head.

"I almost didn't stop," she admitted, starting up again. She felt overdressed in her smart blue Vasari pants and blazer, compared to his ragged outfit. It was a distressing reaction leftover from her childhood, when her mother bought Jane's clothes at Saks while all of Jane's friends wore clothes from Wal-Mart. "Where're you headed?" she asked.

He made a vague gesture. "How far are you going?"

"We're staying in Agrigento."

"I love that place." He put out his hand, then pulled it back. "I'm Dave. But my hand's too dirty to shake right now."

"I'm Jane."

"So who's the other part of your 'we?'"

"My what?"

"You said, *'We're* staying in Agrigento.'"

"Oh. Brian. My husband. He's got the flu."

"Tough."

"I had to drive *all* the way back to Marsala this morning. In the rain. Just because Brian was stupid enough to leave his briefcase at our last hotel."

The rain came down in a sudden torrent. She sped up the wipers but she still could barely see the road.

"There's an abandoned gas station up the road," he said, "You could pull under the canopy 'til it lets up."

She nodded. "D'you live around here?"

"No." He offered no other information.

"Then, where *do* you live?" she persisted.

"I don't live anywhere. I'm homeless."

"But...you're American, aren't you?"

"Yeah. From San Diego, which I dearly love."

"If you love it, why'd you leave it?" She glanced over at him.

"I have a terrible disease. It's called wanderlust." He gave a low laugh. "Sometimes, when I'm sleeping under some godforsaken bush and it's raining like this, and cold as hell, I wonder what I'm doing here when I've got a comfortable house overlooking the Pacific. At least my parents do."

"So...is it worth it? Living like this?"

"You bet!" He peered out the windshield. "Here it is."

As she drove under the sagging roof, the sudden silence made her ears hum. She turned off the motor.

He undid his seat belt and turned to face her. "Your turn," he said. "So you and your Brian are touring Sicily?"

"We're researching a film."

"Where do you live in the States?"

"Los Angeles. But now we live in Montreux. That's in Switzerland."

"I know, dear lady. Been there, done that. It's beautiful. " She undid her seat belt and pushed the button that moved her seat back from the steering wheel, then she turned to face him. Her first impression had been that he was tall and husky. She had assumed he would be college age, bumming around Europe. But now she could see that he was older, mid or even late thirties. He was clean shaven and wore his dark-blond hair in a pony tail. She liked the direct gaze of his brown eyes and the way a smile hovered on his lips.

She could tell from the way he looked at her that he found her exceedingly attractive. Men usually did, judging her by her curly dark hair, pert nose, green eyes and slightly pouty lips. It meant zilch to her that men did this. They knew nothing about her. But then she noticed that he was staring into her eyes, as though trying to probe beyond his first impression of her, with an intensity she found unsettling.

"How long've you been a nomad?" she asked to diffuse the tension of the moment.

He thought a moment. "Well, let's see. I graduated from Stanford when I was twenty-two. First I did all the States, then Canada, then Mexico and part of South America, and I've been criss-crossing Europe for five years. So altogether…twelve years."

She shook her head in amazement. "D'you plan to do this all your life?"

"Why not?"

She felt a sharp stab of jealousy. She remembered feeling the same envy in college when she'd read Henry Miller's "Colossus of Rhodes." Oh, the freedom to wander all alone through Greece, as Miller had, carousing and drinking and dancing half the night.. A young man could do that, but even now, even with women doing almost everything that men did, it still seemed impossible for a young woman to do it. She felt sad that here she was, forty-two, with a son a freshman at Columbia, and there were so many choices in life she never again would have the chance to make.

But she couldn't really complain. She and Brian lived exciting lives. They had a pleasant apartment on Lake Leman with a view across the water of the snow-covered Three Sisters Mountains. They had their own successful film company in Lausanne, making television specials all over Europe for American cable and PBS. On this trip they were scouting locations in Sicily and Greece for a one-hour PBS special exploring the spiritual beliefs behind the magnificent temples built by the Greeks and Romans. She researched and wrote their films while Brian drew up the budgets, hired crews and planned their shooting schedules. She had a marvelous life. Why on earth would she yearn for the uncomfortable existence of a wretched vagabond? It was preposterous.

And yet, was her life really that wonderful? The film business was full of anxieties and daily disasters. Everything that could go wrong, did. Crew members got sick or just didn't show up. Camera equipment broke down in the middle of a shoot, miles from help. Budgets were miscalculated. Rain came when they needed sun. Hotels misplaced their reservations. Shipping companies lost their exposed film. Labs ruined their film. Sometimes sponsors hated their footage and wanted everything re-done.

And then there was the subtle but growing discord between her and Brian, a loss of the intimacy that once had made their marriage so satisfying. Sometimes she felt as though they were on a see-saw: when she was up, he was down, and then when she slammed down, he flew up. They couldn't seem to find the magic balance they once had shared, in the days when they both were on a perfectly even, and loving, keel.

"You have a very expressive face," Dave said with a smile.

"I do?" She felt she had given him a glimpse of herself that she hadn't meant for him to see.

"You looked radiant for a moment, and then...sort of...regretful?"

She was impressed by his perception. "Listen, I hope you don't think I'm prying," she told him, eager to change the subject, "but I guess it's my maternal instinct. What do you do about eating? Do you have any money?"

He threw his head back and laughed with an abandon she admired. "Oh you women! You all sound like my mother." He shook his head reprovingly at her. "I always have what you'd call 'walk around' money. I might hitch rides, but I never have to mooch meals. I do a lot of bartering. I speak French and Italian fluently—thanks to a French mother and an Italian father—so I do some translating. I'm good at fixing things. Sometimes hotels let me shower for a buck or two. And I like sleeping under the stars."

"And when it's cloudy? And raining?"

"Y'know," he confided, "getting wet is highly underrated." He leaned over suddenly and kissed her lips, lingering only briefly, like a bee tasting a flower, then he pulled back. "Don't worry," he said, "I'm just impulsive. I'm not going to rape you."

"I wasn't worried," she said. She had been surprised by his kiss, and even more astonished that she hadn't been in the least offended by it. "Look!" she said. "The sun's out!" They had been so involved in their conversation that neither noticed when the rain stopped and the sky cleared.

The rest of the way to Agrigento he told her about his travels in Sicily and his admiration for the people. "They pay as much attention to tourists as they do to the flocks of birds that alight and fly off. It's when you stay a while, like, when they get to know you—then they start seeing you as a fellow human being. I've been hanging around this part of the island for four months—I go back and forth, sort of like a metronome. That's what's so great about the way I travel. If I find some place I like, I can stay as long as I want."

"From what I've seen of the island, so far," she ventured, "it's a marvelous balance between the natural beauty and the human contributions, you know, the ancient temples and Medieval castles and Renaissance churches. Even their stone farmhouses and terraced fields are beautiful in their simplicity."

He nodded his agreement. "Well put."

"Where should I drop you?" she asked when they entered the outskirts of Agrigento.

"Where're you staying?" he asked.

"The Villa Adriane."

"Good choice. Is your husband still sick?"

"Very. He wakes up long enough to ring Room Service for tea and toast, and then he goes back to sleep. He's impossible to be with when he's sick."

"Then how about having dinner with me?"

"Can you afford it? I mean, can I at least pay my own way?"

"Lady, when a gentleman asks you to dinner, you let him pay, even if he *is* a bum." He looked at his watch—Jane noticed it was a Rolex and she had the feeling that he was accustomed to quality but, at the same time he could take it or leave it. "It's four-thirty now," he said, "how's seven? I've got something spectacular to show you at nine."

"What?"

"It's a surprise." He gestured at her clothes with mild disapproval. "Wear something casual…something you can walk in."

"Sounds good. I love surprises." She pulled into the Villa Adriane's parking lot and stopped. "Where should I meet you?" she asked.

"Right here. At seven. And in your honor, Madame, I'm going to take a shower! The Adriane's manager is a friend of mine." He reached into the back seat for his duffel, then said, "Thanks for the ride," touched her lightly on her shoulder, gave her another brief kiss, and disappeared around the corner of the building.

She found Brian deeply asleep. She looked down with resentment at his familiar face, which was frowning with the discomfort of respiratory congestion. His body was slight compared to Dave's huskiness, but she knew from long experience that Brian's powerful determination gave him the stature of a giant. "What Brian wants, Brian always gets," she often half-teased, half complained when he won an argument with her. She had grown accustomed to his domination, his awesome persuasiveness. In time she even had learned to welcome it, since it relieved her of the need to make difficult decisions. Only now and then, when her desire to have some control over her life flared up, did she challenge the authority that Brian had come to assume was entirely his.

Her forthcoming rendezvous for dinner with Dave gave her a jolt of pleasure. For the first time in years, she was doing something without Brian, something totally unrelated to him. She looked at her watch. She had nearly three hours to savor her delicious secret.

She sat on the terrace outside her room and read Durrell's "Sicilian Carousel" for a while, then she showered and put on designer jeans and a blue T-shirt—the most casual clothing she owned—and walking shoes. She wrote a note in large print with a felt pen—"HAVING DINNER WITH SOME PEOPLE I MET"—and left it leaning on the phone next to Brian's bed. She put on a black windbreaker, shoved her keys into a pocket and was out at her car by seven.

Dave was waiting, wearing jeans, a clean green T-shirt with the Universite de Paris logo across the front, and a light-weight gray jacket. He was freshly shaven, his hair still damp from his shower. He was leaning against the passenger side door, carrying his duffel bag, which he again threw into the back seat. "Now you can shake my hand," he said. "It's clean." He reached out and took her outstretched hand in both of his. They stared at each other for a long moment before getting into the car.

She realized that she never had known anyone who looked so utterly serene and at the same time so exhilarated. Again she felt a jab of the same envy that nearly had seared her soul that afternoon. "Which way?" she asked.

He pointed left. "It's down by the ocean...east of town."

She sighed deeply. "I should have done what you're doing!" she burst out impulsively. "Oh, I don't mean the hitch-hiking and sleeping under the stars necessarily. But I desperately wanted to spend a year just roaming around Europe after I graduated. All during college I worked weekends and summers, waitressing at a coffee shop to save money for it. Sure, now I've been all over the continent for our work, but it's not the same as being young and having all that freedom and absorbing different cultures and meeting all kinds of people you'd never meet at home."

"So why didn't you?"

"Well, I was engaged to Brian and he wanted to get married as soon as we graduated. I felt that both of us should do the Europe thing together, even for just a few months, but he's terribly ambitious. All he wanted to do was start working. We argued about it all during our last year at Columbia, but he finally wore me down."

"How'd he do that?"

"Oh, he's one of those damn pushy Taurus's! So we got married and instead of using the money I'd saved for traveling, we used it to start a small film company." She hesitated. "Oh God, I really shouldn't complain. We have a wonderful life." She threw Dave a resentful look. "But meeting you…it stirred up a lot of old business. A lot of resentment and regret."

"And a lot of suppressed anger, at Brian?" he said carefully.

She nodded. "That too."

"On the other hand," Dave said, "sometimes when I see a happily married couple with a kid or two, I feel all kinds of shoulda's and coulda's. But one thing you have to realize when you're young…you can't do everything. So you make choices. Very, very carefully. It's dangerous to live with too many regrets."

She thought about his words. "I suppose most of us make decisions with our heads, more than our hearts."

"Even if you make them with your head *and* your heart," he said softly, "you entirely forget about the needs of your soul."

Pretentious! clanged loudly through her mind.

"Stop here," he said.

She parked in front of a small café whose rock foundation was under siege by the high tide. Inside were the ubiquitous red and white checked tablecloths and hanging empty Chianti bottles. The owner hugged Dave and shook hands with Jane. He seated them at a rear window table where the waves marched toward them and broke noisily beneath them, each time causing the building to shudder. They grew accustomed to the surf's rhythm.

"The needs of the soul," she repeated.

Dave looked over at her in surprise. "You really paid attention to what I said!"

"Of course I did. Don't you, when you talk to people?"

"Sure, most of the time." He smiled. "It's just that I don't consider myself a very profound person."

"But you are! Everything you say makes me stop and take my spiritual temperature. This life you lead...isn't it a spiritual quest?"

"I never looked at it that way." He shrugged. "Maybe. I just think of myself as being overly inquisitive about the world. Like some kind of compulsive international voyeur."

The waiter came for their order.

"You like seafood?" Dave asked Jane.

She nodded.

He ordered a platter of grilled shrimp, clams, mussels, eggplant and red peppers, followed by fettucine with Sicilian sausage, and a carafe of Mt. Etna red wine.

The waiter brought the wine, a basket of bread and a small jug of garlic olive oil.

Dave took Jane's right hand and turned it over. He traced her life line with his index finger. "Not bad. Mine's shorter."

"You really believe all that?"

"Not for a minute."

She took back her hand. "So what do you want to be...if you ever grow up?" she asked him.

"Can't you see me in fifty years, with a long white pony tail, hitch-hiking through the Himalayas?"

"If that's what you want."

"The mistake most people make is deciding what they want early in life and then never changing. Or, some people never really decide what they want and just keep accepting what life throws at them. So how do I know today what I'll want in fifty years? How do I even know what I'll want tomorrow? The beautiful part of being an American is that most of us have the luxury of changing our minds."

"But aren't you trapped?" She stared at him with concern. "I mean, if you gave up being a vagabond...how would you get back to the States? You can't hitch-hike on a plane."

"My father's VISA card is my insurance. If I get sick, or suddenly decide I want to go home, all I have to do is buy a ticket to San Diego.

But I have a pact with myself. No matter how broke I get, I *never* will use his card for anything but fare home."

"What about girls?" Jane asked.

"What about them?"

"Don't you miss having romantic relationships?"

"What makes you think I don't?" He smiled.

"Do they travel with you? Or, do you stop roaming around and stay with them for a while?"

"Whatever," he said vaguely. "Anyway, for all you know, I might be gay."

She shook her head. "I don't think so."

The food arrived and they both dug in with gusto.

"I like that in a woman," he said when she speared a forkful of grilled mussels.

"What?"

"Having a hearty appetite. Show me a woman who picks at her food, and I'll show you a prude in bed."

She nodded. "Show me a man who's full of preconceived notions about women and I'll show you a man who isn't afraid to make an ass of himself."

He threw back his head and gave the joyous, deeply-felt laugh she had admired in the car that afternoon. "Jane, Jane, I wish I'd met you in high school. Maybe I wouldn't be a crazy bum now."

"Honey-child, when you were in high school, I was a married woman with a baby."

He looked at her carefully. "I don't believe it."

"Believe it."

"It doesn't matter," he said seriously, still staring at her. "Some people are special, no matter what their age."

"If that's a compliment, then thank you." She lifted her wine glass and clicked his glass. "We forgot to make a toast. So, here's to picking up hitch-hikers. I never did it before, and I'll probably never do it again, but I'm glad I did it today."

At eight-thirty they finished the last crumbs of their cannoli and got back into her Jaguar. The sky now was dark, not black but a luscious deep purple, a velvety setting for its thick splattering of stars. "Where to now?" she said. "What's the big surprise?"

"If I told you, it wouldn't be a surprise." He gestured back toward town. "Take a left." She drove and was surprised when he told her to park again at the Villa Adriane. But instead of going into the hotel, he led her along a path through the open fields beyond the building. He held her hand to keep her from stumbling on the rocky terrain while in his other hand he held a flashlight he'd taken from his duffel.

Jane kept looking up at the stars. She could hear the distant surf and realized it had been an undercurrent of sound all evening.

"Watch where you're going," he said when she started to fall and he caught her. "You can look at the stars later."

"Yes, Daddy," she said.

"You do have a childlike quality," he said.

"I? Childlike?" She was genuinely shocked. She considered herself to be utterly sophisticated.

"Not in an irresponsible sense, like I am. It's more..." He searched for the right words. "It's your enthusiasm. I like being with enthusiastic people. Maybe that's why I'm so crazy about the Sicilians. They aren't afraid to show their feelings, once they know you." He stopped walking. "Let's sit here." He pointed his flashlight at a slab of concrete.

He shifted his light onto his watch. "Okay. It's ten of nine. Just relax." When he turned off the light, they sat in utter darkness.

He took her hand again and she liked the feel of his warm palm. She did feel quite ageless in his company, as if they were two truant children off on a forbidden lark. She felt no qualms about being with him in this dark, deserted field. She didn't feel like a wife or a mother or anything but her most basic self, without ties or responsibilities or labels. If she and Dave levitated and floated off into space, she wouldn't have been all that surprised.

She kept inhaling deeply, trying to identify the sharp but pleasant scent that surrounded them until she recognized it as wild sage. From her research she knew that in early spring the area was blanketed with white blossoms from the almond trees, a spectacle she would have enjoyed seeing, but now it was too late, the flowers were gone. God, she was so greedy, she told herself with a touch of asperity. She longed to experience every beautiful sight and taste every delicious food and smell every heady scent. If Dave lived to a hundred he probably would have time to do all that, whereas all she would have, if *she* lived that long, would be a huge list of unfulfilled longings.

Suddenly, Dave squeezed her hand and, in the blink of an eye, what had been darkness was transformed into an astonishing cluster of lighted Greek temples. She never had witnessed anything so magical. Her grip on Dave's hand tightened and a long involuntary gasp came from the depths of her body. He put an arm around her and gave a low, joyful laugh at her reaction to his surprise. They sat quietly for a long time, staring in wonder at the glowing columns against the purple sky.

"My God," she said softly, "what genius thought of lighting them? Painting with light!"

"I don't know," Dave said. "It's always a thrill, even after I've watched it a dozen times."

She felt a profound gratitude toward this man whom fate had thrown into her path and who had made the last few hours so fascinating for her. He had caused her to question her choices in life, which had led her to a new understanding of the ones she had made, even if he had stirred up a pile of doubts, too. And then he had topped it all off with this spectacle.

"Even the brightest moonlight doesn't make the temples glow like this." he said.

"I've been doing a lot of research, for our film," she said. "The Greeks and Romans used to paint the temples and statues with garish colors. I don't think I'd like it."

"Well, it's because we're so used to them being all white. Or gray. But did you ever wonder why pagan temples and Christian churches are so lofty? Soaring toward heaven, I guess you'd say?"

She laughed. "You know, American banks sometimes are like that too. Are they our modern temples?"

"Ever notice that the Greeks and Romans often built their temples on the outskirts of their cities instead of in the center, where you'd expect them to be?"

"You read Durrell!" she gasped.

"Right. I love his theory that the Greeks viewed their temples with fear, like they were filled with a magic that was very intimidating."

"Do you realize," she said softly, "that we've been talking nonstop? All the time we've been together? I never met anyone I enjoyed talking to so much."

He put both arms around her and leaned his head against hers.

When he kissed her, deeply, both of them sinking against each other with total abandon, it seemed entirely appropriate, a part of this adventure they were sharing. He unzipped her windbreaker and removed it, then her t-shirt, and he helped her slither out of her jeans while she unbuttoned his jacket and he slipped off his pants, and that seemed entirely appropriate too. He put his jacket on the ground and she lay down on it. They moved slowly and gracefully, as though their actions were prompted by an ancient choreographer. The air was cool, but exhilarating, all part of this night's spell.

He was on top of her, warming her, exciting her, and they kissed for what seemed hours, letting their tongues play amorous tag. Their hands languidly explored each other's bodies, eliciting sweet little snorts of satisfaction.

He finally let go of her lips and they both took in deep breaths with little chuckles of happiness. "Have you ever made love under the stars?" he asked.

"Never."

"Always on clean sheets on clean beds?" He laughed indulgently.

"Always."

"Do you like it here? On the ground?"

Her upper back and head were on the jacket he had spread, but from the waist down she was lying on wild grass. She liked the way it titillated her skin and the abandon she felt at being so close to the earth.

"I may never do it indoors again," she said.

He brought his mouth against hers once more and she felt him

25

expand even harder against her and her heart and pulses began to pound.

She felt more than erotic excitement. She sensed that being with this beautiful man had released some deep need in her, breaking her inhibiting habit of always making the prudent choices. She trembled with the desire to be swept into his sphere. And when he reached for his pants on the rock and took out a condom, she impatiently tore her lips from his and whispered, "Hurry!"

He slid into her and she welcomed him with deliriously involuntary tremors. By lying perfectly still and letting him move inside of her, she prolonged the insistent grinding rapture that was engulfing her but she couldn't delay it any longer and every part of her imploded at once, and a few thrusts later he, too, erupted, and it fiercely delighted her, as though he were blasting his gift of freedom into her.

They lay there for a long time, letting their pulses slowly return to normal. Now and then he placed soft little kisses on her cheeks, her chin, grazing her lips. Everything felt preordained to her, all of a piece—the illuminated temples, the purple sky, the swarming stars, the warm body of the man who had given her this magical evening.

She wanted to stay there forever. She felt as though she were made of air, ready to float away, anchored to the ground only by his strong, lovely body. After a while, he began to kiss her again, to excite her again, and this time it was different, their bodies more sure of themselves as they joyously paced their mounting pleasure until it deepened and swelled and leaped and mushroomed and flooded them with a silent roar. They lay there contentedly, fused to each other.

"Jane, Jane, Jane," he murmured after a while, "come with me."

"Oh, I wish!" she lamented.

"Why not? You've made me realize what I'm missing."

"What?"

"Love."

She was quiet, visualizing the unfettered freedom of his nomadic existence. It was true: such a life had no room for love.

"I was satisfied having brief flings with willing partners," he admitted. "But it was nothing like this."

It's never been like this for me, either, she wanted to tell him. But...

"Jane, I'll travel any way you want. In cars, staying in hotels...but if you don't come with me...damn it, Jane, I'll never feel...never be...completely *carefree* again."

She knew she couldn't go with him, beguiling though he was. How could she possibly leave Brian? The two of them had created a son together! To her it was a bond stronger than any other in life. To cause a completely separate human soul to come into existence was a person's only chance to be as creative as the gods. No, not even for Dave could she leave Brian. Besides, she was too old for Dave's kind of life. She was addicted to soft beds, gourmet food, marble bathrooms, luxury cars, first class seats on airplanes. She no longer could stay in cheap hotels or drive beat-up cars or sit squashed together flying in coach.

"Part of me will always be with you," she whispered.

"That's not enough, Jane!"

She knew it was a pitifully lame sop and she sighed, at a loss for words.

"Come with me," he whispered again, begging, almost crying.

She was aware that in gaining from him a realization of her own spirit's need for freedom, she had robbed him of his spontaneous *joi de vivre.* Sure, in time he would be happy-go-lucky again, roaming the world by himself, but without the exuberant freedom he had relished before he met her.

She caressed his face, her fingers aching with regret. "I wish I could," she finally said. "Oh, Dave, how I wish I could!" She began to cry.

He held her tightly until the tears stopped. "I know," he soothed. "I know."

Much, much later, he brought her back to the Villa Adriane and they stood beside her car while he retrieved his duffel bag. "I'll be gone in the morning," he told her.

She put her hands on his shoulders and stared up at him, memorizing his face. "Where to?"

"Off to Malta," he said. "There's an art to knowing exactly the right time to say goodbye."

She nodded, overwhelmed by a hopeless panic of loss.

He grabbed her close to him and they kissed, their already grieving bodies frantically protesting against having to part. He took her right hand and held it to his lips for several seconds. When he dropped her hand he again stared into her eyes, then he jerked himself away from her, picked up his duffel bag, and disappeared around the corner of the hotel.

She never saw him again.

But the evening had a profound effect upon her. She never again let herself get upset over the trivial mishaps that plague one's life, or the multitude of disasters that afflict the film business. More and more she drifted away from working with Brian. She hired a new writer to assist him. When Brian objected, she told him she needed more time to pursue her own goals. Making movies had been his idea, not hers. Their relationship became more harmonious and less edgy when they finally stopped working together.

She seemed to float through her days, as though she'd had a permanent injection of tranquillity. She was optimistic and cheerful and yet she felt a little removed from reality. Some small part of her always appeared to be somewhere else. Others found it quite charming, if somewhat disconcerting.

And what about Dave? she wondered. If their hours together had caused such a remarkable change in her, wasn't it likely that they'd had a profound effect upon him too? She felt as though they each had a piece of the other permanently embedded somewhere in their souls, like computer chips, so that every day, as long as they lived, they would long for each other with a bittersweet pang. She was sure that wherever he wandered, he was thinking of her, that knowing her had made him more aware of his own choices and how he spent each day. She hoped that in fifty years he *would* have a white pony tail and be shuffling along a path in the Himalayas…*if that was what he wanted.*

And how she would love to be there so that he could hitch another ride with her!

"Dave," she often murmured to herself. His very ordinary name was, to her, an extraordinary mantra. The brief word set in motion her whole wondrous reverie of memories.

Brian recovered from his flu two days after Jane's night with Dave. The next evening, shortly before nine o'clock, Jane took Brian down the path to sit on the concrete slab where she and Dave had sat. When the lights abruptly illuminated the temples at nine o'clock, she carefully watched Brian's reaction. He blinked, then said, "Nice." He watched the scene for a few more seconds, then he stood up and stretched. "Time for bed." He yawned.

If Jane was disappointed at Brian's reaction, she didn't show it. She did smile down at the spot where she and Dave had made love. She could almost feel the grass tickling her skin and the delicious weight of his body on hers as he impregnated her, not with a child, but with an awareness that she still had the option of making choices.

She took Brian's arm as they strolled back to their room.

"Quite a show," he said, yawning again.

"Yes," she said. "Wasn't it."

The "Gourmet Group" in Paris

They are in their early sixties now, all eight of them, all still members of the "Gourmet Group" as they laughingly call themselves, admitting that they ought to call it the "Gluttons Group." They first met nearly forty years ago in Mill Valley, a hilly, leafy town—now chiefly inhabited by rich ex-hippies—a few miles north of San Francisco's Golden Gate Bridge. Then, they all were in their mid-twenties, all of them attractive and intelligent, all of them members of a cooperative nursery school, all of them with two or three toddlers. In those days the husbands had professions and the women, though college graduates, were stay-at-home moms. Once the children entered grammar school and Betty Freidan became a household name, the four wives woke up and got interesting careers.

Betsy Graham, a tall, handsome, big-boned woman with a headfull of curly blonde hair, worked her way up in Marin County administration and successfully ran for the Board of Supervisors three times before she retired. Her husband Allen, even taller and bigger-boned than Betsy, was a talented designer of starkly modern churches, synagogues and museums. He made partner at his much-in-demand San Francisco architectural firm before he was thirty.

Petite, jolly, outgoing Judy Hobson got a Ph.D. in English literature and became a tenured and very popular professor at San Francisco State University. Her hubby, Glenn, who hugely towers over her and is as gruff as she is cheerful, parlayed his low-level engineering job into one of the top spots in the executive suite at

Lockheed Missile, blasting his way through the phalanx of those senior employees who stood between him and his goal.

Plump, ultra-serious Lucy Adler, famous for her thick, dark hair as voluminous as an "afro," went back to Berkeley for an MSW degree to prepare herself for a career in family counseling. In time she wrote best-selling books on child rearing and became a national TV guru on the subject. Her husband, Bob, is a serious man, madly in love with math. As short and thin as his wife is pudgy, he actually enjoys reading the tiny print in contracts and tax laws. By the time he was forty, he had expanded his accounting firm to a chain of eight busy offices throughout the Bay Area.

Petite Kathy Lipper, the most beautiful of the four women with her long auburn hair and deep green eyes, got herself a loft studio in San Francisco's tenderloin district where she creates huge, splashy paintings on which she uses brooms instead of brushes to spread the paint. Now many of her works hang in corporate offices and contemporary living room walls all over the West Coast. Her spouse, Dr. Kenneth Lipper, an uptight, self-centered man, recently retired as head of Cardiology at one of San Francisco's major hospitals.

So, do try to keep them straight: we have the Grahams, Betsy the County Supervisor and Allen the architect. Then we have the Hobsons, Judy the English prof and Glenn the Lockheed VIP. Then the Adlers, Lucy the child shrink and Bob the accountant. And finally we have the Lippers, Kathy the painter and Ken the heart doc.

Now these "gourmet" couples are all retired, except for Kathy who still paints. All of them live in the same handsome hillside Mill Valley homes they bought in the 1980's, except for Judy and Glenn Hobson who sold their house last year and moved to Paris.

One other remarkable bond the four couples have in common is the quality of their marital relationships. After more than forty years together, each couple still claims to be very much in love. None of them ever committed adultery, not because they are prudes but because they cherish their spouses and don't want to jeopardize their marriages. They have, indeed, led charmed lives in the midst of statistically troubled connubial times.

The eight of them were sincere wannabe gourmets when they first became a group. In those early days, the couples took turns hosting their monthly get-togethers. They had elaborate appetizers and drinks at the hosts' home. Then each host couple arranged a gourmet menu at a restaurant of their choice, usually in San Francisco, often ethnic.

In those days they came together with mega sighs of relief at being out of the house, temporarily away from the responsibilities of parenthood, which all eight of them took much too seriously. At least in those pre-cell-phone times no nervous baby sitters could call them.

Also in those days they drank more: two, sometimes three martinis or highballs before dinner, several glasses of wine with dinner, brandy or cognac afterwards. But the alcohol consumption was spread out over the evening and ingested with a great deal of food. They didn't get drunk, just mellow. Now if they have more than one before-dinner drink and one glass of wine with dinner, they have to haul out the Pepcid.

As the women became involved in their own careers, their cooking abilities went downhill and socializing became more casual. Who had time to plan fancy appetizers and look around for special places to eat, even once a month? Instead of going to exotic restaurants, the group began sharing simple pot-luck dinners, more interested in seeing each other than in what they were eating. Besides, each of the four couples ate out several times a week with other friends, and gourmet meals became commonplace in their lives. What is a special and different meal now is taking their grandchildren to McDonalds.

It didn't take a mega brain for the group to figure out that they might regain their true gourmet status by visiting Judy and Glenn for a week in Paris. With a flurry of phone calls and e-mail, it was all arranged for the last week in May. Judy made reservations for the other three couples at an excellent three-star hotel around the corner from her Paris apartment in the old but again fashionable Marais.

So there they are: four loving couples, all prosperous, all intelligent, all cultured, all still good looking, all affectionate friends, all in splendid health, all spending a week together in Paris. What could possibly go wrong?

"Why the hell did you invite them anyway?" Glenn chews out Judy. "You *know* how much I love my routine. I *love* sleeping late. I *love* going down to the bakery for our breakfast croissants while you fix the fruit and coffee. I *love* our charcuterie lunches. I *love* fucking you every afternoon after lunch. I *love* going out for dinner, just the two of us, and then walking around Paris at night." Glenn is tall and husky with strong, thick legs and the imposing head of a Roman senator, including the curly white hair. Throw a toga around him and he could play Brutus. Somehow, one doesn't expect a man that big to whine.

"It's only for a week, darling," Judy soothes, her years of dealing with the problems of emotional students having perfected her consoling skills. "Our breakfasts will be the same, since the others will have theirs at the hotel. And they'll be doing a lot of sightseeing on their own during the daytime. It's just a couple of lunches together and going out with them at night."

But Glenn is enjoying his pout. The older he gets, Judy realizes, the more of a gruff, anti-social grouch he becomes. She goes to yoga and French class every afternoon while he takes a long nap after their post-prandial sexual romp. She makes friends, and he keeps rejecting them. She is flattered that he still feels so romantic toward her that he wants to be alone with her, but she is very much a gregarious being. She still has a pert little figure and a pretty, sweet face, hardly wrinkled, and her curly dark hair has very few gray strands as yet. She loves parties, but he never wants to go to them.

"You really don't have to go," she keeps saying sweetly. "I don't mind going alone."

When he realizes that she is serious, after she goes by herself to three parties given by her classmates in two weeks, he stops refusing to go but he makes it perfectly clear that he is doing her a big, big favor.

"Truly, Glenn," she insists. "I don't want you to go if you don't want to."

"I don't want you going out alone at night."

"Oh, that's bullshit, and you know it. I get a taxi right in front of our building and it's always easy to hail one wherever I go. It's a lot safer here than anywhere back home."

One thing about Judy: she always is right, and they both know it. He is being a real shit about the gourmet group, but he doesn't care. He enjoys being a shit. He had plenty of practice when he was a big-shot at Lockheed.

"I didn't plan anything special for tonight," Judy tells the six visitors assembled in her living room the evening of their arrival. "I figured you'd all be jet-lagged."

"I never get jet-lag," Betsy Graham bristles. "I eat lightly on the plane, I never drink while flying, and I get right into the rhythm of the place when I arrive. So if it's morning, I stay awake all day, if it's nighttime, I go right to bed."

Does she have to be so holier than thou? Her husband Allen feels an interior rage. *God, she's a pain in the ass!* Allen puts up with Betsy because she is dynamite in bed—when he can get it up—but he wonders why all these nice people have stayed friends with her for so many years. She's always pulling this I'm-so-much-better-and-smarter-than-you-are-act with them and everyone else.

Judy continues, "So tonight, how about going to that little bistro downstairs? It's good, but nothing fancy. I didn't think you'd want to bother getting dressed up after flying all day. Tomorrow night we'll go to our favorite really great restaurant."

She is very aware, and very annoyed, that Glenn is sulking in his easy chair. He hasn't once helped her pour drinks or pass around the platter of finger food she bought at the charcuterie. But she can't be angry with a man who's always so sweet and loving to her in bed. They've had more sex in the year they've lived in Paris than in all the last ten years put together. There is something about this city that keeps their carnal batteries fully charged. Sometimes at night they have a repeat performance. Imagine, at their age! Two fantastic orgasms in one day!

Judy enjoys showing off their apartment to the six visitors, who had a good laugh when they arrived downstairs to find that the ancient elevator holds only two people at a time. And the Hobsons' apartment is on the fifth floor. The men volunteered to walk up the stairway that winds around the elevator shaft while the three women squeezed in together and rode up.

Back home they all live in spacious, quite elegant homes, but the fact that the Hobsons' apartment is in Paris gives it a panache that makes their own homes seem dull in comparison. "We have a two year renewable lease," Judy explains, trying not to brag as she shows them the modern kitchen, the downstairs marble bathroom, the high-ceilinged living room with a wide balcony outside the three tall French doors, and best of all, the dramatic view of Notre Dame, plus a glimpse of the Seine, and the city spread out around them.

Then she leads the procession up a curving stairway to the second floor where they have two bedrooms, each with a balcony, and two more baths. She has furnished the place with carefully chosen French, Danish and Italian pieces that some day she plans to ship back to the States, if she and Glenn ever tire of living abroad.

"You and Glenn must've had a ball, buying all this lovely stuff," Kathy Lipper gushes, her artistic juices roiling with envy.

"Glenn didn't have much to do with it," Judy can't help complaining. "He'd have been happy with a couple of crates for chairs and a mattress on the floor to sleep on."

"Men!" Kathy says.

The hotel where the three visiting couples are staying, just around the corner from the Hobsons' apartment, is a renovated Eighteenth Century mansion. Its spacious suites each have a living room and half bath downstairs, a majestic two-story window taking up an entire wall, and a stairway up to a loft with a king-size bed and a black-tile modern bathroom. All six visitors are impressed and pleased with their accommodations.

But Allen Graham is having a tizzy. "Did you have to play Madame County Supervisor all evening?" he gripes to Betsy when they're alone in their hotel room. "For God's sake, Betts, you're retired now. Don't you know when it's time to shut up? Didja have to brag about never getting jet lag? Like you're some kind of superwoman? Christ! Get the fuck off your fucking soap box!"

"Oh fuck off," she says amiably, pulling off her dress over her head and mussing her short, curly, Clairol-blonde hair. She was the most attractive woman ever to sit on the Marin County Board of Supervisors, and she knows it. She's had a difficult time with Allen's envy of her ever since she first ran for office and won. She bitterly resented his always having been too busy with his architectural work to help her with any of her campaigns. Still, she's as crazy about him as ever. He is even taller than she is and still slender, although he hates any form of exercise. "It's my metabolism," he likes to say when people remark on his ability to eat a lot and not get fat. "It's genetic."

"You should hear yourself," he goes on, taking off his shirt and pants. "Mizz Know It All. Is there any subject you aren't a big expert on?"

"Yeah! What's the opposite of penis envy?"

Allen looks at her naked body and feels a sudden, massive surge of desire. He is so thrilled he almost shouts because his little pecker hasn't been too cooperative lately and he hates taking Viagra. It's such an admission of defeat. He stands behind her and grabs her shoulders, slamming her backwards against his chest while grabbing a breast in each hand and vigorously massaging her nipples until they grow rigid beneath his fingers. When she gasps with delight—she loves playing rough—he throws her on the bed and jumps on top of her. "Bitch!" he grins before giving her a firm, grinding kiss.

She playfully bites his tongue, not hard enough to hurt him, but almost, and grabs a fistfull of his thick gray hair and tugs it. "Bastard!" she whispers affectionately. They give the bed a thorough trouncing, not caring how much noise they make. When they finally collapse against each other, loudly proclaiming their pleasure, they look into each other's eyes and smile with triumph.

She reaches down and caresses his shrinking penis. "Welcome back, you little shithead!" she says lovingly.

"Fuckface!" Allen says, happily caressing her sweaty buttocks.

The Group's second night's dinner returns them to full, glorious, gourmet status. Dressed like Academy Award nominees, they meet at the restaurant. "No before-dinner drinks and no appetizers tonight," Judy announced earlier in the day when they met at a neighborhood brasserie for lunch. "Tonight we're having the special six-course dinner at a Michelin five-star restaurant. We'll be eating for three hours, each course with a different wine. It's costing you six hundred dollars a couple, so be prepared to enjoy every morsel." And they do.

Escargot in filo dough. A smooth venison pate. Wild mushroom soup. Lobster in lobster coulis. Tender baby veggies. Salad verte. Cheese plate. Swirled chocolate and raspberry soufflé. Platters of tiny, delectable tarts. Choice of gourmet coffees. A different wine with each course. They all enthusiastically agree that it's worth every last euro, as the French now call their currency.

Those to whom superb food is an aphrodisiac go back to their beds and indulged themselves. The others take Pepcid and go to sleep.

Judy and Glenn Hobson are among those who feel amorous. For the first time since their friends arrived, Glenn was less sullen at dinner, though still not the charming, humorous raconteur he once was. Judy is so grateful she kisses him passionately all the way up their ancient elevator's slow ascent. When they reach the fifth floor, Glenn holds their kiss and pushes the lobby button. They go up and down three times, still holding their kiss and touching each other in all the right places. It turns out to be another two-orgasm day for the Hobsons.

Judy and Lucy have mid-morning coffee at a neighborhood café while the others go to the Louvre. "Been there, done that a million times," Judy says.

"So have I," Lucy agrees. She and Bob come to Paris every year for a week or two on their anniversary, but Bob has gone along with the others to the museum. Glenn still is asleep.

"I know your specialty is child psychology," Judy begins. "And I hate to impose on your friendship, but I'm worried about Glenn."

"I did some adult counseling before I retired," Lucy assures her. "What's his problem?"

"He sleeps late in the morning, and he sleeps most of the afternoon. Even when he isn't sleeping, he's grouchy. I know that too much sleep is often a sign of depression, but how could he be? We're living in *Paris* for God's sake! We have plenty of money. We're both in good health. Our kids are all happy. What could possibly be making him depressed?"

Lucy sighs, unconsciously scratching her scalp under her big hair. "Maybe he's bored, Paris or no Paris. He was a big-shot executive at Lockheed. He probably misses being in charge. Telling others what to do."

"He sure makes up for it, ordering me around." Judy leans toward Lucy. "Can you prescribe something? You know, like Prozac?"

Lucy shakes her head. "I'm not a medical doctor, Judy. And I'm not even sure that American doctors can write prescriptions here. You'll have to see a French doctor." She touches her friend's arm with sympathy. The two of them always have been closer to each other than to Betsy or Kathy. Their children are good friends and their homes used to be two blocks apart.

"Maybe he needs some special interest. Something entirely different from what he used to do," Lucy muses. "Before I stopped doing individual counseling, I saw quite a few older clients who had trouble adjusting to retirement. Sometimes I suggested that they choose a subject they like and do research on it, you know, like they were going to write a book? And often their interest became so intense after they started doing the research that they actually went ahead and wrote a book. It didn't even matter if they did a book or not. That's not the point. The learning process gave them a goal, an interest. They became experts on the subject, and that's a real ego booster."

Judy is thoughtful. "At Stanford, Glenn majored in European history. He didn't get into engineering until he was in graduate school at Cal-Tech."

"Well, there you are. What better place to study European history than living here? I understand that Paris has some fantastic libraries."

"Yeah, in French. He hates the language."

"There's an English language library somewhere near the American Church, over in the Eighth. And you can always order books in English on the Internet. Anyway, it's just a thought."

"You tell him, Luce. He never listens to me."

"No way," Lucy says. "He thinks I'm a pushy broad as it is."

"What gave you that idea?"

Lucy hesitates. "Maybe you never noticed, Judy, but in all the time I've known you, he always winces when I start talking."

Every night, the group has another gourmet feast. Meal after gorgeous meal. They all compliment Judy on her arrangements. They love their hotel, they enjoy hanging out in the Hobson's apartment before dinner, and there hasn't been one meal they haven't found superb.

All eight of them adore walking in Paris. The weather is perfect, day and night, during the entire visit. Often, after dinner, they walk back to the Marais if the restaurant isn't too far away. Judy and Glenn know every street in their neighborhood and in the surrounding arrondissements too, proudly guiding their visitors past lighted monuments and churches and public buildings.

Cutting across the broad Centre Pompidou their fourth night there, after stopping to admire the square's whimsical fountain, the four women find themselves walking ahead of the men. "There's something about this town," Judy confesses, "that's so sensuous! I don't know if it's in the air or what. Glenn and I are like horny teenagers. I swear, I've never had such orgasms!"

"Me too," Betsy giggles. "Allen and I are like dogs in heat!"

Lucy titters, embarrassed by her friends' confessions. She is accustomed to discussing sex with her clients, but in a more clinical way. Still, she has to admit that she and Bob are "doing it" every afternoon, far more than they do at home. "Yes," she agrees, "it's been fabulous."

Judy looked over at Kathy. "How about you, Kath? Does this place get to you and Ken too?"

"Oh sure," Kathy lies. "It's…amazing." She feels a wave of discomfort. *Orgasms? Dogs in heat? What the hell were they talking about?*

One evening they all take the *Bateau Mouche* and sit sipping wine on the outside deck as the boat glides down the Seine, illuminating the buildings they pass with high-powered searchlights. The guide's amplified voice explains the history or significance of what they are seeing—the Academia, the Pont Alexandre III, the Concierge, Notre Dame, the Ile St. Louis.

Judy feels a wave of self-satisfaction, akin to pride of ownership, as though she were bestowing the gift of Paris upon her friends. She can't help it. She always feels that way when people from back home visit, even her own children. She never considers herself an interloper in Paris, or that she doesn't belong there. She fervently hopes that if there is such a thing as reincarnation, she will return as a wealthy French woman. Anyway, it's the only way she'll ever be fluent in their damn language!

During the days, the visitors all go off on their individual pursuits. Lucy and Bob Adler are only interested in shopping. After all, there are no psychology institutes she cares to see or accounting offices that would be of interest to him. They have three daughters, three sons-in-law, and thirteen grandchildren, and need presents for all of them. ("Didn't you teach your kids about birth control?" Betsy once half-joked to them.) After shopping, Lucy and Bob return to the hotel and quietly make love. They are slow—like half an hour of grinding away—and their climaxes are pleasant if not earth-shaking. They are so afraid that someone will hear what they are doing that their lovemaking is more like a slow-motion silent film than an erotic frolic.

Betsy and Allen Graham do some shopping, but mostly they enjoy walking in different parts of the city so that Allen can study the

Belle Epoch and Art Deco buildings he ardently admires. Betsy is almost as knowledgeable about the subject as Allen is, having taken architecture and design classes when they first were married so that she could discuss his work with him. Was he ever interested in her equally fascinating work as a County Supervisor? Hell no.

Much as they enjoy what they are doing, they bicker about everything—which street to take, which side of the river to explore, where to stop for coffee, which stores to go into for buying gifts. They don't seem to realize that the fiercer their disputes are, the less likely Allen will need Viagra.

One afternoon they come into their hotel suite screaming at each other over a toy she insisted on buying for their youngest grandson. They are too turned on to climb the stairs to the bed in the loft. He throws her onto the couch in their downstairs living room and rips her expensive skirt while wrenching it off of her. These days there is always the suspense of whether or not Allen will get it up without artificial help. But he does! He does! He does it again! "My pecker loves Paris!" he chortles. Their mutual screams of pleasure probably can be heard all the way to the Seine, two blocks away, and they certainly create a racket in the Lippers' suite next door.

Kathy Lipper is in heaven, spending her days in the art galleries on the Rue du Seine. Ken tags along with her because he isn't interested in visiting hospitals or talking to French doctors. "What a sublime combination," she says to Ken, gesturing at the food stalls that are spread along the center of the street while the sidewalks are lined with windows full of paintings and sculpture. "Beautiful food and beautiful art. What more can you ask?" They don't know where to look first. They weave back and forth, sauntering into the galleries and then loitering around the cheese carts, the bakery stands, the seafood displays, the colorful fruits, inhaling the tantalizing aromas and sometimes buying a small portion of an irresistible delicacy.

Unlike their friends, the Lippers don't rush back to the hotel in the late afternoon to indulge in amorous pleasures. Actually, they are annoyed by the passionate grunts and screams from Betsy and

Allen's suite next door. Neither Kathy nor Ken ever were that crazy about sex. At best, when they were young, Kathy submitted to Ken's "needs." When his needs petered out in their early fifties, they simply gave it up. They are terribly fond of each other. It never occurred to either of them that there is anything sad about Kathy's never having experienced an orgasm. And he's a doctor! Shame on him!

As for the hosts, Judy gets up the courage to follow through on Lucy's advice and suggests that she and Glenn do research on the French Revolution and its effect on women's lives. Judy puts it this way. "I'm interested in learning about it, but I need your help, sweetie, since you know so much more about history than I do." She knows Glenn well enough to realize that flattery and his need to be in charge will take over and he'll be off and running with the research. Then she can go back to her own interests, which at the moment happen to be studying French and yoga. She also discovers that two orgasms a day does wonders for Glenn's mood.

Maybe it is Paris, or maybe it is some latent spark in Kathy, but when she hears the frequent sexual fireworks coming from Betsy and Allen's room, and when she recalls the disturbing conversation about orgasms she'd had with her friends the previous evening while walking in the Centre Pompidou, she begins to wonder if maybe she *is* missing something important. Until now, raising the kids and pursuing her painting career and being a doctor's wife has filled every corner of her life.

That night, when Ken gives her the usual peck on her lips and says "Good night," she puts a restraining arm around him. "Let's *really* kiss," she says, and proceeds to press her body against him and titillate his tongue with hers. But she can feel his body stiffen and he pulls his mouth away.

"What's gotten into you?" he whispers, shocked.

"I want to see what an orgasm is like," she says. "My friends talk about them like they're something fantastic."

"Believe me, Kath, they're highly over-rated." He pulls himself away from her and turns onto his side, so that his back is toward her. "Go to sleep."

She sighs. She is too agitated to sleep and has to get up and take an Ambien. But a bug has been planted and it becomes more and more insistent the more it buzzes around in her mind—and elsewhere too.

In the morning, Ken says he's tired of hanging around the art galleries with her. He decides to look up a colleague at the American Hospital in Neuilly who went to Harvard Medical School with him. Kathy knows that Judy, Lucy and Betsy decided the night before to attend a fashion show at the Galleries Lafayette, but she declined, thinking that she and Ken would be visiting more galleries together.

After Ken leaves, Kathy throws on some pants and a cardigan and walks around the block to the Hobson's apartment. Judy taught all of them how to work the combination that opens the building's downstairs door, so Kathy lets herself in and takes the elevator up to the Hobson's floor. She rings the bell several times before a sleep-disheveled Glenn, wearing only green silk pajama bottoms, comes clomping down the interior stairway and opens the door.

"Kathy!" Glenn is astonished, and he stands there dumbly looking at her. "Judy's gone to some fashion show."

"I know," she says, pushing him aside and walking into the apartment.

Glenn closes the door. "So, what…" His words are blocked when she puts her arms around him and brings her lips up against his. He hesitates, in total amazement, and then he pulls her close and lets his mouth respond against hers. He can't figure out what she is up to, except he senses that she is in some kind of desperate need. He always had a little "thing" for Kathy, anyway, but he's never shown it. It's as taboo as incest in their group.

Still mystified, he takes her into the living room and sits down with her on the couch. The pulses in her temples are visibly throbbing and her breathing is ragged. Again, she wordlessly throws herself into his arms.

"Fuck me!" she whispers hoarsely.

It's no time for questions or qualms. Sometimes, he knows, life demands something of you that you don't understand, but you do it anyway. He unbuttons her sweater and caresses her breasts. They are large and white and smooth with delightful pink nipples, like pale little raspberries. He licks them and gently sucks them as they harden, and he enjoys listening to her chirpy little cries. He is filled with pride that he is causing her so much pleasure.

He pushes down her pants and pulls them off. His own silk pajama bottoms slide off easily. He draws Kathy down on the couch, moving ahead slowly, wanting her to relax before he becomes too lusty. He gently kisses her and calmly caresses her until he can feel her tense muscles soften under his hands.

While his fingers excite her nipples, he titillates the rest of her with his lips and tongue all the way down, down, slowly, down over her soft abdomen and down through her patch of silky golden hair and when his tongue slides over and around her turgid clitoris she almost jumps off the couch with shocked quivers. He keeps it all soft and gentle, his tongue lapping and his lips sucking, creating a torrent of her eager, surprised mewings and moanings and when he feels she is ready he enters her, forcefully and purposefully and when she comes he comes too and it is good, good, good for both of them.

Gasping for breath, he stays there next to her with his hand gently lying on her abdomen, feeling her body throb.

After a while she caresses his face in gratitude, then she gets off the couch and puts on her clothes. "It doesn't count," she says. "I mean, we won't do this again. Nobody will ever know. But…I had to find out what it was like."

"What what was like?" he asks, pulling up his pajama bottoms and tying them.

"An orgasm."

"You never had one before?"

"No."

He is aghast. "And Ken?"

"Oh, he used to. But as far as I could tell, they were pretty mild. Just a little heavy breathing. Nothing like this."

"You poor baby." He takes her back into his arms but this time it is not sensual. It is a gesture full of pity. "What are you going to do?"

She moves away from him. "Well, I have two choices. I can stay with Ken and forget about sex, or once in a while sneak in moments like this…" she gestures at the couch. "Or I can leave him and hope to find someone else. Someone who likes sex."

"So…which will it be?"

She gives a somewhat rueful laugh. "Ken says that orgasms are highly over-rated. Right now, I certainly don't agree with him! They're amazing! Absolutely amazing!" She sighs tremulously. "But…I do love Ken. We have a wonderful life together, even without sex. It's a no-brainer. I'll stick with him."

He walks with her to the elevator. He wants to hold her again, to comfort her, but he thinks it would be the wrong thing to do. Right now, he feels more like a benevolent do-gooder than like a man who has committed adultery for the first time in his life.

"Thanks," she says, tearful with gratitude. "You were so kind."

"I was happy to help." He waits out on the landing until she is in the elevator and it moves down out of sight before he goes back into his apartment whistling cockily as he closes the door.

The rest of the week flies by. Saying goodbye is difficult. Judy and Glenn go over to their visitors' hotel after breakfast. The mountain of luggage fills one van, and the six people are traveling to the airport in a second van. They all hug and kiss Judy and Glenn amid cries of "Let's do this again next year."

Judy and Glenn both feel a brief moment of homesickness, knowing their friends soon will be back among all that is familiar and comfortable, back with their children and close relatives and other friends. Conversely, though, the six departing travelers feel a rush of envy that Judy and Glenn are staying in Paris—in Paris!—while the rest of them are going back to such humdrum lives in comparison.

"You know," Judy says, just before the others board the van, "there's no reason in the world why any of you couldn't come live here for a while. You can see for yourselves how great it is."

But Judy knows they won't. They're all too set in their ways, she thinks. They will get back into their busy routines of season tickets for the symphony, the ballet and the theater, art openings, film festivals, volunteer work at hospitals and libraries, charity balls, bridge groups and book clubs, and outings with their children and grandchildren.

When the vehicles pull into the street, for a brief moment Glenn's eyes meet Kathy's through the window. Then the van turns the corner and she vanishes from his view.

"Now, aren't you ashamed of the way you carried on when they first came?" Judy asks Glenn as they walk back to their apartment. "Admit it, Glenn. You enjoyed their visit after all, didn't you?."

He takes her arm and gives it an affectionate squeeze. "Yeah, honey, I gotta admit, I really did enjoy it. More than you know."

Happy Anniversaries in London

Donald and Margaret were both eighteen when they married in London on June 17, 1972, both of them too young, too spoiled, and way too stupid to know how to make a marriage work. Just because they had been crazy about each other since they were twelve didn't mean they always would feel that way. Or did it?

Don's American father was the vice president and head of an international pharmaceutical company's London office. Don's British mother was a bright woman who spent her life at tennis clubs and lunching with "the ladies" to keep from going mad with boredom.

Maggie was an American Army brat whose father was a one-star general and proud as hell of his rank. He was a devoted military man and admirably performed his duties as a military attache at the American Embassy, but at home he swaggered and bellowed out orders which his wife and daughter ignored. Still, God help Maggie if she called him "Daddy" instead of "General." Maggie's mother was a Southern Belle from "'weeziana" who had lived abroad so long that she didn't know that belles had gone out of style a long time ago.

Don and Maggie both lived on upscale Cadogan Place. Their parents' flats faced each other across a private park which was surrounded by a wrought iron fence with locked gates. The park was in the center of the square and only the residents had keys to the gates. The first time Maggie and Don met was on the tennis court within the park, and after a heated argument as to who had been there first—Maggie and her friend Liz, or Don and his friend Freddie.

Then Liz had said, "Why don't we just play doubles?" Liz eventually studied the Law and gained fame as a diplomat during Margaret Thatcher's reign. But long before that, she was Maggie's Maid of Honor at the wedding and Freddie was Don's best man. Nine years later, Liz married...oh wait, that comes later.

That same park was the scene, when Maggie and Don were fifteen, of their first serious sexual encounter. Since they had been "going steady" for three years by then, they had probed, tickled, caressed, sucked and kissed just about every part of each other's bodies, first out of curiosity, then because their libidos were kicking up. Finally, when Don had an erection the size of Big Ben, he didn't even ask. They had been fooling around as they lay on their very private patch of grass, surrounded by shrubbery, and he simply pushed aside Maggie's panties and entered her. He came before she even realized what he had done.

"Yuck," was her reaction as a waterfall of semen came out of her when he withdrew. But she giggled and took off her panties and wiped up the mess and when he re-entered her she wiggled and squeezed and got into the swing of things and liked it even though she still thought it was kind of yucky with all that messy semen. She had a rather overdeveloped fastidious side to her nature.

They both were sophisticated enough to know about teenage pregnancy, and they didn't want to approach their parents, so by lying about her age she got a doctor to prescribe birth control pills. By the time they were married three years later, they had had sex twelve hundred and fifty-three times. Before you tax your brain, that's like once a day and twice on Sundays, including one leap year.

Their parents weren't complete idiots. The four of them had a pretty good idea of what their little darlings were doing in the park besides playing tennis. The specter of teen pregnancy made all of them cringe, so when the kids said they wanted to get married right after they both graduated from high school, the four parents chorused, like a mighty hymn on a great church organ, "YEEESSSSS!"

Maggie and Don grew up with an enormous sense of entitlement.

Both had generous trust funds from their grandparents, which is great if it doesn't turn you into a lazy bum. But you didn't need a Doctorate in Psychology to see all the red flags waving at their nuptials. Both their mothers, who had become good friends, planned the morning church wedding for three hundred guests and a fancy luncheon afterwards at the Savoy. The two women were in their element. *This* was what they had been born to do.

After the church service and the luncheon and all the usual wedding hoopla, Don and Maggie found themselves alone in a limo on their way to the airport to board a plane for Paris and a two-week honeymoon at the Ritz. As the car turned right at Big Ben to go around Westminster Abbey, the clock struck four in the afternoon.

"Mags," Don said, tipsy from too much champagne, "I've got an idea."

She looked at him, her eyes bright with anticipation. Don didn't get ideas too often, unless they involved sex.

"Every ten years, let's meet right here on our anniversary—on the sidewalk under the clock. At four o'clock. Even if we aren't married to each other any more."

"You big jerk!" she screeched.

"Why?"

"You just promised to love me 'til death do us part. How can you talk about not being married to each other in ten years?"

"You gotta be realistic. These things happen. But anyway, Mags, promise."

"Sure. And I'll bring along all the husbands I'll be marrying between now and then too!"

Maggie had no idea how close to the truth that statement would turn out to be.

In case you haven't figured it out, Maggie was a whole lot brighter than Don. They both were good looking kids, tall and blond and gleaming with splendid health. They had a charming apartment in Mayfair, they played tennis on friends' private courts and skied in Gstaad and tore around the St. Albans countryside on horseback with

Don's British cousins. They flew to Louisiana fairly often because Maggie's American cousins were forever getting married and re-married. But through it all, Maggie went on to college and Don...well, Don just hung around, trying to figure out what he wanted to be when he grew up. The trouble was, he still hadn't even begun to grow up. If anything, he had regressed.

Before they knew it, Maggie had a Master's degree in Zoology and a job she loved at the London Zoo and Don was working as a lackadaisical flunky at his father's office, still trying to figure out what he wanted to do "some day." However, it didn't bother him in the least.

It did bother Maggie. She was a bright, mature twenty-four and her husband was like a not-so-bright, immature twelve-year-old. He wasn't even smart enough to see it coming when Maggie announced she was divorcing him and marrying her boss at the zoo.

It was a nasty awakening for Don. He was twenty-four and as lost in the sea of life as an infant. His first reaction was furious anger at Maggie. She was a traitor, a bitch, a quitter, a deserter, and she was cruel. He always had been faithful to her. He felt utterly sorry for himself. But most of all, he was terrified.

Maggie felt a huge sense of relief when she left him. For the last four years of her six-year marriage she had been suffocated by Don, as though he were holding her under water and not letting her up to breathe. What's more, he was a slob, something she hadn't realized when they married. "How could I go steady with you for six years and not know you're like a garbage truck that spews out the stuff instead of sucking it up?" she railed at him.

He grinned. "Because my parents had a maid picking up after me and we don't."

She would try letting his things accumulate, on the floor, on the furniture, everywhere, hoping it would shame him into picking up his belongings, but when she did that, their small apartment became unlivable. And remember, she did have a fastidious nature. That situation is enough to stifle even a marriage of mature adults.

When she wasn't home to cook for him, he ate cold ravioli straight out of the can, too lazy to put it in a dish and heat it in the microwave. He ate frozen waffles drowned in maple syrup without bothering to put them on a plate. He left blobs of syrup on the floor and dribbling down his shirt and he left sticky fingerprints all over the kitchen. He peed carelessly and she was forever wiping up the toilet rim and the floor below it. But, she would tell herself, he was so cute and lovable. And so damn delicious in bed.

Then she met Tony, who was the kindest man she ever had known. As her boss, he shared with her his vast zoological knowledge. He never found fault with her work. Knowing she was married, he didn't tell her how much he admired her and how overwhelmingly much he loved her. She had to make the first move.

Walking away from Don was not easy for Maggie. They had such a long history together. But, she knew that when a relationship isn't working, it's a mistake to prolong it, just for *auld lang syne*. She was grateful they didn't have children. She'd had a miscarriage two years earlier and at the time she had been devastated, and so had Don. She had hoped that fatherhood might mature him.

"Don," she said after telling him she was leaving him, "you're drifting through life. I can't..." She wept, suddenly overwhelmed with sadness for him. She had tried so hard to help him. But the longer he drifted, the more detached she felt from him. "Love needs intimacy to thrive," she told him. "We've just been playmates," she said, "not real lovers."

Still, she had sex with Don almost every day, even after their divorce became final—in fact, right up until the night before she married Tony.

"I don't want Tony to think I'm promiscuous," she told Don, "by having sex with him before we're married."

"Well, he knows you're no virgin," Don said bitterly.

She smiled up at him as he lay on top of her in his bed. "I hate doing without sex," she said. "And since we're already divorced, this way I'm not being unfaithful to anyone."

Maggie and Tony had a baby before their first anniversary. Tony spoke often about his "fellow earthlings," by which he meant his affinity with every living creature in the world. He treated all animals, especially the animals in the zoo, like friends. He killed only insects that were poisonous, and then with the greatest regret. He was kind and utterly accepting of other people. But to him their daughter, Molly, was not just a fellow creature, but a little goddess.

Tony inherited a chic terrace house on Regents Park, walking distance from the zoo. They hired a middle-aged Scottish couple who cleaned, cooked and nannied. Tony was promoted to the zoo hierarchy and Maggie got Tony's old job. Life was sweet.

Every morning Maggie looked at her desk calendar to check her appointments. Thus, when she saw it was June 17, 1982, a bell jangled in her head and she gasped. She wrote down, on the 4 p.m. line, "Big Ben—Don." She was certain he wouldn't be there.

At three fifteen she told her assistant she would be back in two hours and she grabbed a taxi that crept through the crowded narrow streets toward the big clock. She arrived there at five minutes to four, by then feeling foolish because she was so positive that Don wouldn't show up.

But! He *was* there!

She hadn't seen him since the night before she married Tony. Nearly four years! They looked at each other uncertainly, then embraced in tears. They stood there crying in each other's arms for a long time. Tourists and other pedestrians walked around them, slowing to gawk at the spectacle.

Maggie's and Don's tears of sorrow and regret slowly changed to joy at being together again, body pressed to body. They whispered each other's names, longingly, sick with desire. Still crushed against each other, they kissed, there among the throng of onlookers. They kissed and kissed, almost choking each other with their eager tongues.

Wordlessly clutching each other, they walked two blocks up Whitehall to a small hotel Don remembered seeing there. They had little more than an hour together but it was as though all their former youthful lovemaking were rolled into this one frantic hour full of sound and fury, signifying a great deal. It left them elated, yet utterly devastated.

She told him about Tony and Molly. Tears silently welled in his eyes and spilled down his cheeks when she mentioned Molly. He had so wanted to have a child with Maggie. He had married her old friend, no-nonsense Liz, who had dragged him out of his lethargy. While Liz pursued her law practice, he had become a financial advisor and found he had a real talent for it. He was particularly effective in helpings older pensioners manage on their incomes. He felt alive and useful. He was getting quite rich, investing his own inherited funds. He and Liz had no children but they did own a Chelsea apartment and a country house in Kent.

Maggie told him that her father had retired from the Army and he and her mother now lived in Florida. Don told her that his father had been transferred to his company's New York office and his parents were living in Westchester County. Neither Don nor Maggie felt at all American. And even though they both had lived in England their entire lives and were married to Brits, they didn't feel completely British either.

They parted at the hotel entrance. "Oh Mags," he groaned, once more holding her close. "I'll always love you."

"Me too," she sniffled into his neck.

They each took a taxi in a different direction, both of them confounding their drivers by bursting into loud sobs over a string of "if only's." They had made no plans to see each other again. They hadn't even exchanged telephone numbers. It was too late.

Don divorced Liz when Mrs. Thatcher sent her to India to work with their government on the Kashmir mess. Don said Liz was putting her work before their marriage and she said darn-tooting she was. He toyed with the idea of trying to win back Maggie, but he found out that she had divorced Tony, left England, and was living in Paris with a new French husband. Don flew to Paris and stalked her for a couple of days, but from the way she and her new love walked down the street entwined practically like corkscrews, he figured he didn't have a chance. He flew back to London and, now in his thirties, rich and handsome, he tried being a "carefree man about town." After all, he'd been monogamous since he was twelve! It was time to discover what else was out there.

On the morning of June 17, 1992 Don felt faint when he realized what the date signified. After the first shock, he decided there was no way Maggie would come all the way from Paris just to keep that silly little promise she'd made on their wedding day. He had a lunch date with a new girlfriend at his penthouse overlooking the Thames, and afterwards he hoped to consummate their budding relationship. She was a lively little redhead with huge breasts. He was determined to find out if they were the real thing. Or things.

But an hour before she was due at his place, he phoned her and begged off. He felt ill, he told her. What had happened, actually, was that he realized he was honor-bound to be at Big Ben at four. If Maggie did show up and he didn't, she would be hurt and furious and he didn't want that on his conscience. So, even though he was absolutely certain that she would not be there, he was standing on the sidewalk in front of Big Ben as its first BONG reverberated through him. By the fourth BONG, Maggie drove up in a gold Mercedes and motioned for him to get into the passenger seat.

They both were thirty-eight, at the height of their maturity and attractiveness. At the next red light they stared into each other's eyes. Smiling.

"Can you get away for a few days?" she asked.

He was blown away by her question. He recovered quickly. "Sure. With a few phone calls. What do you have in mind?"

She glanced at him, then back at the road. "I have a house on the Thames. Near Henley."

"You said 'I' and not 'we.'"

"Right."

"Does that mean you're not married any more?"

She gave him a brilliant smile. "That's right. How about you?"

"Free. Completely free."

"Well then," she said, "isn't that lovely."

It was lovely. This day, which would have been their twentieth anniversary had they stayed together, was as warm and golden as though the weather were celebrating the day for them. They arrived in Henley in time for the Happy Hour so they sat out on her terrace and watched the river lazily flow past. She prepared a tray of tasty tid-bits and a pitcher of gin and tonic.

Driving out of London, he had expected that they would throw themselves at each other the moment they got out of the car. But no. They both were so relaxed, and so happy to be alone together, that there was no need to rush into the sack.

"Where's Molly?" he asked.

Maggie was pleased that he had remembered her daughter's name, after ten years. "In Florida, visiting my parents. She's thirteen now. A little beauty."

"Does she see her father? What's his name? Tony?"

Maggie nodded. "They're very close. She lives with him and his third wife during the week and goes to school in London. Molly has two little half-sisters she adores. Then on weekends, she comes out to the country and stays with me." Maggie waved a lazy hand at the mass of flowers between her terrace and the river bank. "She's a whiz at gardening. We planted everything ourselves."

They were reclining on two adjacent chaises so he reached over and took her hand. "And you, Mags? Last I heard you were living in Paris."

She nodded. "I left adorable Tony and married Phillipe. It was the most foolish thing I ever did, next to marrying you." She squeezed his hand as a half-apology for the insult. "It wasn't even love. It was a mad infatuation. Phillipe and I had wild sex for six months and one day I woke up and looked at him and I actually screamed. He was gorgeous, but he was like a blow-up doll. There was nothing inside but hot air."

Don felt sorry for her. "And now?"

"I came back here and bought this place. Now I write books about children and animals. I'm alone, except for Molly on weekends. And I love it." She sat up and faced him. "I went steady with you from the time I was twelve. After that, I always was married to someone. I always was a very faithful wife and…"

"Uh-uh," he interrupted. "Aren't you forgetting something?"

She gave him a startled look. "What?"

"June 17th? Ten years ago? You still were married to Tony. Remember what happened?"

She stared at him. Then the memory flooded back to her. She blushed.

"How could you forget?" he asked, hurt.

"Oh Don! It was so long ago. So much has happened…"

"But Mags, that hour together, in that little hotel. It was so special!"

"Yes, it was. Very *very* special." She sighed. "But now, Don, it's wonderful to be free. I can do what I want, when I want, and be with whomever I want, or by myself when I feel like it. Why do we always have to be paired off with someone? Like we're about to board some stupid Ark?"

He raised his glass. "To freedom. And to our might-have-been twentieth anniversary, Mags."

She touched her glass to his. "My god, we were twits when we got married. We were practically still in diapers."

"Remember that first time? In the Cadogan Place park?"

She giggled. "I remember the mess. There was enough semen to repopulate the globe."

"Sex with you was always great," he said.

"Yes it was. So you've heard my life story for the last ten years, Don. What about you?"

"Well, obviously I'm no longer married to Liz."

"I gather not. I'm always reading about her diplomatic missions in the Times."

Don nodded. "I never loved her, but she sure knew how to kick butt and get me moving. I must've been the laziest man in England before I married her." He sighed, then smiled. "I'm like you now. Free, and loving it."

She fixed a simple dinner of fresh veggies from her garden, garnished with cheese for a bit of protein. He opened a tube of rolls and baked them, as proud of his efforts as though he had milled the flour and made them from scratch.

He stayed for five days, until it was time for Maggie to leave for Florida, to see her parents and bring Molly back in time for special summer horticultural classes at Kew Gardens. Don drove Maggie to the airport in her car, parking it there so she would have it when she returned.

They'd had a mellow time together. They both were so relaxed and comfortable with each other that they agreed they might as well be old married folks celebrating their twentieth anniversary. But neither suggested getting together again. She respected his fervent insistence that he loved the single life, and he in turn honored hers.

He kissed her goodbye while a porter collected her luggage. He held her close, not really wanting to let go and she, too, clung to him.

"See you in ten years," he said hoarsely. He could feel tears tightening his throat, stinging his eyes.

"Ten years," she echoed in a whisper, then fled from him and dashed into the terminal.

In the taxi going back to London, he became aware of tears half-blinding him and sliding down his cheeks. Then he surprised the driver by crying in great noisy howls until his throat hurt.

Don couldn't wait another ten years to tell Maggie about his shocking discovery. It happened in mid-July, a month after their five-day idyll at her house in Henly. He was looking through his files of legal papers for his birth certificate, which his health insurance company needed, when he came upon his Decree of Divorce from Maggie. He noticed the date: August 15, 1978. A month later, on September 15th, she had married Tony, as Don remembered only too well: he had gotten pass-out drunk for the only time of his life.

Idly, he wondered what date Molly had been born. Thanks to Liz's influence, he kept a calendar of people's birthdays and anniversaries and he thought it might be a nice gesture if he sent Molly a gift on her birthdays. As an old friend of the family.

He looked through his file of special cards and found Molly's birth announcement. He gasped. Her birthday was April 10, 1979. Less than seven months after Maggie married Tony! Don was sure that Maggie hadn't had sex with Tony until after they were married. He remembered that time so well. Maggie had had sex with him, Don, right up until the night before her marriage to Tony.

"I don't want Tony to think I'm promiscuous," Don remembered her saying, "by having sex with him before we're married."

"Well, he knows you're no virgin," Don recalled saying bitterly.

She had smiled up at him as he lay on top of her in his bed. "I hate doing without sex," she'd said. "And since you and I are already divorced, I'm not being unfaithful to anyone."

Now, Don sat stunned in front of his file cabinet, absolutely certain that Molly was *his* daughter, not Tony's.

Don phoned Maggie, who had returned home from Florida, and said he had to see her. It was urgent. He raced out on the Motorway to Henley.

"I didn't expect to see you for another ten years," she said, greeting him with a bright smile. "What's the emergency?' Then she paled. "Oh Don! You're not ill are you?"

"Nothing like that." He looked around. "Are you alone?"

She nodded. "Molly's at Tony's. You want something to drink?" When he shook his head she led him out to the terrace and sat facing him at a glass-top table. "So, what's up?"

He didn't know how to start. He finally said, "Mags, was Molly…was she born, you know, early? Like, a little premature?"

She looked at him in astonishment. "Premature? No, she was a big, fat, nine-pound baby." Her eyes grew round with horror. "Oh Don!" She shook her head. *"No!* It can't be!"

"Didn't you realize it at the time, for God's sakes?" he asked, suddenly very angry with her.

"No. I mean, we just thought she was a little early." Maggie sat there, shaking her head. "I never paid much attention to my periods, you know, the dates. We…Tony and I…it never entered our minds! Oh Don!"

She looked so miserable that his anger dissolved. He took her hand.

"Oh darling!" she cried out. "If…if it's true, it's so unfair to *you!* And Tony thinks…he's so crazy about her!" She stood up, distraught, looking like she might hurl herself into the Thames.

Don stood and held her close. "Sweetheart," he whispered, caressing the back of her neck. "Listen. Nothing's changed. I don't think we should ever tell Molly. Or Tony. He's been a wonderful father to her."

"But it's so unfair to *you!*" she repeated. "We could get a paternity test…" She began to cry softly. "Oh Don, there were so many times I'd look at her when she was little and she'd have these cute expressions that reminded me of you. I decided it was my imagination. But I never *ever* thought…"

He held her and waited for her to stop weeping. "I have a brilliant idea," he said, still holding her close. "Listen. I never stopped loving you. And this singles life is greatly over-rated. If you'd marry me again, Mags, I'd be Molly's step-father. That's good enough for me."

She started to pull away from him. "Oh, I see! You just want to marry me so you'll be part of Molly's life!"

"You didn't hear the first part of what I said, Mags. I said I still love you. I never stopped loving you. *You* were the one who ended our marriage, not me." He pulled her close again. "Besides," he said, "you've got to admit, we're terrific together in bed. The best. One other thing," he added with a grin, "I'm neat now, thanks to Liz. I pick up my clothes. And I pee carefully. And I no longer leave sticky fingerprints all over the kitchen. But I have to admit, I still like cold ravioli out of the can."

She smiled. "Well, I'll marry you on one condition."

He waited.

"When June 17, 2002 rolls around, at four o'clock I want both of us to go to Big Ben…together."

A Dangerous Man in San Miguel de Allende, Mexico

Sally White knew that Calvin Jensen was a dangerous man the first time she saw him. He was much too ruggedly handsome, a man whom women undoubtedly had spoiled rotten since early childhood. He was tall, lean, virile, tan, dark eyed and white haired, just the kind of man she knew she should avoid at all costs. The safe men usually were shorter, heavier, often bald, even homely, men whose faces reflected their intelligence and their lifelong development of responsibility and good character. Cal looked intelligent too, but that made him even more threatening to her.

Sally had heard about Cal before she saw him. He was her friend Diane's cousin from Seattle. Diane was both proud of him and leery of him. "To be perfectly candid, he's nuts," she told Sally. "His absolutely lovely wife left him two years ago because he screwed around so much."

"Does he work? Or what?" Sally asked.

"He mooches."

"He *what?*"

"Mooches. On friends. Relatives. Rich widows and divorcees. He's charming, so people don't mind if he comes and stays a while." Diane looked uncomfortable. "In fact, he's coming down in two weeks. I feel so disloyal when I talk about him like this."

"Any kids?" Sally asked.

"Two grown daughters."

"He sounds awful," Sally said, and she meant it. But that was before she met him.

Diane and her husband Duane owned a charming hacienda with a four-acre walled garden in the romantic Mexican colonial town of San Miguel de Allende. Sally had been renting the guest house on Diane's property for more than a year. The big house had four bedrooms, six baths, a double kitchen, a fifty-foot living room with a fireplace at each end, an arched loggia and a jasmine-scented terrace, a fruit orchard, a vegetable garden, two maids, a cook, and two full-time gardeners. The one-bedroom guest house was small but also charming, with its own private patio. Both houses had highly-polished terra cotta tile floors, expensive Spanish-Mexican style furniture, dark wood shutters, and stark white walls covered with splashy faux-Fauve paintings.

The two women had been friends in Chicago since grammar school, Diane living in a luxury penthouse on Lake Shore Drive and Sally in a shabby apartment four blocks inland. They went to Northwestern together, Diane living it up at the Tri-Delt sorority house and Sally, on scholarship, commuting to school from home and working Saturdays as a saleslady at Marshall Fields in Evanston. The difference in their financial situations never had been a problem in their relationship, simply an accepted fact.

Duane was Diane's second husband, her first marriage having lasted only seven months after a frightfully expensive wedding. She and Duane had eloped to Las Vegas rather than subject their friends to another round of marriage festivities. Duane was an affable drunk. Diane seemed contented with him. They decided early in their marriage not to have children, which might account for his affability and her contentment.

Sally was a whole other story. She had been madly in love with her husband, Wally, who probably would have looked very much like Cal had he lived long enough for his hair to turn white. But Wally died in an auto accident when he was thirty-two, which surprised no one since he drove like a maniac. He slammed into a concrete pillar on the freeway doing ninety-five miles an hour. He wasn't drunk. He wasn't on drugs. He simply was driving too fast and lost control. He left Sally with two young boys to raise and no money. Since she had a degree in English but no teaching credential, she taught in a private school while going to night classes and getting a Master's and a Doctorate and eventually she became a tenured Professor of English Literature at her alma mater.

Her boys now were grown and married, with children of their own. They adored their mother and thought she was quite perfect. Both were successful doctors and insisted on her retiring early. They sent her a generous monthly allowance to show their appreciation for all she had done for them—giving them happy childhoods, excellent private school educations and putting them through medical school.

Now Sally and Diane, both in their early fifties, were living next door to each other in San Miguel. And Sally was about to meet Cal. The dangerous man.

Diane had "a few close friends" in for cocktails to meet her cousin, forty-seven guests to be exact. Sally, living just across the garden, came in late because she changed her clothes four times, finally choosing a short-sleeved pale green dress with a low neckline that showed off her slim body and oversized breasts and went well with her long auburn hair. She entered the living room through one of the patio doors and slipped in among the other guests.

She recognized Cal at once, from Diane's description. He was at the far end of the room, wearing white shorts and a natty pale blue polo shirt, an attractive outfit that accentuated his bronze skin and sturdy legs and virile body. He was holding a glass of white wine and chatting up a blonde girl young enough to be his daughter, if not his granddaughter. He looked up suddenly and saw Sally staring at him. He left the blonde in mid-sentence and came over to Sally.

Every instinct told her to flee. But she stayed there and smiled at him when he reached her side and they both said, "Hi." She never had been so hypnotized by another person's eyes. She couldn't look away.

"You must be Sally," he said.

"Yes." All she could muster was a whisper.

He grinned. "Diane told me to stay away from you."

She smiled, still unable to speak.

He never took his dark eyes from hers. "So you're a widow."

She nodded.

"A merry one or a sad one?"

"It depends upon whom I'm with," she finally managed to speak. Their eyes still were linked. She tried again to look away, but couldn't.

"Diane told me you're an English professor. I see that you know your who's from your whom's. Even if you did end your sentence with a preposition."

"Actually, I taught English Lit. Not grammar. And you? What do you do for a living?"

"I used to be a stockbroker." He paused, then grinned. "Now I'm just broker."

She tried not to smile at his lame pun. "How long are you staying in San Miguel?"

"'Til Diane kicks me out. Then maybe you'll take me in?" He finally tore his eyes away from hers and looked down at her hands. "You don't have a drink! What would you like?"

She started toward the bar at the side of the room. "I'll get myself some white wine," she said.

He went with her. They waited quietly for the bartender to pour her wine, then Cal took her arm and guided her out to the terrace where they sat on a pair of white wicker chairs.

Their eyes came together again. "I can't wait to make love to you," he said.

She wanted to say something flip, to let him know she wasn't that easily seduced, but she realized her heart was racing and he probably would have seen the pulses jumping around in her neck if his eyes hadn't been glued to her eyes.

"Diane said you've been a widow for more than twenty years."

She nodded.

"Did you ever consider getting married again?"

"No," she said. "I like being free to make love with anyone I want."

He flinched, then smiled. "Diane's been telling you stories about me."

"A few."

"I mean, Sally, that's *my* line."

"I know. But you don't have an exclusive on it." She got up and started for the living room.

"Wait!" He blocked her way back into the house. "Can I see you later? After the party?"

"I don't know. Diane might have other plans for you."

Unexpectedly, he pulled her close. She trembled at his touch, at his lips' pressure on hers and his muscular body fusing into the softness of hers. "Later?" he said huskily.

She didn't agree or disagree. She simply walked away from him.

Sally spent the rest of the party chatting with friends but she always was aware of where Cal was in the room and with whom he was talking. Her entire body was attuned to his, and she could tell from the way he kept watching her that he was alert to every move she made, as though they were the only two people who mattered to each other in the crowded room. Sally felt she had been infected with a hazardous virus called desire and her entire system—body, mind and soul—were in a turmoil to fight it off.

Diane came up to her and whispered, "Stay after the others go."

Sally knew she should flee. Cal is a dangerous man, she kept repeating to herself. He was a threat to her hard-won serenity. She was enjoying life now, after years of bitter grief and anger with Wally for having killed himself. So far she had managed her widowhood sensibly. She never had met anyone she wanted to marry, but the affairs she had had over the years were mostly pleasant ones with kind, responsible men. She never had lived with any of them. The relationships had lasted anywhere from one to four years, and ended amicably. Always at the outset she told the men that she was not interested in marrying again. Some of the men had pressed her to change her mind, and she had to admit that the wealthy ones had been tempting, but she preferred to live alone with modest means than with a rich man she didn't love. Being "in like" was not enough.

Her feelings for Cal were a throwback to the way she had felt about Wally: the instant, overwhelming, heart-stopping physical attraction and the hypnotic eye contact. But she and Wally had been young and he had loved her as intensely as she had loved him. She never had worried that he would love her and leave her, as Cal certainly would. But Wally *had* left her, in the stupidest, most permanent way possible. Even now, after twenty years, she still hadn't forgiven him for carelessly ruining her life and depriving their sons of all the love he would have given them had he lived.

Suddenly her fear of Cal overwhelmed her. She knew she would be unable to resist him. As soon as they were alone together, they would make the kind of love that women dream of and seldom find. But in the end, she would fall in love with him and eventually he would want his damn freedom, and she would be left badly wounded. She couldn't face that.

When Cal went into the kitchen to help Diane bring out more hors d'oeuvres, Sally slipped out of the house as quietly as she had entered it. She ran to her guest house and threw a few clothes and toiletries into a bag and rushed out to her Toyota Prius. She sped away from her house in a mad tire-squealing rush that reminded her of the way Wally used to drive. Her heart was pounding as though a posse were chasing her, but the road behind her was empty. She had made a successful getaway, yet she felt a great sense of loss.

She was out on the highway going south from San Miguel before she realized that she had no idea of where she was going. She went through a mental list of friends in other Mexican places and decided to visit Wally's sister Becky who was married to a Mexican artist and lived in Mexico City. It was a three hour drive. Sally fished her cell phone from her purse and called Becky to make sure she was home and unencumbered with other guests. Then she phoned Diane.

"I'm driving to Mexico City," she told her.

"Why on earth…we wondered where you'd disappeared to. Cal was devastated when he realized you'd left."

"Diane, I just couldn't…I can't handle him."

"Cal? But…"

"I know I can't resist him. And I know it would lead to disaster."

"Oh come on, Sal, he's not that bad."

"Oh no, he's not bad at all. He's too damn *good*. Diane, I can't afford to be hurt."

"What makes you think he'll hurt you?"

Sally sighed. "You told me yourself what he's like. Love 'em and leave 'em. If I fell in love with him, I'd be miserable knowing that eventually he'd leave me."

It was Diane's turn to sigh. "He's the miserable one right now, Sal. He's inconsolable. He just can't believe you left."

"Tell him it was an emergency. And Diane, please don't tell him I've gone to Becky's or where she lives. Tell him it was…tell him I have a sick friend in Guadalajara. And Diane, call me at Becky's when he leaves."

"He's liable to stay all year, waiting for you."

"Then kick him out next week. I can only stand Becky for so long."

Cal phoned her at Becky's the next morning. "Shall I come down there? Or are you coming back here?"

"No. Please. I don't want to see you."

"Believe me, Sally, my intentions are entirely honorable."

"How'd you get my number here?" she demanded, furious with Diane, yet thrilled to hear Cal's voice.

"I charmed it out of Diane," he said. "I've got Becky's address too, so you might as well come home. Or I'll borrow one of Diane's cars and be there before lunch."

"I won't be here."

"Really? Where are you going now?"

"I don't know. Acapulco. Or Merida."

"Sally. Don't make me chase you all over Mexico. Come on home and we'll deal with each other like adults." When she failed to reply he said, "So? Are you coming home?"

She sighed, defeated and elated. "I'll be there before dinner."

"It's a date," he said.

He had dinner waiting when she reached her guest house. He had made Thai shrimp lettuce rolls, chicken mole, sautéed mushroom-polenta pancakes, garlic roasted asparagus, and flan for dessert. And he had left her kitchen immaculate.

"Diane gave me the key," he explained, helping her off with her jacket and hanging it in the coat closet. He made no effort to kiss her even though she had spent the entire three-hour drive trying to figure out how to avoid falling into bed with him the minute she came through the door.

They sat on her private patio drinking martinis with the shrimp rolls. She was very hungry and she realized that she had been so agitated over Cal that she had forgotten to eat all day. Their conversation flowed effortlessly. Again, they seemed unable to stop staring into each other's eyes, except for momentarily looking down at the food. They talked about travel: she explained why Paris was her favorite place, and he felt Rome deserved that honor with its ancient, medieval and Renaissance sites so deliciously woven into the texture of the modern city, but they both agreed that London was probably the most civilized city in the world. New York was a close second.

They talked about food. And about the joys of parenthood and being grandparents—he had four, she had only three. About politics; they both were liberal—she defined it as favoring reform and progress and individual freedom and he concurred—but he was not quite the bleeding heart that she was. They talked about life styles, his being rather reckless and hers being on the safe side, although her willingness to live outside the States made her a bit more adventuresome than most Americans. They talked and talked and stared into each other's eyes and managed to eat the entire exquisite dinner without ever stopping their talking and staring.

When they finished the flan and coffee, he drew her out of her dining room chair and greedily kissed her. She felt faint with desire for him and was about to lead him to her bedroom when he looked at his watch. He told her he was leaving San Miguel in an hour and had to pack. "I'm flying to San Diego tonight with the Addis's, on their jet," he explained. "They invited me last night, after the party. We're taking their yacht to the Galapagos for a month, and maybe the Peruvian coast. But I'll come back here afterwards."

Sally went into shock, but she didn't show it. How could he choose to leave her when she was ready to go to bed with him? It was like a vicious slap to her face. Because he *chose* to leave. He didn't *have* to go. The Addis's wouldn't have cared that much if he changed his mind. So why was she so surprised? She'd known all along what a selfish man he was.

She had a whole month to get over him. The only antidote to Cal was another man. A more suitable man. A man who wasn't dangerous. But where to find him? San Miguel was crawling with single men—Americans mostly, some Brits, and of course wealthy Mexicans. But it was no accident that the English-language newspaper had an entire page of AA and Alenon meetings. Drinking started early in the day and lasted well beyond midnight. She couldn't believe how many alcoholics she and Diane knew.

Sometimes it seemed to Sally that living there was one long party. Day after day she met various people for long, late lunches featuring more margaritas and martinis than food. Then there were cocktail parties. And late dinners with wine and beer and after dinner drinks and drinking and drinking on into the night. Sally had been to more parties this past year than all the rest of her life put together.

Sometimes just standing in line at the food market and speaking English, she would get invited by the people standing behind her to a brunch or a dinner. Jaded and partied out, many of the American and British expatriates constantly were on the lookout for attractive new faces to join their festivities. And if she accepted such invitations from those strangers, she'd get half a dozen more from the other guests when she attended the brunch or the dinner. Sally was unaccustomed to such goings-on. She had had to work hard after Wally died. While the boys were young and she was teaching and going to graduate school, she'd had little time for a social life.

She had trouble with the drinking. If she drank more than two glasses of wine, or two martinis or margaritas, she threw up. It was like an inner monitor. She had learned how to make a glass of wine last for an hour with the tiniest sips imaginable. She also had a secret pact with all the local bartenders to make her a gin and tonic without the gin because everybody here assumed she was in AA if they heard her order a soft drink or juice.

She reviewed in her mind the four men she had dated since coming to San Miguel. She hadn't gone to bed with any of them because all of them had had too many flaws. Multiple divorces were always a red flag. So was bragging about their wealth. So was ignorance about any subject beyond their occupations, or their former work if they were retired. So was being a right wing Republican, though she might be tolerant enough to accept a moderate one if he were charming enough. And although she knew it sounded shallow and petty, she had a strong aversion to men with beards or even mustaches. None of the men she knew were as attractive and virile as Cal.

Driven by her fear of Cal, she began to search for a safe man. She went to bars, sometimes with Diane, sometimes alone. She didn't tell Diane what she was doing. She only told her she was restless.

"So I guess you and Cal didn't hit it off after all?" Diane asked.

"I guess not," Sally said.

"It's just as well," Diane said. "You scared me to death when you ran off to Becky's. What were you afraid of?"

"Oh, I don't know," Sally said wearily. "He just struck me as a dangerous man."

Diane shook her head. "He's harmless."

"That's what I finally realized," Sally lied. "Good riddance," she further lied.

A week after Cal's departure, Sally and Diane had lunch in the bougainvillea-filled patio of the Sierra Nevada Hotel. Sally's appetite had been badly damaged by Cal's abandonment. She picked at the chicken asada in front of her and sipped a margarita. One of her former boyfriends, Dr. Mark Robbins, was at the next table with two much older men. She waved at him and he came over and kissed her cheek.

"How about taking me to dinner tonight?" she said, forcing a flirtatious smile that did not come naturally.

"Love to!" Delighted, he leaned over and kissed Diane's cheek too. They had been friends for years.

"What time? And where?" he asked Sally.

"You decide," she said.

He thought a moment. "I'll pick you up at eight-thirty. As for where we'll go...let me surprise you."

After he returned to his table, Diane raised her eyebrows in an unspoken question.

Sally shrugged. "He's really very nice."

Mark Robbins was a retired cardiologist and a widower. He had one of the loveliest house in San Miguel and a penthouse apartment on New York's Central Park West. Sally had rejected him earlier in the year, after three dates, because she had found him conceited. A bragger. But, she now decided, maybe she'd been unfair. Maybe he had a lot to brag about. Maybe he had tried too hard to impress her. Maybe underneath all the boasting was a sensitive, shy person.

She would give him another chance. She decided she would go to bed with him. Maybe he would surprise her and be an even better lover than she imagined Cal to be. But she was only too well aware that she felt not a drop of the heart-stopping desire for Mark that she 'd felt for Cal the moment she saw him.

The evening proved to be far, far better than she had anticipated. Instead of taking her to a restaurant, Mark's surprise turned out to be dinner at the exotic home of one of the most interesting couples in San Miguel, a much prized invitation eagerly sought by all the town's "in" people. The estate was on a hill, on the outskirts of town, one of the oldest haciendas in the city. The owners had retained the classic Colonial architecture: thick walls, arched windows and a deep colonnaded galleria surrounding the building.

The house was furnished traditionally, but with the most

unexpectedly eclectic art imaginable. Two pale blue Della Robia bas reliefs of the Madonna bracketed one of Father Bill Moore's colorful abstracts. A two-story red Chihuly was hung in a sedate paneled library. Three of Tom Holland's enamel on metal sculptures surrounded a traditional lotus-leaf fountain in the entry courtyard. A circle of Max Fleisher's vivacious dancers pranced endlessly on the dining room's fireplace hearth.

And it worked! The house's dual artistic personality had a merry ambiance that was a fitting background for its owners, Phillipe Bartel and Rollo Grimaldi. The two men, who always entertained in identical white satin tuxedos with royal-blue bow ties, were as unlike as two men could be. Phillipe, a tall, slender patrician, had been a Shakespearean actor in Paris. Rollo, short, fat and bald, had been a successful stand-up comic in New York and had had his own television comedy series for seven years. Both had ribald, rollicking personalities. They tried to shock their guests in French, Italian, German, Spanish and English. Their staff members were all male; rumors abounded that the walled estate was the scene of wild homoerotic orgies.

Sally had a wonderful time. The other four guests were people she knew and liked. Mark was a gentle and attentive companion. Not a word of braggadocio passed his lips. When their hosts brought out an excellent trio for dancing—piano, guitar and drums—Sally was surprised to find that Mark was a strong leader with a great sense of rhythm. The spirited dancing, combined with the wine she had drunk, created a pleasant stir of desire in her.

In bed later, she felt a moment of panic. Gone was the mild desire she had felt for Mark on the dance floor. Now, when it mattered, she felt nothing. Then she flashed onto the way she had reacted to Cal's kiss, and suddenly Mark's body became Cal's and she zoomed into high gear and she came almost at once.

The experience left her utterly confused.

She saw Mark every night for the next two weeks. Since they enjoyed dancing with each other, they looked for every opportunity to do so. They made love every night too. Unfortunately, Sally found that unless she imagined that Mark was Cal, she couldn't enjoy sex with him. Since Mark could manage only one orgasm a night, he always went home soon afterwards. Then for hours Sally would fitfully doze and feverishly awaken, imagining that Cal was embracing her.

When Diane told her that Cal was returning in three days, Sally once more panicked. She suggested to Mark that they go down to the Yucatan for a while. She never had seen the Mayan ruins. Neither had he. They left in his Mercedes the next day.

Sally was becoming exceedingly fond of Mark. He was kind and considerate, generous and quick-witted. She flirted with the idea of marrying him. She always had wanted to spend more time in New York, and she loved his house in San Miguel. She knew they could have a very congenial life together. He loved to travel and he traveled First Class, something she never could afford to do. He talked about spending their honeymoon that summer driving through France, staying at four-star *Relais et Chateau* hotels. The only drawback was that she would have to spend the rest of her life imagining that Mark was Cal whenever they made love.

Driving back to San Miguel after two weeks down south, Sally grew more and more apprehensive the closer they came to their destination. It was after midnight when they reached her guest house. She wanted Mark to spend the night with her to show Cal that she no longer was available, that she was finished with him, but Mark was coming down with a bad cold and he just wanted to get home, have some hot chicken soup, and go to bed.

"Please stay here," Sally said, on the verge of panic. "Let me take care of you."

"I'm a bear when I'm sick," Mark protested. "I don't want you to see me like that."

He insisted on dropping her at her guest house gate. As he drove away, she had a panic attack, but she was too tired to run away again, so she went to bed.

Cal came over the next morning while she was having coffee and fruit salad on her patio. She loved the way he looked—the thick white hair that made her long to run her fingers through it, those dark eyes that hypnotized her, his sensuous lips that kissed so beautifully. Again, he was wearing white shorts and a pale blue polo shirt. She couldn't help comparing his virile body to Mark's overweight, flabby one. She looked away quickly.

"Coffee?" she offered, indicating the carafe on the table, not letting her eyes find his.

He shook his head and sat down across from her. "Did you enjoy the Yucatan?" he asked politely.

"Very much. Did you enjoy the Galapagos?"

"Yes. Well, no." He paused and looked at her, and their eyes, once caught, locked. "Remember how you got frightened and ran off to Mexico City, the first time we met?"

She nodded.

"Well, that's what I did. After that dinner together, Sally, I panicked. I couldn't handle what I was feeling for you. I wanted to grab you and marry you, but I have to admit, I was more terrified of losing my freedom. Still, after sitting on that damn yacht for a month and staring at the ocean, I realized you were worth it."

"So I'm supposed to melt in gratitude and fall into your arms now?"

He smiled. "That's the idea."

"Well, you're too late. I'm marrying someone else." She couldn't keep the triumph from her voice.

"Diane told me about him. Nice, safe Dr. Mark Robbins who will never break your heart. Who can give you every little thing your heart desires."

"I couldn't have put it better myself," she said.

"Is he good in bed, Sally?"

She didn't reply.

"So if you marry the good doctor, he'll support you, right? In the style to which you'd like to become accustomed?"

"Yes, I assume so."

"But if you'd marry me, you'd probably have to support me. Right?"

"Well, since I'm not going to marry you, there's no point..."

"I said IF."

"Not unless you went back to work."

"As a stockbroker? Never! Not even for you. But tell me, why does the man always have to support the woman?"

"Well, in my case, since my sons support me, I'm not sure they'd appreciate being your sugar daddies too."

"Not even if it made their mother happy?"

"It's not going to happen, Cal."

She wanted to end the conversation but she was afraid that if she stood up he would grab her and kiss her and all her resolve would dissolve. She remained seated and poured herself another cup of coffee. "I still don't understand why you panicked, Cal. Why couldn't we discuss it before you went running off for a month?"

He stared at her. "Why are you so angry with me, Sally? Because I love you?"

"Because you've already caused me enough grief, and until this morning I've only seen you twice in my life!"

"God, Sally, it seems like I've known you forever. Why don't you stop fighting me? Let's go to bed."

She slowly shook her head. "Did you ever hear me say that I love you? Did you?"

"Not in words. I can see it in your eyes."

"Well, I *don't* love you. And I never will. I'm going to marry Mark, and that's final!" She stood up and marched into her house and slammed the door. Telling a lie was so difficult for her! Of course she loved Cal. She fell onto her bed and wondered why she was being so cruel to him, and to herself, denying both of them the incredible pleasure that the two of them—together—undoubtedly would generate.

A slammed door is not necessarily a locked door. He followed her into the house and sat next to where she was lying on her bed. He took her hand. "I know you're afraid of loving me," he said. "And I don't blame you. My track record in the responsibility department is pretty dismal. All I have is a small allowance because my sweet ex-wife feels sorry for me and sends it to me. Sally, I have nothing to offer you. Just my love." He sighed. "I guess that's not enough."

She sat up. He still was holding her hand and she looked into his dark, dark eyes. She felt he was trying to drag her down to his immature level. If she let him, the two of them might have to live as irresponsibly as he had been doing on his own. What would they do? Mooch as a couple? Let others take care of them because they were good-looking and charming? What would happen when they were old and had ailments and no longer amused their hosts? No, no, no, she couldn't live that way.

On the other hand, she could marry him and take care of him, as one would take care of a child, which he was. A selfish, spoiled child with a beautiful, adult body. Did she really want that?

There was a third way. They could have a fantastic affair—in the true sense of the word: a fantasy—and when it finally petered out, as it undoubtedly would in time, when the novelty wore off, he would leave her for younger, firmer flesh and she would be sad, but not damaged, because she never would have harbored any unrealistic expectations of permanency. And then, if she still wanted to, she could marry someone like Mark. Because if she chose this path, she would have to give up this particular Mark—dear, kind Dr. Mark Robbins—along with his penthouse overlooking Central Park and his stunning San Miguel house, and the First Class trip to France this summer. Plus, she was taking the chance of never finding another Mark as appealing as this one.

So be it, she told herself. I'll take my chances. Because she knew that if she walked away from Cal, she would regret it for the rest of her life.

She caressed Cal's cheek with her free hand, ran her fingers through his beautiful hair, then she kissed him lightly on his lips. "All right," she said.

"All right *what?* Is that a 'yes' or a 'no?'"

"It's a 'let's see.'" She kissed him again and he let go of her hand and put his arms around her. They lay down together, still kissing, both of them, at that moment, happier than either of them ever had been in their lives.

An Encounter in Rome

Marilyn did not expect to see Scott Wells when she went to Rome by herself. He wasn't on the list of people she knew when she and Lew and their two daughters had lived there, seven years earlier, because last she'd heard, Scott and Kathy and their two daughters had returned to Texas. "Well, you're half-right," Scott said ruefully after they recognized each other at the top of the Spanish Steps. "Kathy left me—took our girls, went back to Dallas. Married a dentist there."

Marilyn remembered Kathy's disgruntlement at being forced to live among all these "foreigners." She never recovered from the culture shock. She'd had screaming rages when her Italian appliances broke down and repairmen failed to show up as promised, or when people rudely shoved past her in a shop. Kathy had tried to duplicate her upper-middle-class Texas lifestyle with three bridge games a week and frequent dinner parties, socializing only with other Americans and refusing to learn Italian.

"So you're still living here?" Marilyn asked.

"Me?" He grinned. "Nope. Living in Cannes now. And hey! I'm a newlywed! Married a French woman three months ago. A widow. Marie-Monique." Scott shook his head sadly. "Damn shame. Lost her husband and two boys last year. Auto accident. Up on the Corniche. Same spot where Grace Kelly lost control."

Marilyn remembered Scott's choppy manner of speech. Short sentences. To the point. No nonsense. They had been friends as couples—she and Lew, Scott and Kathy, always a foursome, and what a high-spirited, good looking group they had been, all of them in their early thirties then, all of them healthy and fun-loving. Dinners at all the best restaurants, dancing at night clubs, Sunday picnics up north of Rome searching for Etruscan tombs with their four girls—the kids knew each other at Overseas School. They were all crazy about Etruscan art and they made frequent visits to the Etruscan museum at the Villa Giullia. Both families had spent a weekend together in Tarquinia tramping through the tombs, so they considered themselves semi-experts on the subject.

Seeing Scott reminded Marilyn of that amazing Sunday when they actually found a tomb in a farmer's field—tipped off by the telltale mound. They dug down three feet and discovered a lintel and a wall made of the same big earthen bricks the Etruscans used to build their tombs at Tarquinia. The eight of them had taken turns with a small folding shovel that Lew kept in their station wagon, digging a trench about fifteen feet long. But when Scott and Lew tried to move several of the bricks—and they were both big, strong guys—they couldn't budge them. They had hoped to get a good look into the tomb and see if there was any loot, like pottery or statues.

Bitterly disappointed, all they could do was take some photos of their find—one of the Wells family standing around the ditch, and one of Marilyn and Lew and their girls—then shovel back the dirt and forget about it. Marilyn still had the pictures in her photo album.

"So...d'you like living in France?" Marilyn asked as she and Scott continued down the Spanish Steps. As always in Rome, she was passionately aware of the clarity of the light, especially at that hour, at sunset, when the ochre walls glowed like pure gold. The radiance made her feel buoyant, as though she were lit from within. Scott took her arm and they walked along the crowded via Condotti.

"Cannes is great," Scott said. "But I miss Rome. Terribly."

"So do I."

He gave her a puzzled look. "So where's...what's his name? Lew?"

"In London. I'm flying there tomorrow morning, then we'll go home together next week."

"I'm leaving tomorrow too," he said. "By train." They both stopped to stare into a shop window featuring a fake fur coat dyed crimson. "So where *is* home now?" he asked her as they continued strolling.

"Well, since we left Rome seven years ago, we've lived in Paris, Barcelona, Mexico City, and now—would you believe it? — Burlington, Vermont."

"Why there of all places?"

"Lew inherited a big house on the lake. But we still travel a lot."

Scott absorbed all this. Marilyn could see the concentration in his eyes as she mentioned each place. "Your girls didn't mind?" he asked. "All that moving around?"

"No, they loved it. They're both at Yale now."

"Yeah? Penny and Karen are at Stanford." He stared at her a moment, and she remembered his flattering way of giving a person his full attention during a conversation. He hadn't changed at all in seven years—he still had a lot of shaggy light brown hair and lazy-looking gray eyes. He always gave the impression of being utterly relaxed. "So…what're you doing here by yourself?" he asked.

"Research. For a novel on expats."

"Yeah, I remember now. You and old Lew're both writers. What's the novel about?"

"Three American women who rent a villa in Fregene for the summer, without their husbands, and all three have a secret affair with their Italian landlord."

"Autobiographical?"

She laughed. "I never had an attractive landlord. But my book is about more than romantic hi-jinx. It also explores how feminism has changed relationships."

"I promise, I'll buy ten copies when it comes out."

"And you, Scott? If you're living in Cannes now, what're you doing in Rome?"

"My company's main office is here. I come down once a month for meetings."

She tried to remember what kind of company he worked for. Biotech? Electronics? "Is your new wife here with you?"

He shook his head. "Marie-Monique's pregnant. Hates to travel."

"So you'll have a whole new family!" Marilyn tried to sound enthusiastic, but the idea appalled her. She'd been so thankful when her daughters left for college. Not that she didn't love them or miss them, but she had grown tired of the day-to-day demands they made on her time.

He stopped walking and faced her. "Listen, I'm going to a party tonight. Embassy friends. Wanna be my date?"

She remembered State Department parties. Noisy, but sometimes interesting. Everyone had just come from some place like Islamabad or was being reassigned to Oslo or Cairo or Lima. Most of them shared the intellectual restlessness of the expatriates she knew, the same searching for new experiences and new people and new ideas that had animated the decision she and Lew made, early in their marriage, to live in different parts of the world.

"Sure, I'd love to," she said. She had planned to have dinner at her hotel and get to bed early, but a party sounded like a better idea. She saw that Scott was wearing a dark blue suit, a white dress shirt and an expensive-looking blue tie. She looked down at the simple green silk sheath and blazer she was wearing. "Am I dressed all right?"

He squeezed her arm. "You look great." He paused, then added softly, "You always did."

She smiled and was reminded that she and Scott had had an undercurrent of attraction for each other. It started early in their friendship when the four of them went to a night club for Mardi Gras and she and Scott danced several numbers together, but in the four years both families lived in Rome, they never acknowledge it beyond a few intense eye contacts, and dancing with each other whenever they had the chance.

"This street is so full of memories." She nodded at a men's shop they were passing. "I remember buying Lew a white cashmere sweater there one Christmas…way too expensive, but *lira* always seems like play money to me." She sighed, suddenly singed with regret. "God, I loved living here! More than anywhere else."

"So did I. But managing the Cannes office was a big promotion for me. I can't remember now…why did you leave?"

She shrugged. "Lew got restless. I wanted to stay here for the rest of my life."

The sky had darkened and the street lamps came on. Shop windows suddenly were flooded with light. Scott and Marilyn continued strolling at a comfortable pace. He still was holding her arm.

"Where's the party?" she asked.

"Near the Piazza Venezia." He stopped walking. "Is that too far? We could grab a taxi…"

She shook her head. "I love walking in Rome."

They turned south onto the Corso and passed the dark stone bulk of Marilyn's old bank and then her favorite lighting store whose windows were vibrant with oddly shaped lamps in bold primary colors. They stopped at a coffee bar for espresso. Sitting at a tiny outdoor metal table, knees touching, she felt strangely exhilarated, as though she no longer were herself. Not that she was anyone else either. She had a wonderfully free feeling of having floated to a new dimension.

He took her hand and held it. His was warm, sending a ripple of titillation through her. Uneasily, she wondered if he expected them to end up in bed together. During twenty-one years of marriage, she never had been unfaithful to her sweet, darling Lew and she had no intention of starting now. Still, when Scott let go of her hand, she felt a pang of disappointment.

She noticed an exquisite white-haired woman sitting at the next table. The woman's hair sat in soft waves around a face dominated by startlingly large lilac eyes. She wore a lavender silk suit that perfectly matched her eyes, I wonder if I'll look that good when I'm older, Marilyn worried. Intellectually, she felt that one's character traits were far more important than one's appearance, yet emotionally she couldn't let go of the need to be judged a pretty woman.

She quickly glanced over at Scott to see if he had sensed her foolish reverie but he seemed deeply immersed in his own musings. She suspected that momentarily they had been far apart, as though their brief period of dual introspection had disrupted the empathy they had experienced during their walk, but then Scott grinned at her—an "isn't-life-wonderful" endearing sort of smile—and their bond was restored.

The party was in a penthouse with a wrap-around terrace overlooking, on one side, the brightness of the Piazza Venezia with its huge white "wedding cake" of a building and the amber-lit Campodoglio behind it, and on the other side a view of St. Peter's dome and the Janiculum Hill across the river. Marilyn hung onto Scott's arm with one hand and sipped from a glass of *pino grigio* in her other hand. They were surrounded by a cacophony of Italian, English, French and German babbling.

Marilyn pointed up at the Janiculum Hill. "We used to take the girls there a half-hour before midnight, on New Year's Eve. We'd watch the fireworks—it looked like the whole city was under bombardment. Then at midnight, the church bells all bonged at once. It was thrilling."

"Yeah, remember how afterwards everyone threw their old dishes and glasses out the windows?"

"It was one Italian custom we adored. Did you do it?"

He laughed. "Sure. Around October, the girls and I started saving up stuff we didn't want. Kathy thought it was silly."

"I couldn't believe how their street cleaning machines came out early on New Year's Day and swept it all up. By noon, you'd never know it happened."

He nodded. "I guess it's symbolic—you know, getting rid of the old stuff in your life and starting fresh in the new year."

They circulated around the terrace as Scott greeted people and introduced her to them until the crowd was a big blur of smiling, laughing, open-mouthed, rapidly-talking faces. After all her years of living as an expatriate, she considered herself pretty adept at recognizing people's nationalities. The Italians had a go-fuck-yourself look. The French had a self-satisfied look (though she loved the way Frenchmen conveyed a flash of admiration and *I'd love to make love to you* in a passing glance). She could spot the harnessed, fastidious, thank-God-I'm-British look a block away. She always felt that the Germans looked more American than the Americans did, except that the Germans usually had better posture. This little guessing game kept her amused at big parties when the screaming noise level knocked out any possibility of coherent conversation.

Scott led her to a quiet corner behind a row of potted yews. "How're you doing?" he asked softly. She was afraid he was going to kiss her and then she felt let down when he didn't. Instead he took her empty glass. "Wait here," he said. He walked off and came back a few minutes later with two fresh glasses of wine. "I just talked to our host—we're going to Passetti's later for dinner," he said.

"Just us?"

"Us and about two dozen others."

They wandered inside the penthouse which was even more crowded than the terrace. A long table laden with tantalizing *antipasti* stood at one end of the living room but the surging crowd around it reminded Marilyn of a feeding frenzy of vultures she'd once seen in Egypt devouring road-kill. Scott looked over at the table and raised his eyebrows questioningly at her. She shook her head and he smiled in agreement.

She felt like she was in a trance, being led by Scott from one elaborate frescoed groin-ceilinged room to another, stopping to admire the tapestried walls, nodding at people he knew and stopping here and there to attempt a few words of conversation. The sound level had grown to an impossible roar but still they roamed, inside, then back outside, then finally down the elevator and out onto the street whose normally loud traffic noise seemed like the most blessed silence.

"I don't know why I bother," Scott said. He gestured up at the penthouse. "I hate these big parties! But I always go."

"They sound like they'll be more fun than they actually are."

"They're barbaric!" He started to take her arm, then reached down and took her hand instead.

"Do we have to go to Passetti's?" she blurted, tired of crowds.

"They'll never notice if we don't show up." He squeezed her hand. "How about going somewhere quiet?"

She nodded and, still holding hands, they walked through the narrow, historic streets leading to the river. "Scott, remember when we all went to the Boca de Verita statue with the girls, and you explained that we each should put a hand into the statue's open mouth?"

"Ah, yes, and I told you that the Mouth of Truth would bite you if you'd ever told a lie?"

"But then, after the rest of us nervously did it, you refused to put your own hand into it!"

"You're damn right. And I still wouldn't!" he said firmly.

"I can't believe you're so superstitious!"

"You're such a goody-goody, you probably never told a lie in your life."

She stopped walking. "Is that what you think of me? That I'm a goody-goody? Whatever that means?"

"It came out all wrong," he apologized. "I think you're a good person. A kind person."

"Thanks. But I still don't understand how you can be afraid of a statue. How could it possibly bite you?"

"I know it's irrational. I'm just an old scaredy-cat."

When they reached the river they stood together at the parapet, looking down at the water. Again, she thought he was going to kiss her, and again she was chagrined when he didn't. Well, why don't you kiss him? the wine she had drunk and her feminist self taunted her. But she didn't want to start something she was unwilling to finish.

They crossed the river on the ancient Ponte Sisto to Trastevere and through a maze of narrow streets. He pointed out a long one-story stone building set into a hillside and told her that generations of artists, mostly sculptors, had been working there for many centuries. She showed him a seventeenth century palazzo that had been gutted so that only the original exterior remained but the inside apartments were totally modern and she knew this because a friend of hers lived there. Finally Scott found the trattoria that he said was his very favorite in all of Rome. When they were seated at an outdoor table,

Scott waved off the menu that the waiter offered. "I know their specialties by heart," he told Marilyn. "D'you trust me to order?"

Marilyn nodded. "I can't think of one Italian dish I don't like."

He chose asparagus and gorgonzola wrapped in prosciutto, deep-fried artichokes, spinach cannelloni, and veal chops with caramelized onion and porcini mushrooms, all of which they washed down with frascati and chianti. The alcohol and the delicious silence around them lubricated their conversation as they each spoke of their early years, hers in Boston with summers on Martha's Vineyard in her grandparent's big house on East Chop, and his in Houston with summers in Galvaston in a beach house on stilts—built that way, he explained, because a hurricane in the early 1900's washed away half the city. They talked fondly about their scattered siblings —her brother in Phoenix and her sister in New York, his two older brothers, one living in Hong Kong, the other in Denver—yet all of them close in spirit, if not geographically.

Marilyn noticed that his language was less choppy when he spoke of subjects that were meaningful to him. His eyes glowed when he talked about his daughters. He visited them often and the girls flew to Europe for most of their holidays, sometimes meeting him in places like Gstaad where they could ski in winter, or sailing on Lake Como or on the Turkish Coast in summer. He let them take turns choosing the destinations.

He spoke briefly of his parting from Kathy. "It was very painful, at least for me," he said. "I still cared for her, God knows why. I mean, looking back, I realize that Kath just wasn't a very loving person. Now I can't even remember what it was that I loved about her."

"I think we all have a love quotient, just like an intelligent quotient. L.Q. and I.Q." Marilyn paused, thoughtfully. "I don't know if we're taught how to love, or maybe we're born with it, but not everyone knows how."

She remembered walking down the Corso with Kathy one September afternoon when they had decided to shop together. Kathy had worn a tight black mini-skirt and a green silk blouse that she left unbuttoned to her waist. She wore no bra. Men walking toward them had stared at Kathy's half-exposed breasts; some leered, some said, "Buon giorno?" with a lilt of invitation in their voices.

"Look at them!" Kathy had complained. "Fucking assholes."

Marilyn had wanted to say, *Kathy, you're asking for it!* But she'd held back.

"I hate them!" Kathy had raged. "I hate this place!"

The two women had been walking past a small courtyard smothered in greenery. An amber niche held a small white marble statue of The Three Graces. "Look, Kathy!" Marilyn had said. "Doesn't that make up for it all?"

And Kathy had cried, "No! No it doesn't!" Refusing to look at it, refusing to let herself see it.

Marilyn didn't tell Scott about her recollection, but she felt a sudden burst of pity for Kathy. And for Scott, too, for having loved her.

"So tell me," Scott said. "Do you miss being an expat?"

"Oh God yes," Marilyn replied. "I mean, Vermont's beautiful and all that, but I hope Lew decides to come back and live in Europe soon."

Scott frowned.

"Oh, I know what you're thinking," she said. "You're wondering how a liberated woman like me lets her husband make an important decision like where to live."

He nodded. "Yeah. Exactly. How come?"

"Oh Scott, it's a long story." She sighed. "Y'know, when you first get married, you're young, so you give in when there's a difference of opinion, because all you want is to make the other one happy. At least I did. And after a while, it becomes a habit. So if I started being the pushy one now, after twenty years..." She shrugged. "I'm okay with it. We have a wonderful life, Lew and I. So why upset the apple cart?"

"I'm no expert, Marilyn. Hell, I couldn't even save my own marriage when Kathy wanted out. But I can't help thinking that you must have a lot of suppressed resentment against Lew. That can't be very healthy."

"I'm happy, Scott. Really." They both were silent until Marilyn asked, "Think you'll ever want to live in the States again?"

"No. But don't get me wrong. I still love being an American. But I'm just too curious—there's so much to *see* here!"

"I know what you mean, Seeing great paintings and sculptures and architecture every day jazzes up my creative juices. I write better when I'm here."

"Maybe it's irresponsible," he said, "but you know how at home, you feel like you *ought* to raise money for charity? Or you *ought* to attend committee meetings? Or join the PTA? Stuff like that?"

"Here, nobody bothers you," Marilyn added.

"I love the way you can re-invent yourself," Scott chuckled. "If you want to pass yourself off as a Harvard professor, or maybe a Hollywood big-shot, who's going to check up on you?"

Scott finished the last of his veal. *"Dolce?"* he asked when they leaned back in their seats, stuffed with all the beguiling food he had ordered.

"I'm not a dessert person," she said rather primly. "But don't let that stop you."

He shook his head.

Marilyn glanced over at the couple occupying the table behind them because they were arguing in English, obviously American, both of them florid, overweight and overdressed. The woman got up and said, "Fuck you! I'm going to the can," and she flounced into the restaurant. The man noticed that Marilyn was watching them. It was a bad habit of hers, eavesdropping.

He got up and started to follow the woman into the restaurant. "I fed the fat cow," he growled to Scott, "now she damn well better milk me!"

After the man went inside, Marilyn and Scott looked at each other, not knowing if it was funny or sad. "Ugly Americans or what!" Scott said.

"Ugly people," Marilyn agreed.

Scott reached into his pocket and gave Marilyn his business card. "Here. If you ever feel like sending me a Christmas card."

She took her own card from her purse and handed it to him. "Sure. Let's stay in touch."

"If I send you a postcard, will Lew mind?"

"He never looks at the mail. I sort it and give him anything he needs to see."

Scott slowly shook his head. "You didn't answer my question, Marilyn. *Would he mind?"*

She shrugged. "Why should he? We're all old friends." But she knew Lew would mind if he knew about this special warmth she was feeling for Scott. And she also knew that if any mail ever did arrive from Scott, she definitely would not show it to Lew.

They sat there quietly, again holding hands while the waiter cleared the table. Finally, Scott signaled for the check. "It's getting late," he said.

She looked at her watch. One in the morning. She felt a wave of disappointment that time had rushed by so swiftly. But she also was swamped with a deep contentment, as though her soul were glowing, as if being there with Scott was what she had been waiting for all her life.

She looked around the café terrace: only one other couple remained. The street was quiet except for a Vespa slowly putt-putting past. Despite the cocoon of beatitude that had enveloped her, she was conscious of a stabbing pain at the thought of leaving Rome tomorrow. She remembered how, as a child, she had hated to leave the Vineyard at the end of summer. She would hang onto the wooden ball at the bottom of the banister on her grandparents' steps and she'd scream, "I won't go! I won't!" And her father would have to pry her fingers off the ball and carry her kicking into the car. But now she had no wooden ball to hang onto.

She remembered the theme of her first, and most successful novel, a theme she had adopted as her own mantra in life: *if you want to be happy, never desire what you can't have...*

"Shall we go?" he interrupted her reverie, getting to his feet.

She wondered if she had imagined it, or had his voice wobbled with his own regret? She forced herself to stand up too.

"I'll get a taxi," he said as they left the trattoria.

"Oh, let's walk!" she said impulsively. Her hotel was off the Venato, on the via Pinciana, facing the Borghese Gardens. His was two blocks from hers. "Unless you're tired," she amended.

"God no," he said. "I love walking through Rome at night."

And so they walked, again holding hands. The air was warm. Strolling through the quiet ancient streets was magical, unforgettable. Like wine-tipsy peeping-Toms, they stared up at lighted rooms and they talked and laughed while she felt gusts of excitement at being there with Scott.

They crossed back over the river on the Ponte Sant'Angelo. "Did you know," she giggled, not sure why she found it amusing but blaming it on the wine, "that the Popes used to chop off thieves heads and nail them to this bridge, like grotesque polka dots?"

"I hear they still do," he said solemnly. "To American women who steal married men's hearts."

She dismissed his words with a flutter of her hand but she felt giddy. They stopped walking in the middle of the bridge and stared, almost mesmerized, at the illuminated crenelated roof of Castel Sant'Angelo. "Y'know what used to thrill me about living here?" she confided, squeezing his hand. "Just going on ordinary household errands, like driving to the produce market near the Ponte Milvio, and passing all these ancient monuments."

"Yeah. My office here is on the Piazza Argentina. I love sitting there and watching those feral cats…can you picture them? Slinking through those two-thousand-year-old ruins?"

They continued walking. "My girls used to say, 'Let's ruin the weekend.' Which meant, let's go look at ruins. Here, or down south…Pompeii, Herculaneum, Paestum, or over at Hadrian's Villa…God knows there's no shortage of them."

"Remember when we all went up to Tivoli?" he reminded her.

"Sure I do," Marilyn laughed. "Your Karen said it was better than Disneyland."

As they walked on, Marilyn was lost in the memory of Tivoli's fountains. She wondered how she would describe the sounds the water made if she were writing about it in a book. Would she say that the water whispered? Or gurgled? Hissed, sobbed and bubbled? Tinkled and roared? Or would it swirl and churn, sibilantly spraying, pitter and patting, gushing, rushing, swishing, lapping, plunging? Oh the magic of it all, she thought, breathless with nostalgia, wondering if she ever would see Tivoli again.

They zig-zagged up the narrow streets, taking her favorite route to the Venato. They both were as familiar with this part of the city as if they had lived there all their lives.

As they approached her hotel, Marilyn suddenly was nervous about how the night would end—with a pleasant goodnight kiss on the cheek and each of them going alone to their hotel rooms? Or would it end, as she ardently desired, and almost as ardently feared, with a kiss of such passion that her twenty-one-year record of fidelity to Lew would end, literally—she couldn't help smiling at the double-entendre—with a bang?

At her deserted hotel entrance, Scott impulsively drew her against him and she realized why she had had such a tug of war with herself all evening, first being afraid he would kiss her, and then feeling regretful when he didn't. It was a kiss of such dazzling power that Scott had to lean against the hotel's stone wall to keep them from falling. They staggered into the lobby and up the elevator to her room, in a daze, still clutching each other.

He held her, standing quietly in the middle of her room in the amber glow of a golden lampshade, giving them time to calm their harsh breathing. They sat on the bed and undressed each other. As he removed her garments he kissed her neck, and her arms, and he lingered over her breasts. "They're as lovely as I always imagined them," he said.

They lay down, bare skin melting against bare skin. Time became a blur of soft moans and sighs, of whispering each other's name. Of mouth upon mouth and body upon body. She felt elated, and exhilarated, and flooded with energy. They kept smiling at each other with delight and gratitude.

Her hotel room was inundated with stripes of sunlight squeezing through the shutters when Scott whispered, "I can't. I can't leave you." But then he said, "If only she wasn't pregnant!" And a minute later: "She's already had too much sorrow in her life." He forced himself to get out of bed and, fumbling, he began to put on his pants. Utterly bewildered, he sat down again on the bed and looked over at her. Then he stood up and put on his shirt and suit coat and shoved his tie into his pocket.

She felt dizzy with fright. She got out of bed and followed him to the door. He turned and clutched her. "Life is so unfair!" he groaned. They kissed, a desperate kiss, swaying together, neither of them willing to be the first to pull away, yet neither of them able to acknowledge that there was an alternative.

She pictured Lew waiting for her in London. Sure he was pushy, but he also was a dear, sweet, kind, lovable man. She knew from experience that he would phone the airline to check her plane's arrival time and then carefully figure out how long it would take her taxi to drive into London. When she knocked on his hotel door, Lew would be freshly showered and shaved and tingling with anticipation of her arrival.

Scott held their kiss while he caressed her back, her neck and her head as though he were frantically memorizing them, and then she was standing alone, naked, shockingly bereft, and the hotel door was closing.

"Wait!" she cried out, but the door already had closed. She was panicked, aware that she just had lived through the most precious hours of her life, that she had been given a priceless gift—that their erotic bond linked her to Scott beyond any vows she'd made to Lew.

She took a step toward the door, knowing she could fling it open and cry out, *Wait! Scott! Come back!* And he would. She was sure he needed only a word from her to tip him in her direction over his own fence of indecision. He would stop before he reached the elevator. He would return to her and they would kiss exultantly, their hearts pounding with relief at being together again, even after so brief a separation. They could live together in Rome. They could repeat these last few hours again and again, day after day and night after night, each time with heightened fervor, for the rest of their lives.

She reached for the doorknob, then stopped. Scott's tragic, pregnant bride was waiting for him in Cannes. And her own loving, lovable Lew was waiting for her in London. If she didn't open the door, no innocent people would get hurt.

She heard the elevator doors clang shut. A harrowing sense of irretrievable loss paralyzed her, making her forget momentarily to breathe. Then she reminded herself of her mantra, her number one rule in life: *if you want to be happy, never desire what you can't have.* She inhaled resolutely, knowing there was nothing left for her to do but go into the bathroom to shower and get dressed, and then pack.

She had a plane to catch.

Honeymoon in Venice

Mark was twenty-eight, so naturally he took charge. Tess, after all, was just a baby, barely eighteen. She was timid and shy, which pleased him mightily. He loved taking care of her.

He had been her high school English teacher during her junior year, back home in Los Angeles. He noticed her the first time he walked into the classroom. She was sitting at the rear, next to a window, with the sunlight streaming in behind her long auburn hair, creating a halo of golden red. Her face was serious, like a contemplative Madonna. He thought, "I'm going to marry that girl." And because he was handsome and intelligent and persuasive and a passionate kisser, he did marry her, the day after she graduated.

Their two-year courtship had been sweet and chaste, except for their abandoned kisses that left her exhilarated and proud and left him with the huge pain of suppressed carnality. They decided—or rather, he decided and she agreed—that instead of spending a lot of money on a big wedding that neither of them really could afford or wanted—they would fly to Venice, just the two of them, get married, have a one-week honeymoon there, and then spend two months seeing the rest of Europe. As for financing the trip, her father was dead and her mother barely scraped by, and his parents had no spare cash available, so it all came out of Mark's savings.

Everyone who knew them thought it was all terribly romantic—his persistent wooing of the beautiful young student, her eventual capitulation to his ardent proposals of marriage, the fact that they both were unusually attractive young people, and their choice of Venice for their marriage and honeymoon; surely few places on earth were more beguilingly picturesque and conducive to *amour*.

Several weeks earlier, Mark had phoned a Venetian lawyer, a Senor Paolo DiLullo, recommended by his L.A. attorney, and asked him to arrange the ceremony. As soon as Mark and Tess arrived in Venice, they went to the Registrar's office where Signor DiLullo met them. Everything was ready, including a bridal bouquet of white roses—her favorites—for Tess, as specified by Mark. They were married in a civil ceremony and afterwards there was much noisy double-cheek kissing and hand shaking.

Mark had chosen to stay at a small hotel near St. Mark's Cathedral. The Albergo Umbria was smothered in wisteria and had a lovely garden leading down to a side canal. It was a two-roof listing in the Michelin Guide and had fourteen rooms, all with private bath. Their room had a *"letto matrimoniale,"* according to the brochure Senior DiLullo had sent Mark. At first Mark thought it meant a bed only for honeymooners, but he learned it was simply Italian for a double bed.

After they were shown to their room and the bellboy left, Mark kissed Tess while gently caressing her back. "Listen," he said softly, "we aren't going to do anything until you want to do…it."

"It," she repeated, giggling. "Tell me exactly what 'it' is."

"Well, first it's undressing. I'll take your clothes off, if you don't mind…"

"And do I get to take yours off?"

He was surprised, but he nodded. "If you like. Then we get into bed…"

"And you put your thing into me?"

He laughed softly. "Honey, first we kiss, a lot, and feel each other's bodies, and I'll kiss your breasts…"

"And do I get to kiss your penis?"

He couldn't help being shocked. After a moment he again said, "If you like."

They did all that, he trying to keep the pace slow and she showing some impatience. When she kissed his penis he was stunned—and amazed—at her gusto, and when he finally entered her she moaned and gasped and squeezed and came before he did.

"Honey," he choked out soon thereafter, "I thought you said you'd never done this before."

"I didn't," she said. "But I sure do like it."

They got all dressed up for their wedding dinner. Tess wore a long pale lavender gown with a sprinkling of pink flowers embroidered randomly around the hem. She arranged her auburn hair into a cascade of curls. She was almost as tall as her six-foot husband. Mark wore a dark blue suit with a pale blue white-collared shirt and a silver tie. They stood together in front of their room's full-length mirror and smiled at each other's reflection.

Mark had asked Signor DiLullo to reserve a table for them at Harry's Bar and evidently the lawyer had emphasized the importance of the occasion for their table was festooned with white roses and a bottle of French champagne was immersed in an ice bucket. Instead of menus they each were handed fancy cards with their names and the date and an elaborate multi-course menu printed on them.

They were seated side by side on a banquette and as the meal progressed, Tess reached under the tablecloth and caressed Mark's penis through his pants. He was so shocked he jumped and nearly upset the table, and when she surreptitiously felt for his zipper he put his hand over hers and put her hand back in her own lap. "Later," he whispered.

Dinner was superb. They started with individual tureens of lobster bisque laced with sherry, followed by shrimp scampi, then enormous veal cutlets with sautéed mushrooms, then a refreshing green salad, and finally a flaky, utterly satisfying dessert. Their menus called the dessert *"Mille Foglie."*

"It means a thousand leaves," Tess said.

She kept astonishing him. "How'd you know that?" he asked.

She shrugged. "I just know."

Mark gave the waiter his credit card without looking at the bill. He knew that the tip was included, but he left a lot of euros as an extra gratuity.

"That was really cool," Tess said, holding onto his arm as they walked back to their hotel through St. Mark Square. It was a balmy June night with just the lightest breeze ruffling their hair. They stopped and admired the horses atop St. Mark's Cathedral. "Pretty neat," Tess said. "Hey, look at this place." She held out her arms and made a three-hundred-and-sixty-degree turn, taking in the entire square. "Did you ever see so many beautiful old buildings? And the way the lights reflect on the water?" She jumped up and down and clapped her hands. "I love it!"

"It's the greatest," he agreed. He was tired, but blissfully happy. He looked forward to getting into bed with Tess and having a gentle bit of lovemaking before falling asleep, but when they reached their room she pushed him onto the bed, unzipped his fly, threw herself on top of him and screwed him…royally!

He was thoroughly perplexed. He didn't know what to make of her. Shy Tess. Timid Tess. Good God, she was a sex maniac! She wanted to stay in bed their whole second day in Venice.

"We can see the sights tomorrow," she said.

"Let's at least get dressed and go out for lunch," he said at mid-afternoon.

She reluctantly agreed and they walked across St. Mark's Square to *Caffe Quadri*. They sat at an outdoor table, watching crowds of tourists criss-crossing the square with the cathedral looming over them. Tess and Mark held hands while they ate their pasta and drank their wine. They went out for a late dinner at *Antico Pignolo,* but the rest of the time they had so much sex that Mark lost count.

The next morning, Mark awoke with a cold. "Honey, I know from experience that if I just stay in bed and take it easy, I'll get over it fast. No sex. You wore me out yesterday and lowered my resistance."

"Oh well!" she said. "*I'm* going out."

She put on a pale orange dress with snaps down the front and a matching broad-brimmed sun hat. The only makeup she used was a smear of lipstick and she was out the door.

Mark slept all morning. He asked the hotel owner for some hot minestrone and tea for lunch, then he napped again. In the late afternoon, when Tess returned, Mark was sitting up in one of the big easy chairs near the window. He was wearing green satin pajamas, a wedding gift from his younger sister, Pam.

He was overjoyed to see Tess, but before he could tell her so, she pulled apart the snaps down the front of her dress and tossed it on the bed. She was naked underneath. She slipped off her shoes and threw herself onto his lap, facing him. Before he knew what was happening, she untied his pajama bottoms, fished out his penis, stroked it to make it hard, and raised herself up enough to slip it into her. She leaned back, her Madonna face the picture of rapture, and slid up and down. Her vaginal muscles were strong and persuasive. She gasped and gave little breathless cries as she moved faster and faster. Her nipples hardened and grew darker and her stomach expanded and when she came with a great howl he could see that her entire body vibrated, but then he was busy with his own orgasm and closed his eyes. His pleasure was so intense it was almost—but definitely NOT—painful.

Mark had had a lot of sex in his twenty-eight years. He had lived with a woman named Ellen for three years. But he never had had a partner as downright erotic, as lascivious, as earthy, as wanton or as adorable as his Tess.

She snuggled against him, keeping his penis warm inside of her. She sighed contentedly, every now and then squeezing her vaginal muscles and giving herself tiny post-coital thrills, which made her giggle. Finally she released him and stood up.

"I had the greatest day," she began enthusiastically as she slipped into a pink silk bathrobe and came back and sat down in the easy chair facing his. "You should see this city! I mean, all you've seen so far is St. Mark's, just on the outside, and we were too excited when we first got here to notice much. This town is a trip! You never saw so many *fabuloso* buildings! So what do you say we forget about the rest of Europe for now and just stay here? Like, getting jobs and living here?"

He stared at her. "Jobs? What kind of jobs?"

"Well, I went back to Harry's Bar for lunch and talked to the manager about working the lunch shift. Since I speak French and Italian…"

"You speak *what?* "

"French and Italian."

"Tess, I've known you for two years and you never told me…"

"It never came up. But my mother was born in Palermo and my father in Lyon. Then, when I was born, my mom spoke to me only in Italian and my dad in French. And I learned English just living in L.A. So…"

"Tess." He sighed. "You're too much. Go on."

"So the manager at Harry's, he said sure, he'd love to have me work there, if we decide to stay.

"But what about me? Where could I get a job? I only speak English."

"Well, I went over to the English language high school. I told them how you had a Ph.D. from Columbia and you've taught for four years at Santa Monica High and they said they'd hire you in a minute."

"But…" He was befuddled. "I mean, where would we live? This hotel is way too expensive…"

"Silly! I thought of everything. The headmaster at the school gave me the name of a real estate guy, and he showed me a really nice one-bedroom apartment in a great old *palazzo,* right near the Grand Canal. It's all furnished and has the most comfy soft bed."

"What did you do, lay down and try it?" He laughed indulgently.

"Well yes, and it's great for making love. Real bouncy. I know because the rental guy fucked me on it." Tess said this with such innocence that Mark thought she was joking. "But I like doing it better with you."

Mark leaned forward. "Tess." He was alarmed and angry. "Are you telling me that you had sex with this man? A total stranger?"

She was surprised at his tone. "Why? Shouldn't I of? He used a condom."

He grabbed her by the wrists. "Married women only have sex with their husbands!"

"But...I didn't know. I thought, you know, once you gave your virginity to your husband, like, on your wedding night, then, you know, it didn't matter." She began to cry.

He pulled her onto his lap and let her cry against his shoulder. "Honey," he said gently, pushing her curls back from her face, "you're only supposed to do it with your husband when you're married."

She sat up and stared into his face. "Nobody told me that!"

He shook his head, bewildered. "Didn't you ever hear of monogamy?"

She thought a minute. "Oh, I guess I heard the word, but I didn't pay any attention. What's it mean?"

"It means that a husband and wife only have sex with each other."

"Oh. So, is that what you want us to be? Monogamy?"

"Yes, dear heart. It's called monogamous."

"Well make up your mind!"

"Both. Monogamy and monogamous. They both mean the same thing."

She thought about it. "But what'll I do if some guy turns me on and you know, wants to fuck me?"

"You tell him you're married and you don't want to."

"But..." she gave him a petulant look, "what if I get turned on and I really *do* want to? I mean really *really* want to?"

"You still don't. You learn to turn off those feelings, except when you're with me." Mark affectionately kissed her chin, then the tip of her nose, then each of her closed eyes.

She hid her face against his neck and sighed.

It all worked out beautifully. He taught from nine in the morning until four in the afternoon and she worked the lunch shift at Harry's Bar. She worked at night only if the dinner staff was short handed, which rarely happened more than once every week or two. Their little *apartamento* was charming, though every now and then, when they were making love, it pained Mark to think that Tess had sexually initiated the bed with that realtor whom Mark never had met and never wished to meet.

Most evenings they ate at little trattorias, discovering dishes they never had encountered at Italian restaurants in Los Angeles. Some nights they ate at home when Tess returned from work with some of the elaborate cuisine from Harry's Bar. On weekends they loved walking around the city, crossing canals to seek out different neighborhoods or taking the vaporetto to the outlying areas of the city.

Every night, and many days when they had free time, they made love. Tess's libido kept amazing him. Her sexual vigor and her imagination left him breathless. "Let's try it with me hanging over the side of the bed," she would giggle. Or, "Let's fuck in the bathtub full of water and make waves." She adored having surreptitious sex in public. Often, when they sat side by side in a restaurant, hidden by the tablecloth she would make him climax with her hand and simultaneously he would do the same to her, and all the while they both kept eating and it worked out fine because he was left-handed. She liked doing it standing up in dark corners of the Cathedral. Or she would sit in his lap on public benches and he would unzip his pants and surreptitiously pull up her skirt—she never wore underwear—and he would enter her from the rear. They both became adept at having the most earth-shattering orgasms, without displaying the slightest emotion, by letting their sex muscles squeeze and writhe independent of the rest of their bodies. She loved double blow jobs, though she hadn't figured out yet how to do it in public. Oh, but she was so imaginative! Mark sometimes thought he would burst with pure joy.

Tess decided to take painting lessons after work. She went to the studio of a Signor Renzo Paolucci, a heavy-set, untidy man of fifty. Often, Mark stopped by the studio after work so that he and Tess could walk home together. Her paintings were surprisingly good, Mark thought. She had a bold, sure stroke and an imaginative sense of color. Signor Paolucci praised her vigorously. Signora Paolucci always joined them when Mark was there. If she had a first name, Mark never heard it. Her husband referred to her only as *"la signora."* She served them campari or frangelica as the four of them lounged around a small garden outside the studio. She was a short blonde woman from Trieste who let the young couple know at once that she was Yugoslavian, not Italian. She spat out the latter word with a contempt that shocked Mark. But it didn't seem to bother her husband who seldom paid any attention to her anyway, other than to bark orders at her.

One afternoon when Mark rang the Paolucci's doorbell, no one answered. He rang and rang and finally, finding that the door was unlocked, he let himself in. Signora Paolucci was nowhere around, so Mark went to the studio, but that was empty too. He glanced out into the garden and was about to leave when he heard a familiar sound from upstairs. He had grown accustomed to Tess's lovemaking noises. She always started with little appreciative grunts of pleasure that intensified in volume and ascended in pitch and ended with loud howling cries. She didn't seem to care who heard her. And now Mark realized that frantic male growls were accompanying her, increasing in volume in tandem with her cries.

Mark was paralyzed. He stood quietly in the studio, unwilling to confront the two of them. Strangely, he felt no anger, only pain and breathlessness, as though someone had unexpectedly thrown a hardball into his stomach. He left the house quietly and walked home slowly and thoughtfully.

She came into their apartment later looking positively ravishing. Her eyes shone, her hair was disheveled, her dress had been haphazardly buttoned and she was breathless.

"So you're fucking that big fat slob!" he shouted.

She ignored him and sat down facing him. "I never knew that love could be so wonderful," she said.

"I thought you loved *me."* He tried to keep the plaintive tone from his voice, but his words came out whining.

"I do, sweetheart. But with you, it's sort of, well, like puppy love. It's fun. With Renzo, it's...oh Mark, it's pure heaven." She sat up. "Don't be mad, honey. I mean, these things just happen."

"What about that dumb wife of his?"

Tess shrugged. "She's gone. I think she went back to Trieste or wherever she came from."

The two of them sat quietly for a few minutes. All at once Mark had a vision of his life with Tess five years ahead, ten years, *fifty* — always having to worry about whom she was fucking. The prospect of his pain, each time she strayed, was wholly unacceptable.

"So what do you want?" he finally growled.

"What d'you think? I'm going to marry Renzo."

He sighed, not so much because she wanted to leave him—he had accepted that with surprising ease—but at the prospect of going through all the red tape that getting a divorce in Italy undoubtedly entailed. But of course—his spirits lifted—there was always Senor DiLullo to help him—for a pile of euros.

Tess got up and brushed her hair and re-buttoned her dress. She went to her closet and got out her suitcase—they each had their own—and started to pack. He watched her with utter detachment. He felt numb.

She rolled her luggage to the door, then came back to Mark. "So tell me, honey, want a goodbye fuck?"

He laughed. He hooted. He roared so hard he choked and had a coughing fit.

She just stood there watching him, totally perplexed. "What's so funny?" she asked when he finally caught his breath.

He shook his head. "You, sweetheart. You."

She shrugged and walked out the door, rolling her suitcase behind her. "Bye," she called out cheerily and left.

"Good riddance!" he gasped at the closed door before the pain in his throat, his chest and his groin rendered him speechless.

Sexual Awakening in London

Until he was sixty-five, Bruce Heller never paid much attention to women. During his junior and senior high school years, he'd had delicious secret sex with Teresa, the family's live-in Portuguese maid, who was in her early twenties. In comparison to her voluptuous woman's body, pubescent girls held no attraction for him. In college, Grace Jordan decided in her Freshman year that she was going to marry him. Since she was a no-nonsense girl who went after what she wanted, he found himself at the altar the day after he earned his Master's degree in Chemistry.

Grace arranged everything: the wedding, their first apartment, a job for herself as a newspaper reporter on a neighborhood weekly, and getting herself pregnant three times (with Bruce's somewhat lackadaisical help) while Bruce worked on his doctorate, became an Associate Professor at M.I.T., and eventually a full Professor with tenure.

Years later, when Grace had a fatal heart attack at sixty-four, Bruce suddenly was a sixty-five-year-old single man wholly incapable of taking care of himself. During their entire life together, Grace had managed everything: the mail, the bills, the mechanics of daily living, their social life, his doctors' appointments, making sure he was fed, clothed and housed, raising their three sons and then staying in touch with them. Had it all been left to Bruce, they would have remained childless and would have continued to live in their first apartment, a one-bedroom walk-up, for the rest of their lives, instead of their comfortable four bedroom Victorian in South Boston. She had prodded him every step of the way to his present prestigious job while furthering her own career as Editor of her weekly suburban newspaper.

She even took full charge of their sex life. She would signal her desire by sitting beside him, unzipping his fly, and stroking his penis. She instructed him step by step, like a coach: "Now, Brucie, take off my shirt and bra and suck my nipples. Ooooh,!" She was extremely vocal when aroused. She grunted and groaned and shrieked. "Now, honey, go down on me—first lap with your tongue and then suck with your lips." And all during this she would use her hands and mouth to make him hard enough and then she would pant, "Now, Brucie, NOW!" and he would slide into her hot, moist, welcoming vagina.

She made it all happen. He barely had to move. She gyrated and slid up and down, moaning and groaning. She had marvelous muscles that practically milked the semen out of him. When they both exploded together, she would scissor her legs around his thighs and throw her arms around his shoulders, keeping him captive while all he wanted to do was go back to his computer. But she wouldn't let him. As soon as she recovered her breath, she would start again, telling him exactly what to do and when to do it, and most of the time their second coming was even better than the first.

Oh, he liked sex all right. He just never thought about doing it until the next time she unzipped his fly.

A few weeks after losing Grace, Bruce looked helplessly at his desk littered with unread papers, books, magazine and students' doctoral theses. Unopened mail had been thrown into an overflowing carton on the floor. Thus, when he received a phone call from London inviting him to speak at an international chemistry forum, he was almost gleeful in his eagerness to get away from the mess facing him.

"It'll just be worse when you get back, Dad," his youngest son, Jerry, reminded him as he helped his father pack..

"Maybe I'll be lucky and the plane'll crash," Bruce grumbled.

Bruce never had been a sociable person. At the parties that Grace had forced him to attend, he usually sat off by himself, refusing to join in what he called the "shit-chat." He only liked to talk about his work, which nobody but his colleagues in the chemistry department could understand, or about his pessimism over the state of world affairs. He was known as a curmudgeon, a sourpuss, a drip, a killjoy, a wet blanket, a sulker, a man who was invited anywhere only because he had such a charming wife.

Still, he was fairly attractive for his age. He had enough white hair to cover his head without having to comb the longer side strands over the top of his head. His brown eyes, while they never had much sparkle, were large and well lashed and his vision was sharp. His facial features were pleasant, if not memorable.

"Now the parade of the Brisket Brigade starts," his best friend, Ira Gross in the physics department, warned him with an amused smile.

"What's that?"

"Widows and divorcees of all ages bearing pot roasts. They can smell a new widower like flies at a hotdog cookout."

"I'm not sure I want to be likened to a hotdog," Bruce said.

"Like it or not, my friend, when they bring over a pot roast, what they're really offering you is themselves."

"I don't know, Ira," Bruce objected, "these women can't be that desperate."

"Just you wait!" Ira chortled. "In a few weeks, it'll be open season on you, Bruce."

Bruce hadn't been to London in ten years. When Grace had dragged him somewhere on their annual vacations, they alternated between going to major European cities and taking cruises to islands he'd never heard of and never had any desire to see. He found all these trips frightfully boring, but Grace particularly loved the cruises. "You wouldn't enjoy it if you were on a galley with Cleopatra," Grace would say, "so we might as well do something I enjoy." She was good at flaking out on a deck chair for hours, and playing bridge all afternoon, and walking a million times around the deck to keep from gaining weight after eating every meal that came her way. Since Bruce refused to dance, Grace competed with the single women for the attention of the ship's staff of attractive "gentlemen hosts" who were hired to make sure no woman was a wallflower.

When he reached London, the international forum put him up at Duke's Hotel, which he found to his taste—in other words, not full of jolly, loud Americans. His room overlooked Green Park and after watching people jogging there his first morning in London, he impulsively found a sporting goods store on Oxford Street and bought running shoes and a couple of blue satin tank tops and stretch shorts. He didn't know what had possessed him; it was a whim, which was a rather odd thing for him to have. He found running so invigorating, even euphoric, that he berated Grace, in a silent tirade, for never having forced him to jog.

His speech was still two days away and he felt lost in this big, baffling city. He phoned a colleague, Sandy Hilla, who was living in London on sabbatical. Sandy was out but Evelyn, Sandy's wife, invited him to dinner that evening. "Your timing is perfect, Bruce," Evelyn told him. "We're having some of our favorite people over tonight, and there's plenty of room at the table for one more."

Bruce picked up a self-guided walking map at the hotel's concierge desk and he spent the afternoon ambling around central London. He was surprised at how little he remembered from his two previous trips to the city. Had he been so blind, so wrapped up in his own little world, as Grace often had accused him, that he never *looked* at anything? Was it possible that he never had seen the massive Buckingham Palace? Never had looked at the Parliament Building? For God's sake, he didn't even remember having seen Big Ben and Westminster Abbey, yet surely he had?

When he tired of walking he boarded a double-decker red bus and got off at the British Museum. Surely Grace had dragged him to see the Elgin Marbles, but he had no recollection of them. Nor of the Egyptian and Greek collections. Most likely, she had taken him there, but all this great art had failed to register on his memory. He began to worry that he was afflicted with a serious attention deficiency. Was it possible that he simply didn't know how to *look* at what he was seeing? That his observational skills were woefully non-existent?

By the time he returned to his hotel room to dress for the Hillas' dinner party, Bruce felt stupid. He couldn't stop scolding himself. How had he reached his present advanced age and noticed so little about the world? He couldn't even remember much about his own neighborhood in South Boston. He knew what his own house looked like, but for nearly forty years he had walked the same four blocks to the T-Station to go to and from the M.I.T campus, yet he couldn't describe one house along those four-blocks.

He blamed Grace. If she hadn't run his life so damned efficiently, he wouldn't be the closed-in person he now was. He felt a stab of grief whenever he thought about her. Mostly he remembered the warmth he'd felt when he plunged himself into her body. He realized that he was more aware of the sensations in retrospect than he had been during all the times he actually had had sex with her. He felt choked up, like he had run out of breath. It made him want to cry, but he didn't know how. He sat by the window overlooking Green Park and tried to think about his life, his future.

He realized he never had felt passionate about anything. Again, he didn't know how. He had read about ardent lovers and their fiery desires in the few books of fiction that were required reading in his college English courses, but he never had understood such feelings. During his adolescent affair with Teresa, sex had been something she did to him. And although sex with Grace had been pleasant, she always had been the one to initiate it. He never had developed any great burning desire for her. Until now.

Even fatherhood had been a cerebral experience for him. He had held his infant sons without an ounce of the pleasure Grace had exhibited, her face exultantly radiant. He never had felt an emotional bond with his children, or even with Grace, nor with anyone at all for that matter.

He had come from an undemonstrative family. Was that his

excuse? Could the whole situation simply be blamed on genes? But Grace also had come from a cold Yankee family, yet she'd had enough warmth and exuberance to propel a jet plane.

He sighed and got dressed for dinner. He wore a suit and white shirt and tie, remembering that the Hillas always dressed quite formally, even for cookouts and clam bakes.

He followed the directions Evelyn had given him, walking to Picadilly Road to catch the Number Nine bus, but he took it in the wrong direction and had to get off and cross the busy street to get the bus going west. He went to the front of the bus's upper level, having discovered that afternoon that he quite enjoyed watching the city go by. In fact, he was so intent on looking at the people and the buildings on Kensington High Street that the bus sailed right past the Safeway where Evelyn had told him to get off. He dashed down the curving stairs and called out to the conductor, "Let me off please."

The conductor shook his head and said, "You'll have to wait for the next stop." It seemed to Bruce at least half a mile before the bus sagged toward the sidewalk and lumbered to a halt.

He walked back in the direction of the Safeway. It was three long blocks to Argyle Street where he turned left and found the long row of white terrace houses, exactly as Evelyn had described them.

His troubles with the bus, at both ends of the trip, made him the last guest to arrive. Evelyn opened the door and said, "Oh poor, dear Bruce. I'm so sorry about Grace." After introductions—he failed to remember even one name of the seven other guests—Evelyn gave him a quick tour of their flat. It was comfortably furnished, with a large living room, dining room, modern kitchen and a powder room on their top level, and three bedrooms and two bathrooms in the basement level, which opened onto a surprisingly large back yard full of flowers, shrubs, shade trees and white curlicued wrought-iron garden furniture.

"Don't ask what this place costs," Evelyn confided as they climbed the stairs to rejoin the others. "You could rent the Copley Plaza presidential suite in Boston for less."

Bruce, who had no idea of what most things cost, went "Hmmm," and nodded.

He made an effort to pay attention to the conversation, which unfortunately happened to be on the relative advantages of Golden Retrievers versus Labradors. Bruce knew absolutely nothing about dogs. His sons had had several generations of dogs and cats and birds over the years, but they no more had impinged on Bruce's consciousness than had the four blocks of houses he'd passed on his way to and from the T-station.

"Any thoughts on the subject, Bruce?" Sandy Hilla said to him quietly but sardonically. "I know how you love this kind of chitchat."

Bruce shrugged. "I guess it's no secret that I'm not a party animal."

Sandy laughed. "I'm surprised you even know the expression."

When the party moved to the dining room, seated on Bruce's right was a woman named Miriam, a very stout, homely, gray-haired professor of Medieval art at one of the California universities. He seldom noticed how people looked, but it crossed his mind that Grace would say that Miriam was built like a "brick shit house." He felt like guffawing aloud. Miriam and her husband, a small bearded man with thick glasses sitting across the table—also a professor, but of Medieval history—were on sabbatical, both of them doing research at the British Museum. On Bruce's left was a petite woman with a pretty face and streaked blonde hair. However her outstanding attraction was amply displayed by her low-cut gown, showing just a hint of two pink nipples. Bruce was reminded that Grace's breasts had been rather small.

He found himself a good deal more aware of this woman's bosom than he wished to be. These boobs were downright distracting and it was all he could do to keep his eyes level with her face. Her name was Josette, she was French and she spoke in charmingly accented English. She had lived in Geneva, Rome, Seville, and now London. "I am zee Geepsy," she laughed. "Every time I get mer-eed, I meree a man from zee different countree."

"And now? You're married to an Englishman?"

"Ah, not now. Vas. My last ex. So here I am, vaiting for zee next country to claim me."

Miriam rather rudely elbowed his arm to get his attention. "Are you on sabbatical too, Professor Heller?"

"No. Just here to give a lecture. And please, call me Bruce." He couldn't believe he had said that. Usually he preferred that people address him formally. He had had a gin martini before dinner and now he was sipping white wine with the salad. It couldn't be the liquor. He was capable of drinking a lot more without being affected by it.

Miriam lowered her voice. "Bruce, I have to warn you. That number on your left can gobble you up for breakfast and spit you out by lunch time."

"I'm a pretty tough bird to be digested that fast," he said, again amazed at the things he was saying.

The conversation became general as the entire group began discussing travel difficulties now that the fear of terrorists meant long searches and waits at the airports. "Coming over, I sat next to a Saudi prince," Bruce told them. (The chemistry group he was invited to address had brought him over First Class.) "This prince was a Harvard man. Had mansions all over the world. I still was nervous. I mean, I kept glancing at his expensive-looking shoes, expecting them to blow us all up."

They all laughed, albeit nervously.

Bruce almost fainted. People actually laughed at something he'd said!

After dessert and coffee, Josette leaned close. "I live at zee Connaught. Come for lunch tomorrow. Vun o'clock."

He didn't know what the Connaught was. "Uh, where is it?"

She took a card from her purse and slipped it into his suit coat pocket. She blew him a tiny kiss. Then she kissed Evelyn on both cheeks, did the same to Sandy, and left the flat.

"Prenez garde!" Miriam shook her head disapprovingly at Bruce.

The Connaught Hotel's stately facade, its white-pillared entrance and costumed doorman intimidated Bruce and made him feel unworthy to enter this grand place. When he found Josette waiting for him in a rosy-hued sitting area, her welcoming smile put him somewhat at ease, all to be undone by the dining room's formally dressed waiters who acted as though Bruce were out of his depths as a companion worthy of Josette.

He found his lack of ease ridiculous. You're a Full Professor at one of the world's great universities, he reminded himself. You've been invited as the honored lecturer at a prestigious international scientific society. Are you going to let a handful of hired lackeys spoil this lovely occasion?

He tried to relax by admiring the room's high-ceilinged grandeur, the graceful blue drapes on the tall windows, the plum-colored carpeting, the sea of fine white table linens, the fresh flowers on each table, the commodious arm chair in which he sat, but added to his discomfort was his horror at finding he still was obsessed by Josette's breasts. He tried to keep his eyes on her face, or on the other diners, but as though on automatic hinges, his eyes would snap down to the very things he was trying so hard to avoid.

They were magnificent. Full, round, with a forward thrust that seemed to beg for attention, and big hard nipples that pressed boldly against the confining cloth of Josette's tight yellow silk dress. Bruce found himself wanting to touch them. He wanted to kiss them. Damn it!—he wanted to slobber over those oh-so-visible nipples and suck on them until she screamed with pleasure. And for the first time since his high-school years with the maid, his penis grew firm of its own accord. Ruefully, he remembered how, in recent years, Grace had had to work with her hands and mouth to make it grow to a useful size.

He felt he would make a fool of himself if he tried to have sex with Josette. He was sure he would be totally gauche without Grace coaching him on what to do. And even though his member was rising to the occasion now, hidden beneath the table and its voluminous cloth, he was sure that at the critical moment of wanting to enter this luscious woman, his penis would shrink to the size of his thumb.

Josette ordered for both of them—a fine creamed squash soup,

Coquille St. Jacques au huitre, a raspberry souffle, a bottle of Pouilly-Fuisse. She tried to put him at ease by artfully drawing him into a conversation entirely about himself.

"Would you care to see my suite?" Josette asked archly as they rose from the table.

"Thank you for lunch," he mumbled. "I have an appointment. Perhaps some other time." He shook her hand without looking into her face and quickly left the hotel.

Cringing with shame, he walked back toward his own hotel. Of course he should have accepted her generous invitation. What a coward he had been! Was there a better way to spend an afternoon, and probably the evening too, than in the arms of that agreeable, voluptuous, generous woman? Surely she was adept enough to help him to a soaring climax, even if he suffered some initial embarrassment. He shivered, thinking of it. And what contentment he could have enjoyed afterwards, lying with her in a sated state while enjoying a sweet little flurry of kisses as they built toward another storm of pleasure.

He turned back toward the Connaught, intent upon changing his fantasy into reality. Surely she would welcome him back? Especially if he flattered her by saying he had decided to cancel his (nonexistent) appointment in order to be with her?

When he approached the desk to ask for her room number, the unsmiling clerk rang her suite and told her she had a guest. The clerk passed the phone to Bruce.

"Josette," he said, "I decided you were more important than any appointment, so I canceled..."

"Oh Bruce, how unfortunate. You see, I too have an appointment. Perhaps some other time?"

He realized that she had icily mimicked the exact words he had said to her earlier. He had hurt her feelings and she was paying him back. He was about to protest, to beg her, when he heard the click indicating that she had hung up her phone.

He walked back to his hotel feeling defeated, certain that he would be rejected by every woman he ever again desired. He realized he was gazing longingly at every female he passed, assessing each face, each body, and especially each pair of breasts.

Then he brightened. He realized that the world was a veritable sea of breasts. Everywhere he looked he saw big breasts, tiny breasts, droopy breasts, standing-smartly-at-attention breasts. What did other men call them? Knockers? Tits? Boobs? Hooters? Bosoms? Busts? The hell with Josette. He had a lot of lost time to make up.

He remembered his friend Ira's words about the parade of the Brisket Brigade. Fortunately, Bruce reminded himself, pot roast was one of his favorite foods. And he certainly would pay attention to the attributes of the "brigadiers" who eagerly brought him his dinners.

He couldn't wait to get home. "Let the parade begin!" he felt like shouting across the Atlantic to the hordes of Boston's lonely widows and divorcees waiting for him.

Lust in Paris

Margo never dreamed that while living in Paris, surrounded by millions of charming Frenchmen, she would have an affair with a fellow American. But one look across a room crowded with cocktail party guests, when her eyes met those of the slender, well-dressed man with smooth dark hair, she was hooked.

He obviously felt the same way because he made his way toward her through the wine-sipping throng, never taking his eyes from hers. She was aware of women looking at him with interest as he moved across the room and she realized that she wasn't the only one who found him attractive. When he reached her, he simply said, "Well, hello."

She said "Hello" back and they stared mesmerized into each other's blue eyes, dazzled and dazed by this swift mutual attraction. He was, of course, taller than she was—who wasn't?—and he gave the graceful yet utterly masculine impression of being felicitously put together. He took her wine glass from her and set it down on a coffee table. Then he held her arm and they left the party without saying goodbye to the host and hostess.

As always when she visited Jean and Mort Eisen, Margo was impressed by the apartment her old friends had bought in the Sixth Arrondissment. She remembered the sense of enchantment she had experienced the first time she entered the Eisen's place through a very old wooden gate on a narrow street off the Boul' St. Germaine, crossed a cobblestone courtyard, climbed a long curving flight of stone steps that feet and time had polished to a satin-like sheen, and walked into the Eisens' starkly modern all-white living room to be visually smacked by a stunning wall of Kandinskis.

Now, leaving the party, Margo was blind to everything but the man who hung onto her arm as though he never intended to let go. He made her feel like a teenager on her first date. She was young for a widow, only fifty-two, though being petite and slender, she looked more like thirty-something.

As they walked down the outside stairs, Margo felt smugly attractive. And sophisticated. God, she'd spent her entire adult life trying to look sophisticated, only she'd found it difficult to overcome her "cute-little-girl" look with her delicate features and curly dark ringlets framing her face. But today, with the help of her magician of a hairdresser, her hair was tamed into a smooth bouffant halo. She wore a clinging blue silk dress she'd bought on the Avenue Montaigne. And as proof of how beguiling she looked, this gorgeous man had chosen *her* from that entire room full of stunning women.

She stretched her neck and imagined a hook on the top of her head from which she was suspended, so that she would look taller and have perfect posture. She had been doing this since she was ten and her P.E. teacher had made the suggestion when Margo played basketball with her taller team-mates.

"Where are we going?" she asked when they reached the street.

"Your place or mine?" He smiled.

"Wait," she said, suddenly nervous about being alone with this stranger. "I'm not sure..." She was certain that the minute they were alone in some private place, they would throw themselves at each other. And she knew nothing about him, not even his name.

He stopped walking and faced her, gently grasping both her arms above her elbows. "Why?" he asked softly. "Can't you go with the flow?"

Their eyes locked again, as though magnetized. "I don't even know you," she said. She felt breathless with desire for him. She never had experienced anything like this, not even with Gil, her late husband. She and Gil had dated for half a year before they went to bed together, and even then it had taken another half year before she learned to enjoy sex. And what if only Gil knew how to make her enjoy it? What if she got into bed with this stranger and what if despite the desire that was so sharp it was almost painful…what if she froze up and felt like a fool?

He took her arm again and started walking toward the Boulevard. "What do you want to know about me?" he asked.

"Well, I'd like to know your name, for one thing," she said.

Again, he stopped walking, bowed formally, and said, "Ben Waller. And I know you're Margo Keyes."

"You do? How?"

"I asked Jean when you first walked in."

They resumed walking. "I'm from Boston originally," he went on, as though reciting a litany. "I've lived in Paris for the last four years, I'm divorced, no children. Before I moved here, I taught high school math in Revere Beach, a Boston suburb. I'm forty-seven, and I make a very good living as a high-priced gigolo for lonely women, mostly Americans widows. What else do you want to know?"

She was shocked by the word "gigolo." She stopped walking and shook her head. "Sorry. I can't afford to pay you."

He laughed. "Come on, Margo. I chose you. I *want* to be with you! I wouldn't accept money from you."

She took a deep breath. Despite her foolish fears, she desperately wanted him to kiss her and then make love with her. And why not have a fling? Isn't that what a widow was supposed to do in Paris? But she felt timid—it was too threatening to her careful, safe life.

"Come on," he said gently. "My apartment is only three blocks from here."

She hesitated, then was shocked when she heard herself say, "All right," before she even had decided what to say. She was not an impulsive person. She usually weighed the pro's and con's of every decision she made.

As they continued walking he said, "I know all about you."

"What did Jean tell you?"

"That you all were friends when they lived in San Francisco, that your husband was an orthopedic surgeon and that he had a sudden fatal heart attack a year ago. That you have a married daughter in Hawaii. That you're much too fragile to be dallied with. That I should leave you alone to your grief." He paused. "Is that last part true? And if so, why are you walking down this marvelous street with me?"

"Because I'm sick and tired of being fragile!" She was amazed at how spontaneously the words had shot out of her.

"I'm just the person to restore your vitality." He put an arm around her and guided her across the wide boulevard, expertly weaving through the rude, bleating traffic. They turned down a quiet side street.

Since arriving in Paris two months earlier, she had been in a strange, dreamlike mood—part joyful, part nightmare. She had come there to escape the stultifying grief that had wrapped itself around her like a paralyzing shroud for the past year, keeping her from her work as a newspaper art critic.

Gil had been eight years older than she was, but still too young to die. His family was riddled with heart problems; both of his parents and all four of his grandparents had been relatively young when heart attacks killed them.

She had loved Gil…still did. But she was trying to get on with her life. She came from families on both sides who usually died of old age, most of them living past a hundred. She could have another fifty years ahead of her and she certainly didn't want to spend half a century indecisively moping through her days, the way she had this past year.

"Do you have sex with the women who hire you?" she asked Ben.

"Sometimes. Why do you ask?"

"Just curious."

"Listen, Margo, relax. Let's just have fun together. Okay?"

"I am having fun. You make me feel…" she groped for the right word, "alive."

"Good. I wouldn't want to make love to a corpse."

They walked in silence along the sidewalk, past art galleries and restaurants and shops with beautiful clothes in their windows but they could have been in the middle of the Sahara for all Margo saw of it. Actually, she saw everything, but comprehended nothing. She was in a daze, like the kind of dream where one loses all control of one's actions. I'm not me, she thought, I'm someone else, and…it's kind of liberating!

Still, she couldn't believe that of her own free will she was about to have sex with a stranger. That she was so *eager*. She never had had sex with anyone but Gil. But even with him, there always had been a slight hesitation on her part, a moment of holding back, of not wanting to do it, even though she enjoyed it once they were in bed. This always had puzzled her, but she chalked it up to the negative signals toward sex she had picked up from her mother.

Ben stopped and opened a wrought iron gate leading into a narrow courtyard. He unlocked the door of a one-story building and flipped a switch that turned on a dim lamp with a saffron-colored Tiffany shade. The rest of the room remained in shadow.

"Home sweet home," he announced as he closed the door behind her. "Won't you come into my parlor?"

"Said the spider…" Her next words were smothered by his mouth on hers. He backed her against a wall and pressed tightly against her from knees to chest, creating waves of tremors that rippled through her like a wild surf. She could feel both their hearts pounding in their crushed-together chests.

Their tongues touched, further jolting their bodies. Still kissing, he two-stepped her into the bedroom where they flung off their clothes and then threw themselves at each other. He reached into a drawer in a bedside table, flipped open a condom package and expertly slipped it on. She shocked herself by coming after a few thrusts, faster than she ever had in her life.

"That was just a little appetizer, sweetheart," he said, affectionately smoothing back her now-disheveled hair from her forehead. "The main course is coming up!"

She awoke in his bed the next morning lying on her back His right leg was sprawled across both of hers and one of his forearms rested on her waist. He was lying on his side, his head next to hers, and he was gently exhaling against her cheek. She turned so that they faced each other. He opened his eyes and instantly gave her a delighted smile. "What a night!" He drew her closer to him.

Their movements were languid, since they weren't completely awake yet, but the power of their responses jolted them into a jubilant sort of vitality. He leaped out of bed and pulled her after him. "Come, sweet, delicious, beautiful Margo, let's shower together and then I'll make breakfast for you."

Their post-sex happiness took the form of silliness, of lathering each other's bodies during a paroxysm of giggles as they stopped to kiss while sliding against each other's slippery soaped-up torsos and playfully bumping each other under the shower head's flow.

"My first Paris apartment, over in the Seventh," he said as he turned off the water and helped her out of the tub, "had a deep, V-shaped tub. Picture it. There was no way to sit in it comfortably. I tried a cheek on each side of the 'V' but I'd slide sideways. I tried kneeling, but human knees aren't designed to slant at that angle. I couldn't even stand up in it. I had to sort of rappel into it."

"So what did you do?"

"I finally settled on bathing on my side. But it was damn painful. The skin over my hip bones got so bruised from holding me up on the hard surface that I was always black and blue."

He insisted on drying her and they ended up back in bed, she with dry skin but his was still quite wet.

He went out to get fresh croissants at the bakery in the next block. While he was gone, Margo explored his apartment. The living room was small but beautifully furnished. The man had good taste—at least it matched hers. A modern Danish couch covered in saffron nubby silk was at one end of the room; in front of it stood a square coffee table made of abstract blue tiles set in rosewood. White leather and stainless steel Barcelona chairs sat on either side of the table. The room's walls were a soft gold. The names of the artists on his paintings were unfamiliar to her but she liked them—two impressionist landscapes and a splashily colorful cartoon portrait of

Ben. Beveled glass art deco doors led to a small garden with a few potted evergreens.

She went back into his bedroom, the scene of such memorable turmoil. Earlier, she had been too busy looking at him to see much of the room. She hadn't even noticed the large fauvist Parisian cityscape above his queen-size bed.

She gazed at herself in his mirrored closet doors. She was wearing one of his white terrycloth bathrobes since all she had with her was her blue silk party dress. Her hair had reverted to its normal semi-wild mass of ringlets but her face, even without makeup, was radiant. Never in her life, not even on her wedding day, had she looked so beautiful to herself.

She went back to the living room and sat on his couch, feeling incredibly at peace with herself. Her months of miserable mourning had abruptly ended in Ben's arms. She was utterly crazy about this man who had given her such profound pleasure. He had brought her back to life! Gazing down at her body, she was astounded at its new-found capabilities. Why had it taken her fifty-two years to discover what a ferociously sensual person she was?

When Ben returned, whistling cheerfully, he went into his small but modern kitchen and made a perfect omelet, soft and moist, with gruyere cheese, sautéed fresh mushrooms and scallions. With it were orange segments, the flaky almond croissants he had bought, and strong coffee. He served the meal on yellow and blue plates which Margo recognized as copies of Monet's dishes she had seen at Giverny.

"Oh, Monet! I love these!" she said, giving him a grateful smile.

"So do I," he said, giving her back a grateful smile for appreciating his taste. He reached over and held her hand while downing the last of his coffee.

"It's the best breakfast I've ever eaten," she gushed. "And I…"

The phone interrupted her. "I'll bet it's Jean," he said rather crossly, "warning me to leave you alone." He walked across the room and picked up the receiver. *"Bonjour,"* he said. He listened a moment, then said, "Yes, she's here." He listened again. "No, I won't let you talk to her."

Margo could hear Jean's shrieks from across the room. She went over and took the phone from Ben. "Hi, Jean."

"What are you doing there?" Jean asked in a frightened voice.

"Exactly what you think I'm doing here," Margo said. "And you don't have to worry. I'm having a wonderful time."

"Do you know what he *does* for a living?" Jean said, her voice lowering almost to a growl with urgency. "He's charming, sure, but Margo, he…he escorts women…for *money!*"

"Yes, I know."

"Margo!" Again, Jean sounded frightened. "Margo…you aren't *paying* him, are you? I'd never have invited him if I'd known…"

Margo couldn't help laughing. "Oh Jean, don't be such a worrywart. I'll phone you tomorrow." She hung up before Jean could say another word. Then she went over and sat on Ben's lap. When the phone rang again, they ignored it.

He put his arms around her. "Why is she so concerned about you?"

"I guess she feels responsible. It was her idea that I come live in Paris for a while. She helped me find my apartment and she introduced me to all her friends…"

"Even so. You're a big girl now."

They went back to bed until they got hungry for lunch.

Margo wore one of Ben's cardigans over her dress when they walked to her apartment in the late afternoon, their hands tightly clasped. Unlike the previous night, when she had approached his house hesitantly but highly-aroused, today she was alert and animated and in a delicious post-coital state. She felt as though her mind were a camera, snapping up everything she saw: every building, every pedestrian who crossed their path, every tree, everything! For the first time in her life, she understood the term, "walking on air," all because this amazing man had made her achieve roaring climaxes that radiated from her groin to every cell in her body.

But she felt more than gratitude to him. Beyond the physical thrills he had given her, a lovely feeling of intimacy had sprung up between them. Since Gil's death, she now realized, she had missed that sense of two people sharing themselves with each other, and while surely sex was the ultimate intimacy, it always led to a heightened closeness, at least for her. She glanced over at Ben. Did he feel the same? His affectionate attitude toward her certainly led her to believe so.

They crossed the Seine and cut across the spacious plaza in front of the ornate Hotel de Ville toward the Rue de Rivoli. "You know why they installed all these raised planters here?" he asked.

"Because they look good?"

"Because every group that has a gripe against the government puts on a protest here, in front of their city hall."

"So?"

"Well, protesters used to storm into this area by the thousands. And mobs are hard for the police to handle."

"So?" she repeated.

He stopped walking and gestured at the square. "The planters make it harder for the protesters to swarm. See? All those raised cement barriers slow the hordes down."

She gazed about her, then nodded. "I get the picture." She took his arm and they resumed walking.

With a terrible sense of horror, she suddenly remembered what he had said when they first met: that he was a *gigolo*. That sometimes he had sex with the women who hired him. "Is this what you do with your...clients?" she asked angrily. "Give them a city tour?"

"I give them whatever they want."

"Like...what we did last night? And all day today?" Abruptly, she pulled her hand off of his arm.

He stopped walking again and held both her arms, bending over so that his face was even with hers. "Margo. Darling. *You* aren't my client. I *chose* to be with you. Now listen carefully and don't jump to conclusions: I take these women sightseeing. Or to fancy restaurants. Or to night clubs. Places where they don't want to go alone. I'm not a gigolo. I'm an escort. And a guide."

"Last night you said you were a gigolo."

"Sometimes I say things for their shock value." He kissed the tip of her nose.

"How much do you charge?" she asked coldly. "By the hour? The day?"

He put his arms around her, a public gesture not at all uncommon in Paris. "Stop being so hostile," he whispered. "I adore you."

He again took her hand and they walked in silence another block to her building. She punched her code onto the small box of numbers outside the door and they went through a marble foyer and into a black wrought-iron cage barely large enough for two slim people. "Made for lovers," he said, holding her close as the elevator slowly rose.

Her apartment, on the top floor, had a large, high-ceilinged living room filled with two massive burgundy velvet easy chairs and a long matching sofa. "The furniture came with the apartment," she half-apologized. "It looks like a whore house."

"How do you know what a whore house looks like?" he asked.

"I was a madam in a previous life," she said, feeling wonderfully clever to have come up with the quip. She led him to one of the four tall French windows at the curved end of the living room and out onto a balcony so that he could see her view of Paris. The square towers of Notre Dame loomed a few blocks to the southwest and a jumble of roofs, treetops, chimneys and spires filled the vista for miles.

"Ever since I can remember, I had this romantic dream of living in Paris," she said. "I took French in high school and college, and then, for years, I was part of an advanced conversational French group at our city college. And *voila!* Here I am."

"Is Paris the way you expected?"

"You know, it was such a nebulous dream. I'd say to Gil, 'Let's go live in Paris for a year,' and he'd just laugh."

"You mean, this is your first time here?"

"Oh no, Gil enjoyed traveling. He took a month off every year and we traveled all over the world, but he couldn't imagine *living* anywhere but San Francisco." She sighed. "I don't know exactly what I expected, being in Paris. I guess I was hoping it would bring some sanity to my disrupted life."

"So what do you do here all day?"

"Oh, some days I rush out after breakfast and I prowl around the city, totally thrilled. I've been to every art gallery and museum in town."

"You said 'some days.' What about the other days?"

She shrugged. "Then I just hole up here in my apartment…almost like having agoraphobia. I get so paralyzed by grief…"

"Are you? Now?"

She laughed softly and hugged his waist. "Well, not today. How about you? Has Paris been everything you expected?"

He put an arm around her shoulders. "Yes. And the more I see of it, the more I'm convinced, it's the only place I ever want to live. I'm just sorry I spent so much of my life anywhere else."

He turned her toward him and licked her lips before kissing her, at first softly and then with growing urgency while he slipped his thumbs between their fused chests and stroked her nipples that eagerly swelled at his touch.

All at once he pulled away and looked at his watch. "Damn it, Margo, I have to go."

She was confused. "Go where?"

"I'm picking up a new client at seven…taking her on the *bateau-mouche.*"

She felt as though he had punched her in the stomach, but she managed to say, "What's that? Some kind of a boat?"

"You know, those tourist boats you see on the Seine all the time?"

She tried to keep her voice light, to hide her hideous disappointment. All the joy she had felt during the past twenty-four hours quickly slipped away. "Sounds like fun," she managed to say.

"They're best at night…they light up the buildings they're passing."

"Is that all? You're just going for a boat ride?" she asked, suddenly hopeful that afterwards he would come back to her.

"Oh no. I'm taking the lady to dinner at Ambrosie, and then to a night club. I'm sorry, darling."

In a daze, she took off his sweater and gave it to him, then she let him kiss her goodbye. At the door, he stopped abruptly. "Oh! I don't have your phone number." He removed a small black leather address book and a pen from his jacket pocket.

For a moment she was so angry that she was tempted to give him a false number. But despite his suddenly abandoning her, despite his being a goddamn gigolo, she desperately wanted to see him again. And again and again and again and again! She gave him the correct number. *When?* she wanted to beg him. *WHEN will I see you again?* But all he said was, "Caio," and he was gone. She heard the clang of the elevator door closing.

She took off her wrinkled party dress and put on pants and a silk shirt and went for an early evening walk. Desolation swamped her. She could hear the slow dirge of her heartbeat in her ears. She never had felt so abandoned, not even when Gil died.

But this is Paris, she exhorted herself, a mantra that often jolted her out of her negative thoughts. And at once, the reminder of where she was gave her a grace-note of buoyancy. She smiled up at the old buildings lining the Rue de Rivoli and she felt like skipping instead of walking sedately. Her earlier feelings of being deserted by Ben dissipated. Hadn't he said he just was a guide? Not a gigolo? Of course he cared about her. Taking these lonely women out for an evening was just a job. They meant nothing to him. *Ben,* she thought longingly. Surely she would see him tomorrow!

Slowing down when she passed her favorite *fromagerie*, she deeply inhaled the escaping aromas. *Roquefort? Camembert?* Next door, her fruit and vegetable man, Phillipe, was in front of his shop, straightening his outdoor displays of succulent-looking pears and plums. He smiled at her and she nodded. They had a private joke: he refused to sell her any item whose French name she didn't know. Sometimes she had to run home and look it up in her dictionary. Her flower lady saw her pass by and ran out to tell her she expected a shipment of pink roses in the morning, knowing they were Margo's favorite.

When Margo first arrived in Paris, she'd been annoyed by all the small neighborhood shops. At home she was accustomed to going once a week to Molly Stone's, with every known food available under one roof. These crazy French, she had thought, they buy only what they need for each day. What a colossal waste of time!

And then she had discovered the joy of having everything absolutely fresh. And the fun of getting to know the shopkeepers, who became her friends. Buying her food became a daily pleasure and a social event. The street was like a small-town village. She found herself raving to friends about the gorgeous trout she had bought that morning, so fresh she half-expected it to jump out of the refrigerator, or the peach that tasted more like a peach than any she ever had eaten.

She found herself in the Place de Vosges, her favorite square in all of Paris. When she passed Ambrosie she stopped to read their menu, sadly wondering what delicacy Ben would choose to eat that night, at his client's expense. Margo had had dinner there her second night in Paris, with Jean and Mort, and had found the food fantastically good, and fantastically expensive. "Clinton ate here when he came to Paris," Jean had boasted, as though she personally took credit for the former president's choice. "It's our favorite too," Mort had added smugly, as though that made him a VIP too.

Margo sat on a bench and gazed around the square, admiring the arcades that enclosed it. The symmetry of it never failed to thrill her, as it had countless throngs for four centuries. The city's history and architectural beauty gave her a feeling of spirituality that she had experienced in no other place she ever had visited—not even the world's most spectacular sites like Yosemite Valley or the Iguassu Falls or even the Taj Mahal. To her, Paris was mankind's consummate achievement.

As dusk settled on the square, she realized how romantic an hour it would be if she were there with Ben. Then the night ahead would be full of heady expectations: the excitement of the city's dazzling lights, its variety of entertainments, its promise of exquisite carnal pleasures. But when she was alone, dusk brought a nostalgia for lost joys and also the painful knowledge that a soul-numbing loneliness would pounce upon her during the long night ahead.

She tried not to think about Ben Waller and the hours she had spent with him. A man like Ben could become an obsession. She wondered how far the word "Love" could be stretched. Had she loved Gil? Well, of course she had! Or…was it the habit of intimacy that she had loved? Was the grief she was suffering over his death actually caused by losing the man himself, or was she missing the pleasant day-by-day life they had shared for thirty years? Could the explosive sex she'd experienced with Ben possibly be called "Love?" Especially since she wasn't sure if she really trusted the man?

All this self-examination reminded her of how impatient Gil always had been of her introspective nature. "Why are you torturing yourself?" he'd explode, his decisive mind rebelling at her habit of analyzing every angle of every action she contemplated taking. "Just decide what you want and for chrissake DO it!"

Easier said than done, she thought ruefully. And because so often she had been indecisive—in fact, downright wishy-washy—she realized that Gil frequently had made decisions for her. When they married, she had just graduated from college while he not only was older, but he already was an established doctor. He had urged her to use her art history major and English minor to become an art journalist. She really had had her heart set on being a political reporter, but he had talked her out of it, insisting that political writers had to be more forceful than she was, more ballsy. "You're too cautious," he'd said. "Too timid. In the art world that won't matter so much." So she had followed his advice. And who knows? Maybe he'd been right. She had to admit, she was good at it, had become accepted by the San Francisco art community as an authority.

Night had come, and the "City of Lights" was living up to its name. The grassy square where Margo sat was softly lit with an amber glow that accentuated every arch of the surrounding arcades. Her serenity was disrupted by a flash of envy of Ben's present companion. Oh the bitch! Yet to be fair, Margo admitted that the unknown woman undoubtedly was some unhappy widow going through the same bereavement she herself had been suffering, and who had come to Paris for the same reason Margo had—hoping the distracting attractions of the glamorous city would somehow ease her pain.

Margo shook off her pangs of jealousy and sat smiling while she let her imagination soar. She and Ben could have such a wonderful life together, once she talked him into giving up being a gigolo, or escort, or whatever he wanted to call it. They could live in his charming house—she loved the idea of it being their snug little love nest—and they could take little trips all over France. They could spend part of the year at her home in San Francisco. She could see them strolling around Union Square, hiking in the Muir Woods, going to all the art openings, plays, operas, concerts. Oh, life could be so good!

Margo walked back toward her apartment, then decided to have dinner at her favorite neighborhood restaurant, *Les Crustaces.* She had eaten in the peach and gold dining room often enough these past two months to be considered an *habitue* by the couple who owned the place, which meant she was greeted as an old friend and given little extra delicacies by the chef—a small sample of *escargot en croute, un petite tranche de tarte champignon, un plat des profiteroles.*

She kept wondering where Ben was at that moment. She told herself she would be wise never to see him again. Look at how he made her yo-yo from joy to despair. But she knew that the moment he called her, she would fly to him, if he didn't come to her first. Her desire to be with him wasn't really like being "in love." Or was it? Or was it simply being "in lust?"

When she arrived back at her apartment, her phone message machine was flashing it's little red light. *Let it be him!* she prayed. "God, Margo, how silly can you be?" she scolded herself aloud, taking deep breaths to slow her heart's sudden rush. She finally pushed the "play" button and she couldn't help the elation she felt at hearing Ben's soft voice.

"Margo. I'm in the men's room at Ambrosie, on my cell phone. Listen, I'll be away for a week, with my client. We're going to drive through the south of France. I'll call you when I get back."

She played it four times. She could feel her face grow pale and clammy. Her pangs of jealousy and disappointment were like physical blows. *She* was the one who should be in the south of France with him! *She* was the one who loved moseying around the French countryside, eating at rural cafés and staying at small hotels. He should be doing all that with *her*. And now he was going to do it with someone else.

She was furious at herself for even thinking that what she felt for Ben might be love. He used people. He pandered to poor bereaved women like herself, whether he took money from them as clients, or used fabulous sex to make them think he cared about them, as he had done to her.

She ordered herself to forget him. She had to stop remembering the thrills she had shared with him. *He's a goddamn GIGOLO!* she screamed at herself. If she fell any further into his beguiling trap, it could ruin her life. He could use her infatuation with him to make a fool of her. He could worm his way into her affections, pull her deeper and deeper into her dependency on him with his brilliant lovemaking, and when she was hooked beyond stopping, he might want to give up his disgusting work and expect her to support him. But in daydreaming about their life together, hadn't she implied that to herself?

He was all wrong for her. But she was obsessed with him. She picked up the novel she was reading, but the words were a blur as she kept seeing Ben making love to fat widows, thin widows, in fancy hotel rooms, on park benches, beneath the tables at Ambrosie. She put down the book and snapped on the TV. She channel surfed and everything looked boring. She alternated between feeling sick with jealousy and furious at herself because she couldn't stop thinking about Ben.

She had known him for only twenty-four hours but he had ruined whatever serenity she had accumulated during her month in Paris. "Oh screw Ben! Screw Paris!" she sobbed, feeling like a fool. She never had felt so miserable in her life.

In the morning, she phoned Jean. Her friend's behavior had been annoyingly intrusive in this Ben matter, but Margo knew that Jean sincerely was concerned about her welfare. She cheerfully assured Jean that her "little fling" with Ben was over, just a one-night stand, it meant nothing, and please, please, for Jean not to worry about her. Margo hung up the phone, ruefully wishing that her feelings for Ben were that simple.

For a week, Margo ran around Paris with a forced cheerfulness that wore her out. Still, her resentment at his going away with another woman was balanced by the promise of his being with *her* when he returned to Paris. At the end of the week she jumped whenever her phone rang and took a deep breath before answering it, expecting it to be Ben. But by the end of the second week, she finally admitted to herself that he wasn't ever going to call her again.

A deep despondency enveloped her, no matter how many times she reminded herself that SHE WAS IN PARIS. Furious at herself, she tried not to think about Ben, but she couldn't stop. And every time he swam into her thoughts, she suffered such a feeling of rejection that it took her breath away. She told herself that she wished she never had met him, but she couldn't lie to herself.

One night, when she was going out to dinner with Jean and Mort, Margo objected when Jean said she had made reservations at Ambrosie. "It's too expensive," Margo said, not really caring about the money but knowing Ben often took his clients there. She was desperate to see him, but not with another woman.

"Oh but you're our guest tonight," Jean insisted. "You paid for dinner the last time we went out together, and I've got my heart set on Ambrosie."

Margo prayed that Ben would take his client elsewhere that night, but unfortunately, when she came into the restaurant with Jean and Mort, the three of them were seated only two tables away from Ben and a plump, red-headed woman. So that's what his clients look like, Margo thought with savage jealousy. Ben nodded pleasantly at them, and the three of them nodded back.

"I'm glad you stopped seeing him," Jean said.

"Mmmm," Margo said, staring at the menu as though trying to

memorize it. It was all she could do to keep from going over to Ben's table, pulling the fake redhead out of her seat, and sitting down next to Ben herself.

She had trouble eating. She took small bites of the divine *poulet de Bresse* she had ordered and had to force herself to swallow. At one point she went to the ladies room and stood in the privacy of the booth taking deep breaths as she tried to quell her self-hatred. *How could she be so stupid as to care about a shallow, stupid, hurtful, miserable gigolo like Ben?*

The evening was a nightmare. She would no sooner start to feel better than her eyes would dart over to Ben and the misery would begin all over again.

Later, Margo sat out on her balcony, gazing forlornly at her dramatic view of Paris. Her feelings for Ben had become more than an obsession; her desire for him was making her physically ill. Why couldn't she stop longing for him? If she were an inexperienced teenager, she could understand such a lack of control over her feelings, but how could a woman her age be so weak?

What is it, she wondered, that makes some men so cruel? Why do they "love us and leave us?" Why couldn't Ben have been considerate enough to phone her and just say, "Goodbye, Margo, it's been fun knowing you, but there's no room for you in my life." Why had he left her dangling? Was he a compulsive sex addict? She had heard psychiatrists say that it was a disease affecting men who spent their entire lives avidly searching for new partners, unable to love any of them. She could pity Ben, if she weren't so furious at him.

She couldn't help mourning for the fabulous life together they could have had, if he had been a better person. If he didn't want her to support him, he could have found a job teaching math again, at one of the English language schools in Paris. "Could-a, could-a, could-a!" she mocked herself out loud. Sure, the life she had imagined for them was pure fantasy, but Damn!!!—it *coulda* been so wonderful!

Impulsively, she decided to phone him, but then she remembered that she didn't have his number. No, better still, she would go over to his place in the morning and confront him. She stood up, elated at the idea of seeing him again, but then she sat down, in a panic of indecision. *Don't you dare go to him!* she silently screamed at herself. *What's wrong with you? Do you want the humiliation of having him reject you right to your face?*

She could hear Gil's annoyed voice saying, *For God's sake, Margo! Stop being such a fool! Just put the guy out of your fucking mind. Period. End of problem.*

In a burst of pain, she phoned American Airlines and asked for a reservation on a flight to San Francisco the next morning. She knew if she waited any longer, she would lose her nerve.

After a restless night, she showered and dressed in her travel uniform, a dark blue pants suit loose enough to sit in for many hours. Packing was easy. She put her favorite clothes in the two suitcases she had brought with her and left the rest of her things for the woman who cleaned her apartment every Friday. Marcelle had a key and Margo wrote a note to her, leaving it with a check drawn on her Paris bank.

She didn't phone anyone, not even Jean and Mort. She would write to them when she got home, and to others she had met while living in Paris, and thank them for their kindnesses to her. All during the flight, she was agitated, worried that the miles she was putting between herself and Ben would fail to end her insane obsession with him. Good God, she thought, where do I have to go to stop yearning for him? On a one-way trip to Mars?

As she entered her house on Russian Hill, which usually filled her with pride, she felt only mildly appreciative of its soothing beauty. She walked from one airy room to the next, pleased with her choices of color and furniture and art but unable to shake a sense of failure. From the heights where her house was perched, she looked down at San Francisco Bay and at Berkeley and Oakland beyond, a view that always had given her a joyful jolt. Yet all she felt now was an overwhelming sadness.

For a whole week, she put off phoning anyone, even her daughter, just wanting to wallow in sorrowful solitude. She stayed indoors and shopped for food late at night, when none of her friends would be at the market. She was too dispirited to talk to anyone.

Toward the end of the week, being home, in the house that she and Gil had so happily shared, she was swamped with rollicking recollections of her years with Gil, as though his spirit were forcing her to remember all the fun they'd had. Like, making love all over the house after Terry got married and moved to Hawaii. Waking up at 3 a.m. and eating omelet sandwiches with raw onion on rye bread. Camping at Yosemite where they tramped on every trail in the park. Winter vacationing at the venerable Death Valley Furnace Creek Inn. Rafting with thirty other adventurous souls down the Colorado River through the length of Grand Canyon. She and Gil always together. Always holding hands, touching, braided together while sleeping, all the physical ways of expressing love. All the verbal togetherness, too, never running out of things to talk about, and the ongoing brainy competition—what's the capitol of Cambodia, who was president in 1842, when was Thomas Jefferson born??? All the loving one-upsmanship. Oh yes, they'd had fun all right!

The memories made her laugh, and cry. But they helped her sort out her feelings. It was as if Gil's spirit were reminding her that life could be so very, very good. And for her to get on with it.

She asked herself, very honestly, whether she would still want to be with Ben if Gil miraculously reappeared and she knew at once that the answer was a resounding NO. She would give everything she owned to have Gil return to her, even for an hour. Even five minutes! But she had been trying all year to accept the fact that his death was final, *that Gil wasn't ever going to be with her again.*

Then she asked herself, was she going to let one stupid man keep her from enjoying Paris, after all the years she had dreamed of living there? She already had paid the rent for four more months on her Paris apartment. Her friends there were waiting to visit more art galleries with her. The owners of *Les Crustaces* would be concocting dozens of delicacies for her to taste. Paris had hundreds of streets that she hadn't yet explored. And, she reminded herself, France had hundreds, thousands, even millions of charming men she hadn't yet had a chance to meet. A new love interest certainly would put a quick end to her desire for Ben.

So enough's enough, Margo, she scolded herself, *it's time to get your silly ass back to Paris! It's time to get on with your life.*

On her return flight to Paris, she asked herself what she would do if Ben ever called her again. Would she see him? Or would she be sensible and refuse? With a terrible sigh, she had to admit that despite all that had happened, despite all the misery he had put her through, she still would be unable to resist him.

And then she had so brilliant an idea that she whispered a soft "Oh!" She would get his phone number from his Herald Trib advertisement and hire him for a week's trip through Provence! Then, during their week together, either he would fall desperately in love with her and they'd live together happily ever after. Or, she would find him an utterly self-centered bore and she finally would get over her foolish obsession with him.

Grinning, she leaned back in her seat, thrilled because she was going to see Ben again.

Zinging in Zermatt

I

Thirty-three years ago, four babies were born many miles apart. Then they all met. And...WOW!

Daniel Sawyer was an only child, born in Chicago to Sadie and Irving Sapperstein when they were both in their early forties. They had been married sixteen years, had tried without success to get pregnant starting right on their wedding night. Then, after they had given up all hope of ever having a child, out came Daniel.

Of course they wanted the best for him, including a nice American name to go with the nice American life they envisioned for him. But what do you do with Sapperstein? Sap? Sapp? Sapper? Stein? Well, at least they kept the S.

So Sadie became Selma Sawyer, and Irving became Ian Sawyer, and they joined the local Episcopal Church. Yahoo! Instant Wasps.

Alison Sawyer, nee Clark, was the fourth of seven children. Her parents had no talents, except for reproducing Clarks. She had siblings almost old enough to be her parents and sibs almost young enough to be her kids, but none very close to her own age. She grew up rather lonely inside the family, even though she was quite pretty, and quite smart, but quite un-noticed, which was why she always had to work harder than other kids to get the same grades. Still, in her quiet, dogged way, she managed to graduate from Newark High as salutatorian, get a scholarship at Columbia, study pre-med, and only when she'd earned her MD.did her family take some notice of her. Quiet little Alison? A doctor? Who'da thunk it?

So she left her native New Jersey, did her pediatric residence at the Michael Reese Hospital in Chicago, got a job that didn't pay all that much doctoring black kids at a clinic on Chicago's south side, shared an apartment with three U of Chicago women graduate students. At the wedding of one of her roommates she met Daniel, who had an MBA from Northwestern and a high-powered job with Searles Laboratories' marketing department.

Alison married Daniel six months later. Whoa!

Now leap from Chicago to Houston where baby Kessler, first name Reinhard, a third-generation German-American, was born, not with a silver spoon in his mouth, but with one that was solid gold and studded with diamonds. Or rubies. Or whatever gems cost the most. He was the oldest of three sons who inherited the same ambition genes that had made their great-grandfather stinkin' rich. Don't ask how. Great-granddaddy diversified. Oil, lumber, ship-building, utilities. But Reinhard and his brothers wanted to "make it" on their own. All three got into the computer explosion, Reinhard as the Texas version of Bill Gates, his brother Deiter as a hugely successful hardware designer, and youngest brother Hans with a chain of computer super-stores.

Then Reinhard, as the oldest, inherited his Uncle Hugo's electronics conglomerate in Munich, Germany. Reinhard and his wife Trudi moved themselves from a penthouse in Houston into Hugo's palatial Munich mansion near the former Dukes of Bavaria's palace and the young American couple transformed themselves into ersatz German nobility. Reinhard even learned how to click his heels and give a little bow and Trudi let her inborn haughtiness come to full flower.

Speaking of Trudi, she was the fourth baby in this quartet, daughter of a fat Austrian couple who owned a small inn outside of Aspen, Colorado. They were modest people, short, solid and stolid.

They didn't know what to make of their little girl who acted like a princess from the day she was born. Trudi grew tall and regal, smart and shrewd, beautiful, talented and athletic. She taught herself to ski before she began kindergarten. Her mother let her help make meals for their guests, and Trudi became a fabulous gourmet cook. Her school teachers were in awe of her abilities, in subject after subject.

Of course she quickly outgrew Aspen. She outgrew Colorado. She outgrew and outgrew until she became the most Senior Vice President of Reinhard Kessler's giant Houston enterprise, second in command only to Herr Boss himself. *Yavold!* And in no time at all— you guessed it!—she became the wife of Reinhard Kessler. Who was the boss now?

So, here we are, with just the basics on Daniel and Allison Sawyer, both working hard to better themselves in Chicago, and Reinhard and Trudi Kessler, who already *had* bettered themselves in Munich. I mean, how much better can you be than everyone else? How did the two couples meet? Be patient. I'll tell you how.

II

Alison stared up at the chair lift in panic. How did she get into this terrifying situation? She was bundled up in thick garments, her feet encased in heavy boots that were locked onto a pair of skis. Adding to her misery was the frigid air that made her nose run. Just because Daniel's company was trying to make some deal with Herr Kessler's company, did she have to suffer like this?

"Come," Herr Kessler said gently but firmly. He put a strong arm around her and the next thing she knew, they were sitting side by side on the lift as it marched up the side of the mountain. She clung to the pole that held up her seat while her alarm grew. And grew. She was afraid to look down. Up there, at the top, she would have to jump off the lift and if she didn't fall down and suffer a multiple fracture, she would break her neck, her spine and both hips trying to ski down the mountain. Why hadn't she just said NO, I DON'T KNOW HOW TO

SKI? And then refused to go? But she was so damn meek. *You're a fucking doctor!* she screamed at herself. *You're not supposed to let people push you around.*

She decided that enough was enough. When they reached the top, she would simply refuse to ski down that stupid mountain. Cautiously, she glanced down, and caught her breath. It looked so easy, and so…WONDERFUL!!…all those skiers skimming in great slaloms across the snow. But she couldn't. She wouldn't! She would stay on the chair lift and go back down. Maybe she would try the bunny slope, even if all the little Swiss tots laughed at her.

She looked down again and recognized Daniel's green ski jacket and Trudi's white parka with white fur trim. They were skiing side by side, passing everyone in sight. Lucky Daniel! His parents had been lesson-crazy: piano, guitar, tennis, golf, swimming, and of course skiing lessons every winter, in New Hampshire, in the Rockies and the High Sierra, in Canada, one year in Gstaad. Their darling little Danny had to have the best of everything. Alison felt a vast exasperation with her parents-in-law. They had created an aristocrat who didn't know how to live in a world of mortgage payments and utility bills and taking out the garbage.

As they approached the top of the mountain, Alison took in a deep breath, summoned her courage and said, "I'm not going to…"

But as she spoke, Herr Kessler swept her off the lift and side by side they were flying down, down, he was holding her, their skis like four parallel lines, and it was…heavenly! She was screaming with the thrill of it, too crazy-high to care about anything else in the world. Just this, this soaring, no longer earth-bound but soaring like a butterfly caught up in the wind.

The cold air made her eyes tear and her lungs freeze, but it didn't matter. She felt not so much safe as without a care, with Herr Kessler's arms guiding her. Nothing else mattered. Just this. She felt disembodied, ecstatic.

Reinhard turned her just enough for their four skis to brake, and they stopped. They smiled at each other and then she laughed like a delighted child. She flashed onto a memory of her father throwing her little self into the air and catching her—"more, daddy, more?" she'd beg—but he'd quickly lose interest. Now she wanted to say it to Herr Kessler—he had asked her to call him Reinhard but he seemed so forbiddingly formal, she half-expected him to click his heels and bow like German generals she'd seen in movies. Of course she couldn't ask him to take her up again. He'd been kind to give her as much of his time as he already had.

"That was…exhilarating," she said, trying to tame the lilt in her voice.

He did bow, slightly. Formally. Together, they joined Daniel and Trudi at a sunlit table on the ski lodge terrace where they could look up and gaze at the Matterhorn. Alison felt a rush of happiness. She was delighted with the luxurious ski lodge and this resort town without cars, and the tinker-toy train that had carried them up to this never-never land from the railroad station far down below where they had parked the Kessler's Mercedes after driving there from Munich.

Daniel never had seen Alison so animated. She looked positively stunning—not only happy but pleased with herself. She was always so serious, so often preoccupied, and he admired this in her; it had attracted him in the first place. He disliked frivolity in a woman. He never had dated girls with too much makeup or provocative clothes.

But Trudi Kessler was something else. She was so flamboyant, so totally gorgeous, so damn sexually exciting…but he couldn't see himself ever having the nerve to go to bed with her. Even if she were the aggressor. And there were moments, like on the chair lift when she had put her hand on his upper thigh and left it there. Even through his heavy ski pants and her glove he had felt a flash of heat.

He wondered why he felt unworthy of her. He wasn't her equal in wealth, but he could hold his own as a human being. He was good looking, excellent at sports, educated, intelligent, personable. He knew all that, but despite all the lessons his parents had provided for him, they had given him something else without realizing it: a sense of unworthiness. Why, he couldn't figure out. His parents also educated and attractive, yet they were extremely picky about their friends, their food, their home and it contents. They were too critical of other people's possessions and lifestyles and much too smug about their own good taste. They hardly ever approved of Daniel's friends. "They're not good enough for you," was their usual refrain. Even Alison hadn't made the grade. Daniel had been able to tell from their faces that they didn't like her, though they had smiled and acted pleased to meet her.

But in time, Alison had earned their respect, if not their love. He looked over at her. She was quiet, but not from shyness. He could tell. No, she seemed to be nursing some inner pleasure.

He smiled at her. He wondered if he really knew her, even after seven years of marriage. He brushed away the thought. Of course he knew her. No doubt, he concluded, she was happy that she had managed to ski down the mountain without breaking her pretty little neck.

"What d'ya think," Trudi asked Reinhard later, in the privacy of their ski lodge chalet. "Will they go for it?" She removed her parka and sweater and bra and ski pants and panties in that order and dropped them on the floor. She loved to walk around naked.

"I'm not sure." Reinhard grabbed her from behind and gently caressed her nipples, one in each hand.

She wiggled with pleasure. "So how do we present it to them? Should we be subtle? Or come right out with it?"

He turned her around and kissed her deeply before answering her. "Most Americans are weird about sex, my darling. They love to look sexy, but deep down they're prudes. I think we'll have to be careful." He removed his own clothes, left them on the floor and kicked them out of the way.

She went up to him and rubbed herself against his newly-exposed penis that was beginning its elevator act. "Just in case it doesn't work with the Americans, how about some fireworks of our own right now, *mein herr* ?"

"You know my motto, darling. Never say 'no' when you can say 'yes!'" He grabbed her roughly, throwing her down onto the bed, knowing she enjoyed his cave-man tactics. Though they had been married for nine years and had shared every type of sexual act known to man, and woman, they always went at it like two snarling animals intent on devouring each other.

"So what d'you think of them?" Daniel asked, taking off his wet ski pants and carefully hanging them over a chair in their chalet.

"They seem nice." Alison removed her jacket, sweater, ski pants and thermal underwear, folding them on a table but leaving on her bra. She was uncomfortable about exposing her large breasts, even though Daniel had seen her naked thousands of times.

"Nice? *Nice?* They're two of the most high-powered, important people you'll ever meet."

"Okay. They're two *nice* high-powered, important people. I'm impressed." She wanted to add, *I think Trudi's a bitch and Reinhard's divine.* Alison didn't trust women who were classic beauties, and whose blonde hair, makeup and clothes were always impeccable. A little flaw would have made Trudi more approachable. And how the hell did the woman ski down a mountain and end up on the ski lodge terrace with every hair in place? Alison knew that her own auburn hair, when she took off her parka, had looked like a bird's nest.

But Reinhard was something else. Flying down the mountain with him was the most thrilling experience of her life. Afterwards, she had felt a rush of desire for him. He was the handsomest man she ever had seen. Not that she put much stock in looks, especially in men. Fabulous-looking people tended to be horribly conceited. How could they help it with everyone fawning over them just because their genes had been thrown together in a haphazardly attractive way? She preferred to admire achievement. Nevertheless, Reinhard turned her on as she never had been turned on before.

"Are they really Americans, Danny? They seem so German."

"It's an act," Daniel scoffed. "I knew Reinhard in Houston. His family's German—you know, German-American—but in those days he was one hundred percent Texas-American."

"A breed unto themselves." Alison began brushing her hair. "Anyway, Reinhard and Trudy have their 'I'm a snooty aristocrat' act down pat."

"Want a little nooky?" Daniel interrupted her.

She hated the term, but it was one of Daniel's favorites. She also disliked turning him down unless she didn't feel well. If anything, she already was feeling amorous because of Reinhard. But, she fretted to herself, was it fair to have sex with one man when another man put you in the mood in the first place? You have to understand, Alison is a jerk when it comes to scruples. To paraphrase Gertrude Stein, an orgasm is an orgasm is an orgasm. What the hell difference does it make how, who or what turns you on?

"Sure," she said. She went over and kissed him, wishing he would put a little effort into some simple romantic foreplay before posing his annoying "nooky" question. She closed her eyes and let her imagination take over. Now it was Reinhard caressing her, not Daniel, Reinhard kissing her. Reinhard caressing her. *Ohhhh Reinhard!*

The four of them met for before-dinner drinks in the living room of the Kesslers' ski lodge chalet. They were seated in a comfortable circle around a coffee table crowded with Japanese sushi, Thai lobster rolls, Italian prosciutto and melon, French brie, and Norwegian jumbo prawns with a dill dipping sauce. All four of them had martinis in hand and nobody touched the food. So much for offering fancy hors d'oeuvres to skinny people.

Reinhard changed his mind about being subtle and decided on a direct approach. "There's an old German custom," he began, "called *fasching*. It used to be that on Rose Monday, which is today—the day before Fat Tuesday, or Mardi Gras as you probably know it—everyone went to a masked ball in costume. For the next twenty-four hours, husbands and wives were free. They could sleep with anyone they wanted, and afterwards, no questions were asked. It's pretty much gone out of style, so Trudi and I have streamlined it. No costumes. No masks. No balls. We simply swap partners with whomever we're with." He flashed a smile at Alison while Trudi threw back her head and gave Daniel a challenging smile. "Anyone interested?"

Alison and Daniel looked at each other. She just had had lusty sex with Daniel by imagining he was Reinhard. Did she want to try the real thing? You bet! But she was afraid of hurting Daniel's feelings if she admitted it.

Daniel told himself that he would give a year's pay for a chance to ball the luscious Trudi, but how could he let Alison submit to Reinhard? The poor little thing was adamantly against adultery in any form. At least, he was pretty sure she was. Come to think of it, they'd never really discussed the matter. He stared into her eyes and...was he going crazy? She actually looked eager. He couldn't believe it! Her shining eyes, her smiling face, her entire body, was silently screaming, *"Yes! Let's do it!"*

Daniel was torn between outrage at Alison for wanting another man and his own frantic desire to make love to Trudi. He looked over at Trudi who was smiling at him seductively. He groaned aloud and quickly covered it with a cough. He cleared his throat, still furious with Alison. He looked at Reinhard who was watching him with supercilious glee. Finally, Daniel realized that all three were staring at him, waiting for his verdict. "Is it up to me?" he managed to croak.

"Oh come on, Daniel!" Trudi said impatiently. "When in Rome..."

"Do as the Romans do?" Daniel rasped. "Is that what you're saying?" He looked over at Alison. "What d'you think, Ali?"

"I'll do whatever you want," she said. *Say YES, you fool!* she wanted to scream at him.

"Well, okay," Daniel finally murmured.

Needless to say, none of them ate dinner that night.

They agreed that Alison and Reinhard would spend the night in the Kessler's chalet while Trudi and Daniel went over to the Sawyer's chalet, fifty feet away, and they'd all meet in the lodge dining room for breakfast at ten the next morning. There was an awkward moment when Trudi and Daniel went to the door and Alison and Reinhard followed them and the two couples didn't know whether to kiss their spouses good night. They finally got sorted out and Reinhard closed the door and turned to Alison. He clicked his heels with a slight bow and said, with a broad smile, "At your service, Madame. May I get you something to drink?"

"I think I've had enough," she said, sitting down on the couch.

"Allow me to surprise you." He went into the chalet's kitchen and emerged five minutes later with a tray holding two big steaming mugs.

Alison took one and looked into it. "Hot chocolate?"

"Yavold! Mit creme schlage. Real whipped cream. None of that crap we get back home that you spray out of a can."

She sipped it slowly to hide her nervousness. This beautiful man turned her on, but she never had had sex with anyone but Daniel, not before their wedding and certainly not since. She felt shy about undressing in front of him and almost terrified of having him touch her. And yet, the silly little goof was shaking with desire for him.

He came over to the couch and sat beside her. He took her half-finished mug from her and set it on the coffee table. When he took her in his arms and kissed her, all her fears dissolved. Unfortunately for Daniel, Alison's lovemaking with Reinhard was so fantastic that she couldn't believe it was the same act she had been performing with her husband for seven years. As for Reinhard—the sophisticate, the man of the world, the hot-shot lover—he was stunned too. He'd had sex with at least three dozen, maybe four dozen women in his life, but nothing, *nothing* could match this. Sex with the others had ignited his sex organs, but sex with Alison had exploded in his heart. Or soul. Or somewhere in that vicinity.

A dilemma? You bettcha!

Meanwhile, pan over to the chalet where Daniel and Trudi were naked on the king-size bed. From the POV of the chandelier above them, it looked like a wrestling match. Trudi was super-aggressive, bouncing him all over the place and when they finally consummated he came too fast and left her high and, well not dry, because she was covered with his semen. He apologized profusely, which is hardly a romantic thing to do, and he offered to blow her away. She agreed but he was embarrassed and she was pissed and it took longer than either of them expected.

They put on robes and went out to the living room where they had a couple of Scotches on empty stomachs, not a good idea after their earlier martinis. When they returned to bed, he couldn't get it up and she didn't give a damn by then, so when he said he was tired, they turned in opposite directions and tried to sleep. Since neither of them could, Daniel looked in Alison's cosmetic bag and found a bottle of Nembutal and they each took one and finally fell asleep.

It was a whole different scene in the Kessler's chalet. Alison and Reinhard couldn't leave each other alone. They made love all night and it got better and better and by morning they knew they were soul mates and all that jazz and they decided to stay together forever. Yes, they felt sorry for poor Daniel. Yes, they pitied poor Trudi. But what the hell, you only live once. More than likely, anyway.

Surely you can imagine the rest? The tears? The screams? The recriminations? And please, please, don't forget the lawyers who made a ton of money on the mess.

Is there a moral to the story? Yeah. If you want to save your marriage, stay home and don't go to bed with strangers.

Taking a Chance in Prague

In all her thirty-eight years, Julie never had felt so alone as she did standing on the Charles Bridge, just before twilight, watching people cross the bridge, some walking quickly, others strolling languidly. Coming to Prague had been a big mistake, she decided. During her first three weeks there she had kept busy sightseeing. But now she had seen everything in the guidebooks. She had gone to every art gallery. She even had visited the famous old Jewish cemetery simply because it was on the list of tourist attractions, although she hated cemeteries. In fact, the fallen tombstones, stacked like outsize playing cards, had saddened her.

She was in Prague because she had inherited a lovely small house there. A great aunt she never had met, her grandmother's ninety-year-old sister Helene, had died and left everything she owned to Julie. Julie had to keep suppressing her guilt at never having visited her Great-aunt. All Julie's life, Aunt Helene had sent her generous birthday and Christmas gifts and fervent invitations to visit, with offers to pay for the trip, but Julie always had been too busy. Too busy with school. Then too busy trying to build a career as a stockbroker after she graduated from Columbia. And mostly too busy with lovers, either in the rapturous beginning of a new affair or in the letdown of the ending. Now it was too late to meet Helene. Julie was overwhelmed with remorse.

Still, she always had felt close to Aunt Helene, the two of them the "old maids" of the family. Julie often wondered about this mysterious lady who had left her not only the house but enough money to live on very comfortably if she never worked another day in her life. Had Helene ever had a lover? Many lovers? Or none at all? Could she have been a *lesbian?* The photographs of Helene in a leather-bound album on her coffee table showed a woman of great beauty, and Julie felt a jolt of vanity when she realized that she and Helene could have been twins.

The books in Helen's house, in Czech, English, French and German, indicated an educated, sophisticated mind. Her collection of Czech art was quite exceptional. Where had her money come from? Julie had a feeling that Helene never had worked. Nor had the money been inherited because Helene's sister, Greta, Julie's grandmother, had complained endlessly of their deprived childhoods. Yes, Julie concluded, Helene's wealth had to have been accumulated from men who had loved her.

Now Julie's grandmother and parents were dead and Julie didn't know where to turn to find out more about Helene. Julie still was going through Helene's house, trying to find more clues about her benefactor's life. But she had come across no letters or journals or anything that would reveal the woman to her, beyond the photos. She even had called Helene's lawyer, but he knew no more about Helene's personal life than Julie did.

Julie hadn't had a decent conversation since she left home. At least back in New York she had friends, plus her book group, her bridge group, her gym, her job as a broker for Merrill Lynch where she had been with the other employees and clients all day long. Here in Prague, she spoke only to shopkeepers and even then, if they didn't know English, she had to point to things she needed or stumble over the Czech words in her English-Czech dictionary.

She knew she should sell Aunt Helene's house and go home. But since she had come over intending to stay at least six months, she had rented her Chelsea condo to a couple and had given them a six-month lease. She decided not to rush into any rash decisions just because standing on the beautiful bridge on a lovely June dusk was making her feel desolate.

She knew that many of her friends back home felt sorry for her. Even in these days of liberated womanhood, being thirty-eight and never having been married still carried a stigma. She could see that appraising look in people's eyes as they wondered if she might be a lesbian. When rude people brought it up with prying questions like, "So...were you *ever* married? Or engaged?" she liked to smile enigmatically and simply not reply. She had learned early in life that you don't have to answer every question put to you.

She had been promiscuous since her teens, and she had loved every minute of it. But the price she now paid was an inability to love any one man. She never lived with any of her lovers because she knew that sooner or later someone would come along whom she would find more attractive. Sometimes she juggled more than one man at a time in her life. She had absolutely no desire for a long-term relationship. In fact, she carefully avoided men who had that "it's time to get married and settle down" look in their eyes.

What her married friends didn't understand was the thrill of falling in love, over and over again. The intoxication of beginning a new relationship gave her life an addictive, provocative spice. She thrived on those enthralling first dates of "getting to know you," of confiding the half-truths that made up her past. What fun she had, again and again recreating herself for each new man in her life. She couldn't imagine having sex with the same man year after year, or even for too many months. Oh sure, she understood the profound bond that could develop in a long-term loving relationship, but did it compensate for the loss of enthralling variety?

She sauntered along the bridge, glancing at the crafts and paintings for sale. She was more interested in the vendors than in their wares. Most of them were young people, bantering cheerfully among themselves, getting ready to pack up for the day. She wondered, scanning their faces in the waning light, where each would be going now. Home? Clubs? Night jobs? Did they have lovers, spouses, children, parents? She enjoyed looking at strangers and trying to imagine what their lives were like, just from the expressions on their faces.

She hadn't felt lonely until this evening on the bridge. A few times since arriving in Prague she had considered going to a bar to meet men, but being in a foreign place had thrown her into an unaccustomed shyness. She had traveled before, to many places in Western Europe, but living here in a house instead of a hotel had somehow induced this feeling of timidity.

"Hello lady!" Her reverie was interrupted by a slender, clean-shaven man holding up a small watercolor painting of the bridge. "Take a bit of Prague home with you? Only ten dollars."

She stopped and took the painting from him. It was unframed, but was held firmly taped to a piece of cardboard. Actually, it was good. "It's worth more than ten dollars," she told him.

He laughed. "You're supposed to bargain."

"All right. I'll give you fifty."

He shook his head, as though she had said something unfair. "My counter-offer? You must have a drink with me and then I shall give you the painting free."

She looked at him more carefully. He was dressed in a gray sweatshirt and black pants. His face was tan, contrasting with his pale blond hair. He had blue eyes and rather feminine, beautifully delineated lips...and he was at least ten years younger than she was. She laughed, suddenly having fun. "Isn't that the craziest bargaining you've ever done?"

"Definitely. Did I make a sale?"

"Not quite. I'll accept your offer, but you must let me pay for the drinks. And dinner afterwards."

He put out his hand. "It's a deal."

She took his hand and he held onto hers longer than a handshake should last. He slipped the painting into a protective plastic bag and she took it from him and put it into her oversized shoulder bag.

He gathered together his six other paintings displayed on a large easel which ingeniously folded up into a plastic case with a shoulder strap.

"Pretty neat," she said.

He took her arm, briskly leading her toward the Old Town

Square. They didn't speak until they were settled at a small outdoor café table where the waiters all seemed to know him. "Two of the usual," he called to one of them.

"How do you know that I'll like whatever 'the usual' is?" she asked.

"You will." He studied her face. "Are you Czech?"

"Half."

"Oh you Americans! Half this, a quarter that." He smiled. "How many fractions are you?"

"Does it matter? We try not to make a big deal about who came from where."

He shook his head. "Quite the contrary. With most Americans I meet, it is, I am French-English, or I am Scotch-Irish, or I am German-Swiss, or I am Jewish. As if Judaism were a nationality and not a religion."

"Judging by my Jewish friends, it's a state of mind."

Their drinks arrived in tall glass cups. She looked at hers, then took a sip: coffee with some sweetish liqueur she couldn't identify—Irish cream? Frangelica?—and thick whipped cream swirled into it. Heavenly.

"You see? I knew you would like it." He stared at her face again.

"Now what are you looking for?" She was somewhat annoyed.

He smiled, drinking his coffee concoction slowly, still gazing at her. 'I look at people closely to see if we are soul mates."

"So? Are we?"

"I am not sure." He nodded slowly. "I can tell you this. When you smile, there is sadness in your eyes."

Again, she was irritated. "You are very presumptuous. Do you by any chance know what that means?"

"Of course I know."

"How did you learn such good English? You have almost no accent."

"I learned it in school, from an early age. Then I was an exchange student for one year in high school. Omaha, Nebraska. You know it?"

"Never been there."

"Too bad. A nice city. I am, you might say, one-thirtieth American, because I spent one of my thirty years in America."

She finished her coffee, feeling slightly tipsy. "So...do you make a living, selling your work?"

"I also paint houses. Every afternoon. You know, walls, ceilings, sometimes furniture. No, don't look sorry for me. I find it very satisfying to take old walls and make them look fresh. It is a different way of creating beauty." He took his last sip of coffee. "Tell me, why are you here? Somehow you are not like a typical tourist."

"Are you psychic?"

"I would say...perceptive." He smiled slyly. "Do you know by any chance what *that* means?"

"Touche."

He indicated their cups. "Would you like another?"

She shook her head. "They're too strong. You'd have to carry me home."

"That would be a great pleasure." He took her hand. "My name is Bruno."

"Mine is Julie."

"A very nice name."

"So is Bruno. It sounds...well, strong."

"Where are you staying?" He still was holding her hand. "The Intercontinental?"

She shook her head. "I have a house." She wondered how much she should tell him. He could be a thief. Or a murderer for all she knew.

"You are renting a house? You are planning to live here?"

"I don't know yet if I'll stay. I inherited the house from an elderly aunt." She knew she was blabbing too much. None of this was his business.

"I can see in your eyes that you don't trust me, Julie. And you are right, you should not trust a stranger, no matter how charming he is. I might come and murder you in the middle of the night if you told me where you live.

"Yes, you might."

"I would rather come to you in the middle of the night and make love to you."

She was quite certain that she and this Bruno could have fabulous sex. He had just the right combination of virility, vitality, good looks and sensitivity to make a great lover. But should she take a chance on a random pick-up like this? Usually, she refused to go to bed with men the first time she met them. The few times she had, they were men who had been introduced to her by good friends whose judgment she trusted.

"I can see in your face, Julie, that you very much want to make love with me, but you are afraid. I am a stranger. Who knows what I might do? But remember, you are a stranger to me, too, but I do not fear you."

"Of course you don't. We're not the dangerous sex."

"Oh yes you are! You harm us in worse ways."

"Maybe, but we aren't likely to strangle you in the middle of the night."

He looked sad. "Julie, please don't be afraid. I could make Prague so memorable for you."

"Don't you have a girlfriend? Or maybe even a wife?"

"I have many women. But no, I am not married." He still was holding her hand.

"What do you mean by 'many women?'"

"Many women want to make love with me. Some are beautiful, some are plain. We have fun in bed. But we are not in love. We have no strings, no hard feelings when an affair ends. We part friends."

"Always?"

"Of course there are exceptions. Sometimes they fall in love with me, but I never fall in love with them. It is not in my nature to stay with one woman only. Monogamy is for fools."

She laughed, thinking how much alike they were. "I couldn't agree more."

"Ah, Julie. You need to be loved. You need me to make your body soar once again."

She looked up at the dark sky, full of stars. She hadn't had any sex for three weeks, not since leaving New York. Now she could feel desire coursing through her. Her nipples were hardening in anticipation of having his lovely mouth tease them. Her lips trembled, wanting his kisses, and her tongue tingled at the thought of dueling with his. She could feel her vagina tighten in its eagerness to have him enter her. Why not? her body begged her. Why the hell not?

He moved his chair closer to hers and gently pulled her head toward him so that their lips touched. Oh, he was good! His mouth had just the right pressure to thrill her and yet soothe her fears. His kisses said, trust me. I'll take you to the moon and bring you back safely, and oh so happy.

When he finally drew his mouth away from hers, they smiled at each other. "Listen," he said softly, "my place is near here, and you won't have to worry that I'll steal your aunt's silver."

She nodded her agreement, too aroused to speak.

Again, he walked briskly, holding her arm and guiding her across the softly lit square and down one side street and then another. Every now and then he stopped and drew her close and kissed her, keeping her heart in a steady uproar.

His apartment was up three flights of dimly lit stone steps. He flung open his door and led her inside. He flipped a switch and a row of baby spots came on, glowing against a wall of his larger work. She could see that he was talented. But this was no time for an art critique.

They kissed standing in the middle of the room. They kissed leaning against a wall. They kissed lying on his bed, in an alcove off the studio. They kissed while removing their own and each other's clothing. At last he kissed her impatient breasts and entered her eager vagina and what happened afterwards was one of the sweetest, most powerful eruption of pleasure she ever had enjoyed.

The next day she took him to Aunt Helene's place. Now he spends every night with Julie in the big ornate bed in her charming house. He spends every morning painting in his studio, and every afternoon painting houses, and the rest of the time he spends with Julie. He had to give up selling his work on the bridge; there just wasn't time, but she is trying to get him a show at a New York gallery managed by one of her old lovers who remained her friend.

As for Julie, she keeps busy with Czech language lessons. She is learning how to cook. She revived her childhood interest in playing the piano, inspired by Aunt Helene's Steinway grand in her living room. Julie derives enormous pleasure from playing Mozart and Chopin and Bach and Beethoven and all her other favorite composers. She has no illusions about becoming a famous concert pianist, but she knows that Bruno loves listening to her.

One great change in Julie's life is her willingness to be with one man and forsake all others. At least for now. If Bruno still has other women in his life, she doesn't know and doesn't want to know.

He was right about what he promised her their first evening together. As he said he would, he does make her body soar. She does the same for him. She seldom thinks about the future. Both of them are deeply aware of how satisfying it is to live for each day.

Julie knows, and Bruno knows, that when one or the other moves on to a new lover, it will be painful for the one who is abandoned. They both admit to being more deeply committed than ever before. They secretly gaze at each other and wonder who will be the first to get restless. And yet every time Bruno takes Julie to the moon and brings her back safely, and oh so happy, they both become less and less convinced that monogamy is for the fools of this world.

Mellowing in Cannes

Clara left Chicago in a rage. A short, plump woman with an enormous voice and a rat-a-tat-tat delivery, she had been a rebellious child, had had two abortions as a teenager, had completely alienated her sister Flora, and had not spoken to her son Henry and her daughter-in-law Lil for two years. Clara made friends easily but most of these relationships ended bitterly. Still, none of this had mattered too much because she'd had Herb.

After thirty-two years of marriage, she and Herb still had been crazy in love. They'd had fun together. They'd worked together. And they'd talked, practically nonstop. They both enjoyed movies, plays, concerts, baseball games and eating out, although he was one of those insufferable people who can eat a six-course dinner with two desserts and not gain an ounce. Their sex life had been robust: they'd given their bed a good pounding four or five times a week. Whenever one of her relationship with a girlfriend had ended with a crash, Herb always had been there to comfort her. And now he was leaving her for a younger woman. *What a crock*, she raged to herself. *Did he have to be so corny?*

When Clara was badly wounded, her big voice disappeared. "Who is she?" she whispered when he told her.

He hesitated. "Well, her name is Sally. Sally Robb."

"I mean, *who* is she? Where did you meet her?"

He hesitated again, longer this time. "She's…one of Lil's girlfriends."

Clara was astonished. "You mean, you still see Henry and Lil? After the way they treated me?"

"Sure I see them. I'm not the one they're mad at."

Clara was too deflated to continue the conversation. She felt defeated, utterly alone. She bolted out of Chicago and landed in Cannes.

She had plenty of money. Herb had said, "don't worry, I'll be generous." Generous with what? she thought bitterly. She always considered the money they had as *their* money. The house was in both their names. So were all their stocks and bonds. They were partner, co-owners of their furniture store. He took care of the business end but it was her taste as buyer and her outgoing personality in the showroom that made the company successful. So all of a sudden everything was *his* to be generous with?

When she left Chicago, in a hurry, she told the travel agent to get her to Paris. Once there, she realized it was too big, too difficult to navigate by herself, so she boarded a plane to Cannes. It was a good choice.

She opted to live in a pension, a pretty town house on a narrow side street two blocks from the Boulevard de la Croisette and the ocean. She didn't want a car. Everything she needed was within walking distance. She liked being with people and not all alone in an apartment. She made friends easily. She was the only permanent guest at the pension; the others were tourists who stayed for a few days but she enjoyed talking to them, getting to know them a little. They were mostly Europeans but many of them spoke some English and Clara was learning French. Now and then a few Americans stayed there.

She had a back room on the second floor with windows looking out onto an enormous tree. A big upholstered chair and a small glass table sat in front of the windows. The room was not very large, but her private bathroom was huge with its own bank of windows facing the greenery. She enjoyed taking leisurely baths in the big old-fashioned tub, something she never had had time for at home. There it always had been rush, rush, with a quick shower, a hurried breakfast and off to the store, then dinner out most nights with friends and maybe a movie or a play and then home late. Who had time for relaxing baths?

Here in Cannes she enjoyed a late unhurried breakfast in the pension's dining room, a cheery yellow room with white lace curtains and fresh flowers on every table. She also had most of her dinners there, excellent meals; luckily for her the portions were small, because she was a lifelong member of the clean plate club. Put it in front of her and it was goodbye food.

She had a structured day. On weekdays, after breakfast, she walked two miles along the Croisette to her French class, which lasted for two hours. Then she walked back, stopping for lunch at various little brasseries and cafés. Afternoons she walked again; she felt addicted to ambling around the beautiful waterfront city on its lovely bay with the mountains rearing up behind it. She kept no food in her room except for a little fruit. And because it was her nature to be ebullient, friendly and talkative, she was warmly accepted by the local people she met. They enjoyed her attempts to speak their language and were happy to help her with it.

She realized one day that her clothes were loose. She was so accustomed to wearing comfortably roomy pants and big overblouses that she couldn't tell at first that everything was really, really loose. She went shopping for new clothes and found to her delight that she could get into fitted pants and even tuck in the tops. Her round face had slimmed too, revealing attractive cheek bones that hadn't been visible since her high school days. Herb used to call her "pudgy," a word she hated. Well, you asshole, she wanted to tell him, now I'm svelte!

She had a private telephone installed in her room and kept in touch with those friends back home whom she hadn't fought with before leaving. She sent her address and phone number to Herb, in case of an emergency, though she made it clear she had no desire to communicate with him, ever again. She had to admit, to herself, that she sorely missed their conversations. How free-ranging their talks had been! Both of them were witty and intelligent, using rapid repartee to entertain each other, like jugglers using their talents to beguile an audience.

She got in the habit of having a mid-afternoon cappuccino at a waterside café near the pension. The ocean was soothing. For the first time in her life, she became introspective. Since she had no one there with whom to have a meaningful conversation, she began having them inwardly with herself. One by one, she reviewed her crashed relationships. Take her sister Flora. Flora was the family beauty—not that Clara wasn't attractive—just that her entire adult life she had been, well, overweight. It hadn't seemed to bother Herb, except for his affectionate teasing, so she never had worried about it.

When Clara's parents died, first her father and a year later her mother, the two sisters' inheritance was substantial. The will stipulated that the money was to be split down the middle, and that was no problem. But the personal property was not mentioned in the will. Their mother's death was sudden so Flora, whose Fort Lauderdale home was five miles from their parents' condo, had cleared out everything of value before Clara could get on a plane and fly down.

"It's my payment for taking care of them all these years," Flora'd said when Clara objected.

"What d'you mean, all these years?" Clara had snapped. "You've lived here less than a year. And they had a live-in housekeeper to take care of them."

"But I had the responsibility," Flora insisted. She never admitted that she had behaved unethically. She refused to give Clara any of her loot, and it drove Clara crazy.

Now, in Cannes, Clara concluded that no doubt Flora was a selfish, grasping bitch, but Clara asked herself if it was worth being angry with her over a bunch of *things?* Except for a few family heirlooms, there wasn't one item in their parents' house that she couldn't afford to go out and buy, if she wanted it. Was that worth losing a sister?

She phoned Flora that evening and apologized, even though she knew in her heart that Flora had been wrong. But, so what? They both cried on the phone and pledged eternal sisterhood. They spoke for an hour. When she hung up, Clara felt such a flood of relief that she sat by her window and cried some more.

The next afternoon, while having her cappuccino at the café, a man asked if he could sit with her. "I've got to talk to someone, or I'll burst!" he said in a low, grim voice.

"American?" she said.

"From Boston."

"Some of these Europeans speak such perfect English," she said. "I'm always assuming they're American."

His name was Simon Woolf, he was a professor of Political Science at MIT, on sabbatical, living with his new wife in Cannes. He was of medium height, not tall like Herb, and he was on the stout side, not slim like Herb. But he had a nice face full of laugh lines and he had youthful eyes, and she always judged people by their eyes and how comfortable she was holding eye contact with them.

She introduced herself with a minimum of information. Name. City of origin. Residential status.

"So if you've got a wife to talk to," Clara said, "why talk to me?"

He took a deep, ragged breath. "She's too stupid."

Clara caught on and began to hate him. "Young?"

He nodded.

"You left an older first wife for her?"

He nodded, looking miserable.

"I have no sympathy for you," Clara said coldly. She got up and walked back to her pension, leaving her unfinished cappuccino.

She saw him sitting in the café the next afternoon so she turned around and found a different place for her cappuccino break, though why she called it a break she didn't know. What was she breaking from? She was thoroughly enjoying her life of leisure. Too many years of work, work, work had been unhealthy. She had started working Saturdays and summer holidays while a junior in high school and continued to do so in college. She hadn't had to work— her parents had had plenty of money—but she'd had a huge desire for independence. Except for the two weeks a year she had insisted that she and Herb take off every August, she never had stopped working until the day she left for France. She owed herself. Big time.

Simon found her at her new café. He sat down at her table and said, "Why won't you talk to me?"

"Am I the only American in Cannes?" she growled.

"You look like you'd understand," he said.

"You're damn right I understand," she said. "You're a fucking bastard."

"You look like such a lady," he said disapprovingly.

"Forget it!" She got up and again left her cappuccino half-finished. "Stop bothering me!" she said as she walked away.

He had the nerve to come after her and grab her arm. "Why are you so angry with me? You don't even know me."

"I know all I care to know, mister."

"I told you, my name is Simon. Simon Woolf."

She jerked her arm from his grasp. She kept walking and after half a block she glanced back. He still was standing there, looking down the street after her.

She didn't see him for a week and found she missed him, rat though he was. He's just another Herb, she thought. Any man who'd leave a perfectly good first wife for a juvenile piece of ass was no damn good. She was better off without Herb, and she certainly would be out of her mind to befriend this Simon. *Don't you ever learn?* she asked herself. *So why are you missing him? Idiot!*

She spent all the next day trying, in her mind, to unravel her feud with her son Henry and his wife Lil. Who'd started it? She tried to remember. It had something to do with a present. Yes! Two Christmases ago. Had she bought Lil some jewelry? Then she remembered: she had given Lil her grandmother's amber brooch. Now it all came back to her. The brooch originally belonged to Clara's Grandma Dorothy. On Clara's twenty-first birthday, Grandma Dorothy had given her the brooch with great ceremony. It was the only family heirloom Clara owned, since Flora had grabbed everything else.

Clara had put the brooch in a sparkly silver jewelry box, left over from a bracelet she'd bought at Marshall Fields, and dolled up the box with a porcelain rose instead of a bow. Lil had picked up the little package from under the Christmas tree with an exclamation of admiration. But when she opened the box and saw the brooch, she frowned. "Nobody wears antique brooches any more!" she said petulantly.

Clara, Herb and Henry were silent. Embarrassed.

"It's really cheap of you to give me your old cast-offs!" Lil continued, so uncharacteristically outspoken that the other three stared at her in amazement.

"Give it back," Clara said shortly. She reached over and grabbed the brooch from Lil.

"What are you doing?" Lil cried out.

"I'll get you something else," Clara said in quiet fury.

"Mom," Henry started but Clara turned on him.

"Keep out of it! There's nothing more to say. I'll get her a gift certificate from Neiman's."

"But why'd you give her that crappy piece of junk in the first place, Mom?" Henry was furious. "You know Lil hates old things!"

Suddenly there was an uproar, Herb shouting at Henry to be quiet and Henry screaming at Lil for being so tactless and Lil hollering that Clara was always trying to impose her taste on her and then Henry and Lil had grabbed their gifts and rushed out of the house. The sudden quiet had left Clara breathless. "What just happened?" she asked Herb.

He shook his head. "Beats me, honey."

She hadn't spoken to Henry or Lil since.

Clara relived the entire scene while having her afternoon cappuccino at still another café that Simon hadn't yet discovered. She hurried back to her room, picked up the phone and dialed Henry's and Lil's number. She still knew it by heart, though she hadn't called it in over two years. It was Saturday morning in Chicago, they might be home.

Henry answered with a "hello."

"Hi, sweetie-pie." She always used to call him that.

"Mom!" The surprise in his voice was mingled, she thought, with gladness. "Are you back?"

"No, darling, I'm still in Cannes. I've had a lot of time here to think. I want to apologize to Lil for that whole business with the brooch."

"Oh, the hell with the brooch. Mom, it's just so good to hear your voice."

"Yours too." They always had been close. She'd always loved him wholeheartedly and unconditionally, not because he was her only child, but because she admired him. Until Lil came along.

Lil was Henry's choice and Clara tried to respect that. Lil was everything Clara was not. Clara was fiercely independent, Lil was a clinger. Clara was fearless, Lil was afraid of everything, including motherhood. Clara was witty and articulate, Lil spoke slowly and hesitantly. Still, Clara reminded herself, I tried. God, how I tried! And then she asked herself, you tried *what*? Did you ever call Lil and ask her to have lunch, just the two of you? Did you ever sit down and talk to her, not as a mother-in-law but as a fellow human? Did you ever try to really like her? And the answers were no, no, and no.

"Darling," Clara said to her son, "I've missed you so. People who love each other *never* should stop talking. I'm so sorry I let it happen."

"It's my fault too," Henry said. "Hold on a minute, Mom."

She heard him call Lil to the phone.

"Why Clara," Lil murmured, her voice saturated with surprise. "How…how are you?"

"Lil, I'm fine. Listen, I love you. For being who you are. And I love you for making my son happy, and I am so sorry, so very sorry, that I let two years go by…" She stopped, hearing Lil weeping on the other end.

"It was all my fault," Lil sobbed.

"Darling girl," Clara soothed, "it doesn't matter who was at fault. It was everybody's fault. So let's start fresh. How about you and Henry visiting me soon? I can get you a room here where I'm staying.

You can spend a week or two in Paris afterwards if you'd like. I'll pay for the whole trip."

"Oh Clara, I've never been to France. I've never been to Europe. It's my dream!"

"All right, that's wonderful. Figure out a time and let me know."

Clara hung up the phone feeling beatific. She couldn't stop smiling. During the next few days she made many more phone calls, first compiling a list from her address book of all the names of friends she had crossed out with an angry "X." One by one, she called them. She apologized to each, even to those who had been egregiously at fault. Some accepted her effort to make amends, and others rebuffed her. She didn't hold it against them. It was as though all the vindictiveness had drained from her body. She felt euphoric.

She went back to having her afternoon cappuccino at her first, and favorite café. When Simon approached her, she said, "Sit down," indicating the chair next to her. He gave her a look of amazement, but sat beside her and ordered a latte.

"So tell me," she began, smiling at him. "What was your first wife like? A real bitch? A two-hundred pound horror?"

"She was nice," he said. "She was beautiful. I still love her."

"So? Go back. Apologize. It'll do you both a world of good."

"I can't," he said. "She married someone else." He sighed. "I'm stuck with Merrilynn. You know? What they call a trophy wife?"

"A student of yours?"

"No. She's too dumb to get into MIT."

"Go ahead," Clara said kindly. "Get it off your chest. Tell me what happened."

He looked at her suspiciously. "Why this change of attitude? Does some doctor here give niceness shots?"

"I'll ignore that, Simon."

He gazed out at the ocean while he spoke. "It's such an old story. A trite old story. A young man and a young woman fall in love, they marry, they establish a home, they have kids, they're happy, they still love each other, and one day a beautiful young woman comes along and figures out that if she marries a young man, she'll probably have to help him establish himself and work toward financial success. She's shrewd enough to know that if she can get an older man who's already been through all that, she can have the money right off the bat. She's young, she's sexy, and maybe the older man is beginning to have a few problems in bed. He gets the hots for the girl, she solves his problems, with her he can get it up every time. So he leaves his wife, marries the girl, and pretty soon he has no one to talk to. The only conversation she knows is telling him what she bought with all the credit cards he gave her. Meanwhile, he realizes how much he used to enjoy talking to his first wife. They both loved politics, books, art, concerts, plays, movies—and Wife Number Two is interested in None of the Above. He misses the laughter he shared with Wife Number One. He misses the fun they used to have with their kids, and their grandkids, because now when he visits his children, there's a strained coldness on their part. He knows they think he's an old fool. But nobody knows better than he does how much of an old fool he is." He stopped and sipped his latte.

"So how do I figure in all this?" Clara asked.

"You look like someone I can talk to," he said. "I'm desperate for some good conversation."

He took her to dinner and they sat out on a bench afterwards, looking at the lights across the water where the shoreline curved. Clara had almost forgotten how much she enjoyed talking with someone who shared her interests. Although these past two months she had been with people much of the time, at the pension, and in shops, and during her French class, none of those people had had a meaningful dialogue with her.

She and Simon began having lunch and spending their afternoons together. They both liked to walk, and to sit on benches and look at the ocean, and to attend movies which afterwards they analyzed to death. Simon had a car so some days they drove to Nice, or St. Tropez, or up to St. Paul de Vence to see the art galleries. Evenings he reluctantly went back to Merrilynn, his young wife.

Clara realized one day that she was getting too dependent on Simon for her own peace of mind. She wanted to be with him all the time. She started imagining passionate kisses and the inevitable lovemaking. She knew she was on dangerous ground.

She got a wedding announcement from Herb. He had married his Sally Robb. Clara felt not an ounce of pique or anger. She felt nothing. She was proud of herself...until she realized that all the emotional maturity she displayed over Herb's marriage was totally absent from her feelings about Simon. She was, she had to admit to herself, crazy about him. Mad for him. Not since her college days when she went through the heady madness of falling in love followed by the crashing misery of breaking up had she felt such a whirlwind of passion monopolizing her mind and coursing through her body. For all the good sense she had shown in mending her broken relationships, she was showing the opposite in her feelings for Simon.

One night she went to the Negalescu Hotel for an after dinner drink with a couple from Buffalo who were staying at the pension. As they entered the lobby and went toward the lounge, they came face to face with Simon and a young blonde beauty whom Clara assumed to be his Merrilynn (stupid name!). Clara and Simon nodded at each other, but didn't stop, and the encounter left Clara in total misery. Maybe Simon couldn't talk to his new wife, maybe Merrilynn was as stupid as he said she was, but she sure looked eminently fuckable with all that luscious smooth skin, those perky breasts, that body that moved as though it had just been oiled and lubed.

Clara tried to speak cheerily with the Buffalo couple, but she couldn't wait to get back to her room and wallow in self pity. Despite all his complaining, there was no way Simon was going leave a beauty like his young wife for an old bag like Clara.

For the next four days she stayed cooped up in the pension. She was certain that Simon didn't know where she lived. They always met at "their" café, usually at one o'clock so they could have lunch together.

"What does your wife do, while you're with me all afternoon?" Clara once asked him.

"She shops."

"Every day?"

"Well, she has her spa days, and her hairdresser and manicure and pedicure appointments, and other young American wives she goes to lunch with." He shrugged dismissively.

Clara went regularly to a spa and a hairdresser and had her nails done too, but she never made a whole day of it. As for shopping, if she needed something she went and bought it. She never had been one to just go moseying around the stores. She couldn't understand the attraction.

On the fifth day of her seclusion, she decided to go to her French class. After all, she was hiding from Simon, and she never had bumped into him that early in the morning. But coming back afterwards, she turned a corner and there he was.

"What're you doing here?" she blurted, flustered.

"Clara!" He put his arms around her, there on the street, and kept saying her name. "I've looked everywhere for you," he said, his voice breaking. "I even checked the hospitals, the police…" He still clung to her and when she tried to move out of his embrace he wouldn't let her go. He kissed her, and a shiver of desire radiated all through her.

When he finally released her they both were trembling with relief at being together and their yearning to go beyond kissing. She took his hand and led him toward her pension. He gripped her hand so hard it began to hurt so she pulled it from his grasp and held his arm instead.

The pension was usually quiet in the late morning, the guests having gone out sightseeing or shopping and the staff busy with cleaning and cooking. When Clara reached her room it already had been made up as she knew it would be. The maids always cleaned her room as soon as she left for French class.

She was aware that what she was doing could be dangerous to her peace of mind. She knew that for every ounce of joy she was experiencing now, she would pay with a pound of misery when they parted. If she had been longing for Simon before, making love with him would make her desire for him monumentally greater. *Was it worth it?* she asked herself as she undressed. But she had no choice. Her desire wouldn't let her put her clothes back on and walk away from him now.

With Herb, and with her boyfriends in college, she had been so completely immersed in the act itself that her partner's identity had become incidental, a body that was enabling her to reach a frenzied climax. But with Simon she found that his presence was the primary factor in her rush toward pleasure, that *his* face hovered above her, that *his* body writhed against hers, that *his* penis plumbed her depths, and that it was Simon, Simon, Simon who created the intense spasms deep inside her.

He collapsed on top of her and she welcomed his weight, his closeness, his presence there. They both opened their eyes and stared at each other. "I never..." he gasped.

"I never knew..." she whispered.

"So incredible..." he murmured.

"Simon," she breathed.

"Clara," he groaned, ecstatically.

She threw her toiletries and some underwear and two dresses into a suitcase and they left Cannes a short time later. "I'll buy whatever I need," he said, not wanting to go home. He left a message on Merrilynn's answering machine that he would be gone for a few days.

They drove the short distance to Vence and were fortunate, without a reservation, to get a room at Chateau Saint-Martin, set in a lush garden. They were given a small private villa but despite the beauty of their surroundings they only wanted to look at each other.

"Remember," he laughed, "how you called me a fucking bastard? That first day we met?" They were lying in bed, flushed with pleasure.

"You were," she said. "And it was the second day."

He tightened his arms around her. "Did you ever dream we'd end up like this?"

End up? she thought, suddenly somber. *Who knows how we'll end up?*

He sensed her abrupt mood change. "Live in the present," he coaxed. "It's the only way to fly."

They explored their hotel's glorious gardens and they lollygagged through the narrow old streets of Vence. They drove to the outskirts of town to see the amazing chapel and stained glass windows designed by Matisse. But mostly they stayed in their villa and ate in the hotel's garden. They didn't know if their happiness made the food seem especially delectable, or if it truly was sensational, but they feasted on hot fois gras and delicate pastas and imaginative seafood dishes and wonderfully seasoned sea bass, marveling to discover that whatever they ate was, for both of them, all at once their favorite dish.

They didn't want to leave. For a week, he phoned excuses to Merrilynn's answering machine as they postponed their return to Cannes. Finally one day at lunch he said, "I guess we better go back."

"Not yet," Clara begged.

"Clara." He leaned over and put a hand over hers. "Sooner or later we have to decide what we're going to do."

"I prefer later than sooner."

They sat there holding hands while the waiter brought them a chocolate charlotte to share.

"You eat it," Clara said, her appetite gone.

He ate in silence, smiling up at her now and then.

"So what are we going to do?" she said when he finished. She faced him and locked eyes. "Tell me the truth, Simon. Are you staying with your doll-bride?"

"Don't be silly. I can't stand her." Still, he looked worried.

"But...can you get rid of her? She hasn't given you grounds for divorce."

"All it'll take is money."

Drinking their coffee, they both looked longingly at the blooms growing all around them. "Do you have enough money to buy her off?" Clara asked. "Because I have tons of it."

"You got a good settlement?"

"Not a settlement. I earned half of everything we owned. Though to hear him tell it, he owned it all and I robbed him blind."

They had to force themselves to pack, to walk out of their little villa, to get in his car and drive back to Cannes.

He dropped her in front of her pension and said, "Meet me at our café tomorrow at one." She wrote out her phone number and gave it to him. He leaned over and gave her a light kiss on her mouth. As soon as she got out of his car, he sped away.

Somehow, as soon as he drove off, she knew that he wouldn't show up the next day at one o'clock. She didn't know how she knew, she just did. She waited at "their" café for an hour, then she walked back to her room and lay down. He didn't call. She had no phone number for him.

She tried to remember if she had suffered this much when Herb left her. But then she had been more angry than hurt. She tried to recall if any of her college romances had made her this wretched, but she knew they had not. Anyway, in those days she could blame her pain on immaturity, her own and the boy's. Now there was no excuse. She should have known better than to trust a man like Simon. She had called him a 'fucking bastard' the second time she saw him, and now he had proved that she was right. Any man who could leave a lovely, loving first wife would certainly have no qualms about jilting a woman with whom he'd had only a brief fling.

She talked to herself for days, castigating herself for stupidity, then telling herself that at least it had been fun while it lasted. Every time her phone rang, her hope rose like a rocket, but it always was some friend from Chicago, or Henry or Lil. Once, she felt a flash of hope that maybe Simon had been in an accident, that he was lying unconscious in a hospital, but she knew it was most unlikely.

She saw him two weeks after their return from Vence. He was walking with Merrilynn on the other side of the Croissette. He had an arm around his young blonde wife. He was laughing at something she was saying and he was gazing down at her adoringly. If I had a gun, Clara thought, I would shoot him. And the blonde too.

Clara went over to the balustrade and gazed out at the ocean. She had to laugh at herself. The thought of her shooting anyone was so absurd! After all, if she had learned anything from all that had happened to her since she first came to Cannes, it had been acceptance of other people's faults. And her own faults too. All of her apologies—to Henry, to Lil, to Flora, to her alienated friends back home —had made her a happier person.

Simon, too, had taught her a lesson. It was, sadly, that if you trust someone, expect to be disappointed. If you love someone, expect to be hurt. But if you can't trust anyone, and if you're afraid to love anyone, what was the point of living?

She knew she wouldn't achieve true contentment until she let herself forgive Simon. And Herb, too. A surge of fury reminded her that she wasn't ready to pardon either one of those cruel men. Not by a long shot.

And yet! What was the point in not forgiving them? Making her peace with all the others in her life definitely had lightened her soul. Did she want Herb back in her life? Never! Nor did she want to have anything more to do with a sonofabitch like Simon. They both were hurtful, selfish men. But they had taught her a lesson, and she could take that lesson two ways. She could hang onto her bitterness and hate all men for the rest of her life, or she could believe that some day she might meet a man who was kind, thoughtful and loving. And if such a man didn't exist? So be it. She'd already proved that she could be happy by herself.

"Okay, Herb, and you, too, Simon," she called out toward the ocean. "I forgive both of you bastards!" She paused, then added, "And I also forgive *myself* for being stupid enough to fall in love with fucking assholes like you."

Regression in Portugal

When he was a fully grown man, and then some, Elliott Norton succeeded in regressing himself to the age of ten—a very precocious, sexy ten. Wearing white shorts and tank top, an outfit that displayed his tanned, sturdy legs, his muscular arms and his virile torso, he sat on a bench overlooking the estuary of the Tagus River. Behind him was the old Portuguese fishing town of Cais Cais (pronounced Cash-Keish). It was a fine warm June afternoon, with a cloudless sky, a royal blue ocean.

The town was buzzing with locals going about their business and tourists ambling along the boutiqued pedestrian streets and calling everything "quaint" and "picturesque." Just west of Estoril, the winter resort favored by wealthy Brits and deposed royalty, Cais Cais was ideally situated on the water, only twelve miles from Lisbon, with a high-speed train making frequent trips into the capitol.

Elliott watched three German women tourists as they came down the steps of a nearby waterfront café. They were all blonde, all curvaceous, all eminently fuckable. He could close his eyes and go "eeny-meeny-miney-mo" and be perfectly happy with any one of them. His groin tingled, imagining how it always was with a new woman: the first sweet kisses suddenly growing more fervent, her initial self-conscious undressing, the ardent pressure of his firm, eager, naked body against her more pliant, more tentative one, his skillful caressing guaranteed to thoroughly ignite her, her quick breaths and delicious little grunts and sighs of pleasure, and then his masterful escalating thrusts and finally-finally-finally, like plunging off a cliff, the astonishing, miraculous, mind-blowing culmination. Lord! He never ceased to be amazed by it.

Four months earlier, on his 60th birthday, Elliott had gone alone for lunch at Le Vallauris, the pricey French restaurant near his home in Palm Springs. He'd ordered a Sapphire Bombay martini and a lobster salad, and silently communed with himself. He was in his third marriage then, the first two both having started with great hoopla and both having ended in divorce after too many years of dissatisfaction, at least on his part. Had his wives been difficult? Had the divorces been entirely his fault? All he remembered was that each time he began to feel miserable almost as soon as the honeymoon was over. By then he no longer enjoyed making love to his wife; instead he'd had exuberant sex with every willing woman who crossed his path.

After his second divorce, he also realized that he disliked the work he had been doing most of his adult years as manager of a lucrative medical testing laboratory. His only real pleasures in life boiled down to frequent casual sex and his avid interest in painting. There wasn't an art gallery or museum in all of Southern California whose paintings he hadn't voraciously studied and absorbed into his memory. And, over the years, his seven vacations in Europe and his frequent business trips to New York and Washington had consisted of marathon museum visits.

His third wife, Linda, had thoroughly enchanted him for half a year before they married. She was a tiny, startlingly beautiful forty-year-old woman, a successful pediatrician, with the bawdiest sense of humor he ever had encountered in a woman. She was a daredevil, forever challenging him to ski down the most difficult slopes, to swim across broad lakes, to climb high peaks. But by that day, on his 60th birthday, it was the same old, same old. Three months of marriage and suddenly he was utterly bored with Linda, despite her marvelous energy. Or maybe because of it. And he hated his work more than ever.

What the hell is wrong with me? he had fretted, sipping his birthday martini. How could he be so good at a business he despised, and so unable to live in wedded bliss with his lovely, kind, intelligent wives? And what, he demanded of himself, did he really want? When was the last time he had been truly happy? Totally, blissfully satisfied with his life?

His mind slid back over the years like a snake undulating across a rocky terrain. His entire adulthood had been a mess. He'd always felt that he was with the wrong woman, doing the wrong work, wasting his life, with contentment forever beyond his grasp. Sipping the last of his martini and toying with the lobster salad, he thought back over his teen and college years.

Ever since junior high, school had been a struggle for him. He wasn't a great student and always had had to push himself to get passing grades. Why had he bothered? Because his older sister, Julie, was a Superior Court Judge and his two big brothers, Bart and Hal, were successful lawyers, as were both his parents. What was he going to do? Be the family drop-out? Be a box boy all his life? No, he stuck with it and after enormous effort he graduated from college. He couldn't face law school so he got an MBA instead. He had a natural affinity for the business world. But that didn't mean he enjoyed it.

His mind went back to his teen years in Milwaukee. One thing he'd had that his older sibs lacked was arrestingly good looks. When he walked into a room, all eyes turned to him and stayed there. Tall and slender, he had marvelously thick hair, the color of honey. Even now, at sixty, his few white hairs were only an attractive silvery tinge above his ears. His large gray eyes were heavily fringed by long dark lashes. By the time he was fifteen, he'd instinctively learned that women loved eye contact. He remembered his elation when he first looked intently into the eyes of a girl named Elise and it jump-started her interest in him so swiftly that within a half hour they were having sex behind the empty stage in the high school auditorium.

From that time on, girls had spoiled him rotten. He sometimes had felt that he could walk through the school hallway and, if he smiled at them invitingly, the girls would throw themselves on the floor and spread their legs, begging him to "do it." And he had "done it" plenty, not ever on floors but at girls' homes when their parents were away, and best of all, in the convenience of his own apartment after he started college.

This eagerness to have sex with him eventually jaundiced his view of women. Although he was mighty glad for the sex, and he knew it was basically unfair to these women, he still had a certain amount of contempt for females who had the hots for him solely because of his flashy appearance when they knew nothing about what kind of a person he was. Worse, he himself never was sure about what kind of a person he was.

Only when he went back to remembering his tenth year did he recapture a feeling of satisfaction with life and a complete lack of self-consciousness. At ten, he hadn't yet begun to worry about grades. And he hadn't given a damn yet about girls. He'd had his few good buddies and he never was concerned about whether or not they liked him. In those days, he was totally focused on how he felt about others, not at all on how they saw him.

He remembered, at ten, the feeling of being utterly, deliciously free. He'd get up in the morning without any preconceived ideas about what to do with the day, except for a few hours in classes during the school year. But after school, and on weekends and vacations, he was open to whatever came along. A pickup baseball game? Sure. A swim at the public beach on Lake Michigan? Sure. Skateboarding on the hilly streets near his house? Sure. Moseying around downtown? Sure. A movie? Sure. The days had rolled by easily. He seldom had done anything he didn't want to do.

Sitting there eating his 60th birthday lunch, he suddenly was jolted, as though the San Andreas had kicked up a monster quake. *That was the answer! He had to recapture the feeling of being ten again!* He could do it! He had enough money conservatively invested so that even if he never worked another day in his life, he could still live quite comfortably on the interest. He also would have enough money left over to give Linda a fair financial settlement—actually more of a token forfeit, an admission of his guilt, since she had much more money than he had.

He had to admit that when he married Linda, he sincerely had hoped they would grow old together (granted, he had a 19-year head start) and achieve the kind of beautiful bond he often saw in elderly couples who had managed to stay in love all their lives. But, he concluded, he just wasn't the type for that sort of monogamous relationship. During all three of his weddings, he had winced inwardly at the minister's words, "forsaking all others," realizing, even as he said "I do," that he was perjuring himself.

Linda was furious when he told her he was leaving her. She hadn't seen it coming. "I feel sorry for you!" she cried out. "You don't know how to love! You fucking asshole!"

What could he say? She was right on all counts. So he walked out and Linda proceeded to divorce him. He resigned from his position at the lab, he sold his two-year-old Lexus and gave away everything else he owned except for a few favorite clothes and his toiletries. The house belonged to Linda.

With one small suitcase, he flew out of Palm Springs and eventually he reached Lisbon. There he bought a motorcycle and roared into Cais Cais on it. Why Portugal? Why Cais Cais? Because a Canadian woman he had been balling for two weeks before he left Palm Springs had mentioned that it was a relatively inexpensive and fun place to visit. The odd name had stuck with him.

His plan was working beautifully. He lived in a small oceanfront hotel that once had been a wealthy family's mansion. There, he had a large corner bedroom and a bathroom tiled with colorful Portuguese *ajuelos.* From his balcony he could see not only the ocean but also a blow hole that spouted dramatically with every incoming wave. The name of his street tickled him: *Estrada da Boca do Inferno* —the Street of the Mouth of Hell.

All he had to do when he got up each morning was shower, shave, dress in his uniform of white shorts, tank top and sandals, and go down a broad marble staircase to the flower-filled ocean-view dining room for an enormous late breakfast. Lunch was a piece of fruit he bought at the produce market. Dinner was with whomever happened to present herself. He never had to go searching for female companionship; the women came to him.

The truth was, he simply adored women. Actually, he preferred short, cuddly, shy ones, but even though he didn't care as much for the bold, pushy types who made the first move, he was perfectly willing to fuck them.

He tried never to hurt a woman's feelings (except the ones he married). He was adept at making snap judgments about the ones he wanted to go bed with, steering clear of those ultra-romantic types who would fall in love with him after the first kiss. He was one hell of a good kisser. No cave-man tactics for him. Never would he shove his tongue half-way down a woman's throat. For him, a kiss always started tenderly, gentle yet titillating, and then escalating in fervor—undoubtedly the most important part of his expert foreplay.

Often, when he looked in the mirror, he was amused at the random genes that had produced such an attractive face and body. What would his life be like had he been born short, fat and homely? He couldn't imagine it. But he felt that everything in life was a grab bag. Weren't some of us born rich and others poor? Some smart and others stupid? Some good and others evil?

On a whim he bought an easel and canvas and some basic acrylic colors and began painting. It was an amusing strategy to meet some of the nicer, more intellectual women who hesitated coming up to him and boldly starting a conversation, like the pushy broads he'd been balling. He hoped that the more timid women would watch him paint for a few minutes and then feel comfortable enough to start talking to him. Actually, a dog would have served as the same kind of ice-breaking, woman-attracting ploy, but his hotel didn't allow pets.

IT WORKED! First Renee, an attractive, thirty-something school librarian from Dallas, quietly watched him paint. Elliott liked her bright yellow pantsuit—it went well with her long black hair. Only, he thought, her lipstick was too red. Someone ought to tell her to switch to pale rose...

"Are those acrylics or oil?" she asked shyly, pointing at the tube of blue paint he was squeezing onto his palette.

"Acrylic," he replied. "Easier to work with."

He slashed his brush across the canvas, happily aware of her breathless scrutiny.

"D'you live here?" she asked.

"MmmHmmm." He put on an act of being intensely involved in his work.

'Ooooh! Lucky you!" She sighed enviously.

For a few minutes he became so involved in his seascape that he forgot she was there. A waft of her perfume—he recognized Estee Lauder's "Beautiful?"—reminded him of her presence. Reluctantly, yet tingling with sexual stirrings, he put his painting paraphernalia into his portable wheeled locker.

"Drink?" he asked, nodding at the waterfront bar nearby.

They ended up in her hotel room after dinner, by which time she was relaxed enough for a sexual romp. Elliott knew that women who at home would refuse to make love on the first date were willing to hop right into bed, as though being on vacation sped up time and made it okay. His virility never faltered. After Renee there was Judy, then Debra, then Alison. He enjoyed sex so much that his joyful zeal usually loosened up even the most tight-assed females.

Parting was seldom a problem, either. Since he hated to hurt anyone's feelings, and since most of the women he chose for intimacy were tourists, he made sure they had non-refundable, non-changeable return airline tickets. That way, he could part with them after a few days of mutual pleasure without anyone feeling jilted. He liked to think that he was doing these women a favor. He saw himself as a strewer of sexual satisfaction, with his partners returning home thrilled by the memory of their delicious orgasms, thanks to him.

Despite his busy sex life, he spent more and more time painting. He was surprised one day when the manager at his hotel, seeing him carrying two of his paintings, asked to display them in the hotel lobby. Elliott was aware that his seascapes did indeed catch the illusive gleam of sun on water, or the dramatic effect of storm clouds and high winds on furiously churning waves. He realized he had an instinctive sense of composition. His colors were rich, imaginative and masterful. His work had the free, uninhibited quality of a child's drawings combined with an adult art connoisseur's years of accumulated knowledge. The two paintings he hung in the hotel lobby sold overnight for five hundred dollars each! He was stunned. He put up six more, each with a price tag of a thousand dollars, and they sold in two days.

He suddenly remembered how much he had enjoyed sketching when he was a kid. He had filled his notebooks with pictures of everything he saw: people, animals, houses. He had been sent to the principal's office more than once for drawing caricatures of his teachers when he was supposed to be doing math. How could he have forgotten?

But then, in Junior High the kids were required to take a class in "Art." What a downer. The teacher had given them "design" assignments with strict rules that had taken all the creative joy out of drawing. That, plus the stress he had put upon himself to keep up academically with the rest of his family, had left no time or desire to draw any more. Until now. Had trying to be a ten-year-old brought it back?

What's more, he was delighted to have a talent that nobody else in his family possessed. He became obsessed with painting everything he saw. He awakened early, wolfed down a small breakfast, and was out with his brushes, canvas and paints while most people still were lolling in bed. Instead of hoping to attract women with his painting, he now became annoyed with kibitzers, no matter how attractive they might be.

He sold his motorcycle because he found it awkward to carry his easel and canvases on it and he bought a used Renault truck with a camper shell. He roamed up and down the coast in it, away from the tourist areas, compulsively painting the ocean. Some days he drove up the mountains behind Cais Cais to Sintra to paint the castles and the quaint old cobbled streets where the Kings of Portugal once had spent their summers. Other days he drove into Lisbon to paint cityscapes and visit art galleries.

He fell in love with the jewel-like Gulbenkian Museum whose collection was small but every item in it was choice. He began painting people, chosen at random. He realized one day that he hadn't had a piece of ass in two weeks! Ever since he was fifteen, he never had gone that long without sex. But he was too busy painting to go looking for someone and too busy to return the flirtatious looks he did get.

In an Alfama art gallery near Lisbon's 12th Century Cathedral, he saw a big coffee-table book with photographs of Rodin's sculptures. On an impulse, he bought it. He did a four by five foot painting loosely based on "The Kiss," but his lovers were depicted impressionistically, their naked bodies erotic slashes of bright, fleshy colors against a bluish purple surf and sky, that beguiling color that often permeates the earth at dusk, a time that the French call "L'heure bleu."

Elliott's paintings now were hung all over his hotel's lobby and dining room, so when the owner of a major Lisbon art gallery stayed at the hotel one weekend, he took a few of them back to Lisbon and sold the "Kiss" painting to a wealthy exiled Iranian ("I'm Persian," the man hastened to tell him). Iranian or Persian, the man paid him seventy thousand dollars for the painting. From then on, Elliott's reputation took off in the art world. Several art magazines had stories about him. He was photogenic, and so were his paintings. He had to change hotels to keep from being bothered by reporters and admirers. All he wanted to do was paint. He didn't care that much about the money. And he certainly didn't want the fame.

But he did buy a tux for the fancy formal dinner in his honor at the estate of the Iranian/Persian who had bought his version of the "Kiss." Elliott gasped when he saw it in the buyer's mansion, in its own alcove. The walls had been painted a pale peach, a perfect background for his painting's colors.

In the midst of all the fine food, and the approving comments by the men, and the women gushing their praise, he suddenly realized he wasn't feeling like a ten-year-old any more. Other people were intruding on his time. And on his life. The next morning he packed his paintings into his truck and headed for Spain's northern coast, stopping in Lisbon to consign his work to the gallery owner who had "discovered" him.

There was no way Elliott could stop painting now. It was in his blood and it permeated his thoughts. He hoped to find a small town, maybe near the Altamira Caves in Santander, where he could rent a private little beach house and just paint all day. Yes, he certainly wanted people to buy his work and validate what he was doing. But he would let the Lisbon gallery owner, who had connections with galleries in Paris, Rome and New York, do all the selling. He himself would stay out of the limelight.

He again looked forward to meeting new women. He was getting horny as hell. Then he had so shocking a thought that he almost lost control of his truck.

"For God's sake, Elliott," he shouted at himself, "ten-year-old boys don't get horny or even think about women!" It was one of the blessings of that innocent age. To be true to his new-found inner child, was he going to jeopardize that innocence? He scowled. Sure, he loved living the carefree life of a kid, but he loved sex too. Then he laughed with relief—a big guffaw. After all, who the hell was in charge here?

"Listen kid," he yelled out loud at his ten-year-old persona, "you have no choice in the matter! From now on, you're gonna be one goddamn precocious brat for your age! You're gonna fuck every willing broad who crosses your path! And that's that!"

Still, Elliott vowed, never again would he paint in public as a come-on to women The painting process was his ten-year-old's private joy, in no way to be exploited. No! This time, to attract women, he would find himself a cute little puppy dog instead.

Stupid Broads in Sorrento

Lisa Braverman has been living in Sorrento for the past year. Why? Because that's where she left her husband, Kevin. They had saved their money, both of them working hard for four years so they could take off a year and see Europe while they still were in their twenties. Lisa was a third grade teacher at an Oak Park, Illinois, school and Kevin was an emergency room doctor on leave from one of Chicago's west side hospitals.

Although originally it had been Lisa's idea to see Europe, Kevin always had seemed equally enthusiastic about it. In June two summers earlier, they bought a Volvo in Sweden, paid for by Lisa with some of the money she inherited from her maternal grandmother, They toured Scandinavia all that summer, then they slowly zigzagged through Great Britain, Holland, Belgium, France, Germany, Switzerland and Austria, with forays east to visit Prague and Budapest and a loop west around Spain and Portugal. They made their way south, criss-crossing through Italy, with Lisa loving every last kilometer they explored and Kevin quietly growing more impatient.

"You know," he finally exploded, "we're wasting our fucking lives here!"

They had stopped at a small outdoor café in Sorrento for a mid-afternoon cappuccino after spending two heady days exploring Pompeii. Just before Kevin spoke, Lisa had been sipping her drink with a deep sense of contentment, feeling utterly blessed by their life of unhurried wandering, like sitting here beneath a leafy bower, gazing out across the bay at Naples in the distance, and sharing it all with the man she loved. She'd been feeling damn good about herself too, knowing how spiffy she looked in her travel "uniform," a pink silk shirt and a short denim skirt and jacket, with her long red hair swinging around her head whenever she moved.

Jolted to her core by Kevin's shocking words, she stared at him as if he were some new, unappetizing species. Yes, he looked like her Kevin, the same restless blue eyes, the same curly brown hair, the same green t-shirt with a white "Yale" emblem, but the Kevin she'd married never would have said what this antagonistic stranger just had said.

"Wasting?" she demanded, carefully lowering her voice so it wouldn't sound shrill. "You call the thrill of exploring Pompeii *wasting?* You call the last nine incredible months *wasting?* Are you stupid? Or just plain crazy?"

"Yeah, call me all the names you want. Nine fucking months, Lisa! We coulda used the money as the down payment for a house. We coulda used the nine months to make a baby. What the hell is wrong with you? This isn't living."

She was devoured by rage. How dare he invalidate the most precious months of her life? In just a few minutes, he had transformed himself from a loving fellow adventurer to a conventional, unimaginative jerk, the kind of man she had avoided since she started dating at fifteen. Then she stunned herself by experiencing a sudden gust of gleeful freedom. "Goodbye," she said cheerfully, almost cackling. *"Arrivaderci,* you shit!"

From her blue tote bag she took his passport and his Rome-to-Chicago return airline ticket and threw them onto his lap, then she grabbed the car keys from the table where Kevin carelessly had flung them. She calmly walked to the Volvo and dragged his suitcase out of the trunk and set it carefully on the sidewalk, then she took his jacket from the back seat and neatly laid it on top of his luggage.

Kevin watched all this, at first with a bemused smile which quickly changed to stunned outrage. As he abruptly rose from the table, knocking it over, Lisa got into the Volvo and drove away. She hasn't seen or heard from Kevin since. Only from his lawyer.

She now lives in a charming hotel on a Sorrento clifftop overlooking the Bay of Naples. She is pampered by the owners, two elderly British men who bicker like a long-married couple. She teaches European history, her college major, at an English language international high school in Naples. It's a nice life. She's never at a loss for companionship, since the hotel is listed in a popular guide book, in seventeen languages, as a "best bet." Travelers of various nationalities stay there, and many of the single men ask Lisa for a date. She is popular because she is attractive, bright, friendly, and gives a damn good tour of the Amalfi peninsula in her Volvo. Sometimes, depending on the man's degree of attraction, she throws in a rousing night or two of *amore.*

One evening at dinner in the hotel's garden, four American women were seated at the table next to Lisa's, all of them grossly over-dressed and over-bejeweled for the informal tourist surroundings. Being an avid eavesdropper, Lisa ascertained that they all worked in a Manhattan dress manufacturer's bookkeeping department, that they had been co-workers and friends for fourteen years, that they had saved and scrimped all that time, giving up yearly vacations for this one-month tour of Europe.

Their trip had started in England where, they loudly complained, the food was lousy, the weather was damp, the people were snotty, the toilets smelled bad, and everything was expensive. They had been to France where they grumbled about all of the above, except they reluctantly admitted that the food was fine but they found the people even more hostile. In Germany they put the bad-smelling toilets at the top of the list and the food was too heavy. Now, in Italy, well, they had to admit that the food was really quite, quite good, and the weather had been mild, well, really quite beautiful, and the scenery was nice and the people were friendly enough, but the four of them were terrified of being robbed in the streets and the shopkeepers tried to cheat them and really, the toilets could be cleaner…

"Basta!" Lisa shouted over at them.

They stared at her, their mouths open with shock.

"That means 'shut up!'" she added.

They remained speechless.

"You dumb broads," Lisa continued, taking her half-full cup of coffee and dragging her chair over to their table, "you should hear yourselves."

"You've got your nerve," said Rita, a heavyset woman with frizzy red hair who was the first to recover her wits. "Who the hell asked for your opinion anyway?"

"You're going to get it whether you want it or not." Lisa scolded. "You make me ashamed to be an American."

Rita and her three companions glared at Lisa but remained quiet.

"Listen, you idiots," Lisa went on, "you're so busy with your stupid complaints that you missed the whole point of being in Europe."

"Which is?" Rita growled.

"Did you go to the British Museum in London? And the National? And the Tate? Did you say a prayer in Westminster Abbey? And walk along the Thames?"

"Of course we did!" said Gloria, a thin, blonde, African-American woman wearing gold-rimmed, oversize glasses.

"And?" Lisa prompted. "Weren't they magnificent? Worth all the crappy food and the bad weather?"

The four friends shrugged. "Our Metropolitan and MOCA are just as good," Rita maintained.

Lisa groaned. "How about the history? Like, walking through the streets of Stratford-on-Avon. Didn't you get goose bumps, visiting Ann Hathaway's cottage and knowing Shakespeare had been there?"

Eve spoke next. She was pale, with exceptionally alluring gray eyes offset by an unfortunate receding chin. "Yeah, we saw all those places. But the tour bus didn't stay long enough to do anything but grab a pub lunch and use the john."

"The only thing that gave me goose bumps was their toilet paper," grumped Estelle, an aging blonde Barbie-doll with an arm full of clattering bangles. "It's about as absorbent as wax paper."

"In Paris did you sit in St. Chapelle and let the beauty of those stained glass windows sear your soul?" Lisa asked in a disheartened voice, certain they had not.

Gloria snorted. "The only thing that seared my soul in Paris was getting charged fifteen bucks for a lousy *croque monsieur.*"

"Oh, you're impossible!" Lisa slammed her coffee cup onto its saucer and fled to her room.

At breakfast, Rita, Gloria, Estelle and Eve came and stood beside Lisa's table. Lisa was reading a novel and looked up, surprised not so much by their presence as by their broad smiles.

"May we sit with you?" Rita asked politely.

"Sure." Lisa closed her novel and watched them settle into their chairs.

"We stayed up half the night, talking about what you said," Eva told her. "You were right. We were awful fools."

"So," Gloria said, "we have a proposition. Are you free for the next week?"

"Yeah, my summer vacation started last week. Why?"

"If we leave our tour, we don't have to fly back to New York for another week yet. So, would you travel with us, at our expense, and teach us how to do it right?"

Lisa was intrigued. "Where do you want to go?"

"Well, the tour is going to Greece for the final week, and then they're coming back to Rome for the flight home." Rita shrugged. "We'll do whatever you want."

"Did you see much of Rome?" Lisa asked.

"Yeah," Eve snickered. "They rushed us through the entire Vatican Museum in two hours, with five minutes in the Sistine Chapel. I don't know, we saw three other museums, maybe four, I lost count, and God knows how many churches and most of our meals were rush-rush at the hotel so we could board the damn bus and hurry somewhere else."

"Here's what I suggest," Lisa said. "Go see Greece next year. But now, let's drive back to Rome in my car and we'll do it right."

"Can we get rooms? In the busy summer season?"

Lisa nodded. "The guys who own this place have a small hotel near the Spanish steps. They always keep a few rooms for friends."

She took the coast road and stopped at the American Army cemetery near Anzio. As they walked through the sea of graves, they all were moved to tears by World War Two's tragic cost in human life. They restored their equilibrium by enjoying a leisurely lunch, with wine, at an outdoor café on a nearby beach. As they relaxed, Lisa noticed that the four New Yorkers' faces looked less pinched with stress. When they smiled, they weren't a bad looking bunch.

In Rome, as arranged by her Sorrento landlords, they registered at their hotel near the *Piazza de Spagna*. As soon as they unpacked, Lisa led them to the via Condotti to window shop, and then to the Spanish Steps where they bought flowers for their rooms. That night they walked leisurely along the via Babuino to dal Bolognese, in the *Piazza del Popolo,* one of her favorite restaurants. They ate slowly, with plenty of *vino,* savoring the *lasagna verde de Bolognese,* the *ensalada,* the *scampi,* the *mille foglie* for dessert.

"The trick," Lisa explained, "is to be aware. Of everything. The buildings you walk past, *slowly,* the people you see—really *look* at them like you're going to write a two-page description. Memorize the colors of the flowers on window ledges, pay attention to every single bite of food you eat, and eat *slowly.* Relish it. And enjoy. Let yourself be a sponge sopping up whatever you see and do. You can't do that if you hurry. It's better to see a few things well than to rush through, trying to see everything at once, so that the trip becomes a big blur."

Afterwards they stopped at a night club in a Renaissance mansion where they sipped Frangelica while listening to a jazz trio. A huge Nigerian in colorful native dress asked Gloria to dance. That broke the ice and soon Lisa was doing the rhumba with a grinning Italian college kid, Evelyn wobbled on her too-high heels in the arms of a Brazilian salesman, Rita was jabbering in Yiddish with an Israeli soldier and Eve was doing a two-step with a man from the Bronx who lived half a mile away from her.

Lisa taught her four "students" how to go through a museum without wearing themselves out. "Be selective," she said. "You don't necessarily have to stay together. Go at your own pace. I always enter a gallery room, stand in the middle, and then take a closer look only at those paintings or sculptures that appeal to me. Then again, some people, like my ex-husband, prefer to look at every last item and read every last information card. So do it whatever way you like, and we'll meet for lunch out front in two hours. Longer than that at one time is too much of a good thing, like eating too much sugar. If you finish earlier, find a café and have a cappuccino. Don't be afraid of talking to strangers. It's often a memorable chance to exchange ideas with people you'd never meet at home."

She took them to churches and taught them not only to appreciate the beauty of the building and its art, but also how to sit meditatively and let the tranquillity of the place invade their souls. "You don't have to be religious to enjoy a church," she pointed out.

Their leisurely lunches always were at small trattorias, often outdoors, where she suggested that they try the chef's specialties. At night they dined in style, trying the cuisines of Italy's various regions. They drank more wine in that week than in two months at home. And they walked. They admired fountains. They strolled around *piazzas*. They stood beneath the balcony where Mussolini had shouted his fiery speeches. They nervously stuck their hands into the opening in the *Boca de Verita*, the Mouth of Truth, which, according to legend, bit off the hands of liars. They traipsed through the Forum and, giggling, imagined being Vestal Virgins. They climbed the steps where Brutus did in Caesar and cornily, in unison, proclaimed, "Friends, Romans, Countrymen, lend me your rears."

During their leisurely meals they exchanged heart-felt stories about their lives. Rita cried when she talked about the year-old daughter she'd lost to meningitis, and how the grief had sent her husband spinning out of control and out of the marriage. Eva confessed that she only enjoyed sex with black or Asian men, that white men reminded her too much of a cousin who had raped her repeatedly all during her teen years and had kept her from betraying him by threatening to harm her parents. Gloria talked of her hopeless, secret love for her sister's husband and how it had kept her from loving other men for nearly twenty years now. And Estelle confessed that she had lost custody of her son and daughter after her ex-husband found out about a foolish affair she'd had with a man she hadn't even liked.

One day Lisa drove them out to Tivoli, where they "oooh'd and Aaah'd" like gleeful schoolgirls as they were lightly showered by the imaginative fountains in the spacious steep gardens. At nearby Hadrian's Villa, Gloria's shoe scraped some dirt and revealed a mosaic. All five of them excitedly pushed more dirt aside with their shoes until they had exposed two square feet of a lovely floral design when a guard came running up waving his arms and screaming "Non! Non! Non!"

"But look what we've found!" Lisa cried out in Italian.

"No," the guard scolded while pushing back the dirt with his hands. "The dirt is there on purpose! It protects the mosaic from the sun!"

Everywhere they went, Lisa taught them to feel, to deeply *experience* each place, to imagine and to absorb a sense of history, not as a list of dates and battles but as places where people had lived and died and suffered and rejoiced.

Above all, they laughed. Relaxed and relishing every experience, they were at their best. Gloria had a wicked, irreverent sense of humor, Rita taught them hilarious-sounding Yiddish words for every man they saw, Eve had an amazing memory of every joke she'd ever heard and loved repeating the best of them, and Estelle had a nose for bargains when they poked around the shopping streets.

At the end of the week, when Lisa drove them out to the airport to meet up with their former tour-mates for the flight home, her four charges cried when they parted from her.

"I've learned so much from you, *boubala*," Rita gushed. "I'll be grateful to you for the rest of my life."

"It's not only when traveling," Eve told Lisa. "I mean, in my everyday life, I'll try to get the most out of everything I do."

"I'll never again gobble a meal without really tasting it," Estelle vowed, "even if it's just a hamburger. Like you said, I'll *saaavor* it."

Gloria simply threw her arms around Lisa's neck and sobbed on her shoulder.

Driving back to Sorrento, Lisa was stunned to find that she acutely missed being with the four women. At the beginning of the week, her attitude had been impersonal and even a little arrogant, like that of a stern teacher toward her errant students. Now she realized that sometime during the past seven days, Rita, Eve, Estelle and Gloria had stopped being her pupils and had become her very dear friends.

A Lesson in Rome

"Carla! Carla *bella! Vieni qui!*" Daniella's sweet, clear voice sang out to Carla from beneath her bedroom window. Daniella had been calling to Carla this way for six years, ever since Carla moved to Rome with her parents, in 1954, when Carla was thirteen.

Carla waved from her second-floor balcony. "Be right down!" she called to her friend. But she paused to look out at the view.

Their hilltop apartment building was in Vigna Clara, an enclave of modern high-rises sheltering wealthy Italians and expatriate Americans. Beyond them, to the north, the Latium countryside began abruptly, giving them a dramatic vista of forested ridges and golden meadows.

Carla glanced down to see what drama was taking place that warm August evening in "the village," a deep gully below them where three families lived in crumbling stone huts and conducted their primitive agrarian chores with stunning disregard for the surrounding 20th Century buildings whose shadows daily engulfed the gully in a premature dusk. Today, a woman in a long black widow's dress was scrubbing sheets in an outdoor vat while a young girl hung shirts on a clothesline. Had they ever heard of washing machines? Carla wondered. For six years she had been watching the men herd sheep and cultivate the ground with antiquated hand tools and the women drudge through their domestic chores, all of them living 18th Century lives right in the shade of a busy modern city.

"Carla!" Daniella's voice sharply reminded Carla. "Are you *pazzo?* Hurry! We shall be late!"

Carla took one quick look in her bathroom mirror to check the mascara she was wearing for the first time, then she ran for the front door.

Her mother was in the marble foyer, glancing through her mail. "Going out, dear?" she asked absently, not looking up.

"Yes," Carla said, hoping her mother wouldn't notice the mascara. Carla considered her mother to be hopelessly conservative about the way Carla looked, treating her like nine instead of nineteen.

"Don't be late," her mother said automatically.

Downstairs, Carla and Daniella locked arms and ran toward the bus stop. "Where are we going?" Carla asked. "Why'd you tell me to dress up?"

"I am taking you to a party."

"Where?"

"Near the Villa Borghese. At the home of my father's uncle."

"Then why don't we go with your father? In his Mercedes?"

"He is in Paris." Daniella laughed shyly. "You will finally meet my cousin Nardo."

"Is he really as handsome as you always said?"

"You will see for yourself." Daniella touched Carla's face. "You look beautiful, Carla."

"So do you!"

They stopped running and stared at each other with admiration. Like twins, they both were five-foot-five, both long-haired although Daniella's was darker than Carla's, both brown-eyed, both slender and full-bosomed, both nineteen, both virgins, and both of them Rome street brats. During the early years of their friendship they had prowled the city as freely as the wild cats that frequent Rome's ancient ruins. Carla's parents traveled throughout Europe on her father's pharmaceutical business. Even when they were in Rome they only gave lip-service to caring about what Carla did. They were too wrapped up in each other and in enjoying their sybaritic life abroad.

Daniella too had remarkable freedom, especially for an Italian girl. Her mother had died when Daniella was ten, and her father, an

190

overworked member of the Italian Senate, left his daughter's upbringing to a series of servants whom Daniella bribed to ignore her father's strict rules.

The streets of Rome were safe in those days, night and day. The two girls often took the bus out Nomentana, down to EUR, up Monte Mario, to Parioli, or across the river to Trastevere. Wherever they went, they fell in with Italians their age. They downed enormous amounts of *pasta* and *vino* and *gelati* in neighborhood *trattorias*. Then they roamed the streets with their new-found friends, all of them singing sentimental Italian songs.

It was summer, early August. Daniella and Carla were home for vacation from the Swiss college they both had attended for two years. Daniella had been oddly subdued all summer, as though she were worried, or frightened of the future. They both were aware that in September they would have to separate, Daniella to return to Switzerland, and Carla to spend her last two years of college at Boston University, her parents' alma mater.

Carla was not eager to live in the States again. This Eternal City, which she loved, was her home. She was completely attuned to the Italian rhythm of life. She was fascinated by the ever-present sense of history. For her, the Caesars, the Constantines, the Caravaggios, were still alive. She saw their faces daily on the streets of Rome. She was delighted by the seemingly endless variety of Renaissance *palazzos* and Baroque churches sharing their cobbled streets with time-mellowed ancient walls and dazzling new glass buildings. She loved the long siestas, the late-night festivities, the boisterous street noises, the impassioned language, the Italian flair for impetuously enjoying the moment despite an underlying chronic sadness. Above all, she revered the incredible wealth of beauty stored in the city's museums where, at will, she could gorge her senses like a chocoholic running amok in a candy factory.

As they waited for the bus on the Via Flaminia, down the street from the handsome red brick building where they both lived, Daniella suddenly said, "Carla, don't go.

"To the party?"

"No, *stupida,* to America." Daniella clutched Carla's arm. "Why are they forcing you to leave Italy?"

"They're not forcing me. They're bribing me…with a car."

"A car! What kind?"

"A brand new blue Thunderbird. My Aunt Helen in Washington ordered it for us."

"Mannagia Madonna!"

"Besides, they want me to find an American husband."

"No, Carla! We shall find you an Italian one instead."

When they reached Daniella's great-uncle's villa, Carla was shocked to find it as sumptuous as the Quirinale Palace, where Italian Prime Ministers live.

"Stop being so American," Daniella whispered to Carla as they walked through a frescoed galleria. "It is gauche to look so impressed!"

As Carla caressed a marble pillar, her eyes filled with stinging tears. She didn't want to leave Rome! She was being thrown out of Paradise. Here in Rome, anything could happen. You could turn a corner and find a fountain, and perhaps romance. Here, life was full of surprise and promise. But as long as her parents were supporting her, how could she go against their wishes?

Carla glanced disdainfully at Daniella's prim lace-collared gray dress, then down at her blue silk shirtwaist dress. "We look like schoolgirls," she complained.

"One should, until one is married."

"One-one-one!" Carla mocked. "Then, after one is married, one is expected to look like an old lady!" Boldly, Carla unbuttoned her dress half-way to her waist. "I'm tired of being a goody-goody, Daniella. I want to have some fun."

"Carla, you must wait until you are married to have fun."

"You can wait, Daniella. I want to have fun now…*and also* when I'm married."

"You mean, you will not be faithful to your husband?" Daniella's voice was a shocked whisper.

"Of course I will. The only reason to get married is because you love someone desperately. Then you're both faithful to each other because you want to be. And you can have fun together."

Daniella smiled faintly. "You are a dreamer, Carla."

"Why not dream?"

"Because it is unhealthy," Daniella insisted. "You will always be disappointed if you expect a lot from the man you love. It is not in their nature to be faithful."

"You're wrong, Daniella. There are plenty of men who are willing to be faithful."

"And if you never meet such a man?"

Carla shrugged. "Then I'll become the world's greatest art museum curator and console myself with fame and glory...and lovers."

Daniella snickered. "It would be easier to marry the greatest curator and let him bring you the glory."

"That's how you crazy Italian women think," Carla said. She stopped when she saw how troubled Daniella's face had become. "What's wrong?"

Daniella hesitated. "When you talk like that, Carla...well, you see, my father is arranging...for me to be married."

"Daniella! Why didn't you tell me?"

"Because if the negotiations fail..." She looked frightened.

"Who is he? Do you love him?"

"Yes, I love him very much. But Carla, I cannot tell you who he is. If I tell you, and then I do not marry him, I would be so ashamed." Nervously, Daniella took Carla's hand. "Promise, you will not tell anyone what I just said."

"I promise."

"Besides, even if all goes well and I become engaged, we will not marry for at least a year."

Together, they went into a salon where clusters of well dressed people politely conversed in English, French and Italian. Everyone was holding a crystal flute glass while uniformed waiters with magnums of champagne and trays of antipasto passed quietly among the guests.

"There is Nardo," Daniella whispered proudly. For six years she had boasted about this second cousin of hers: how clever and witty he was, how charming, how handsome, how rich. Now, at twenty-nine, he was rising rapidly in the Italian Foreign Office. "Some day," Daniella constantly bragged, "we shall have a Prime Minister in our family!"

As Daniella led Carla across the room toward her cousin, Carla suffered waves of shyness. She had had little actual experience with men, despite a long history of unrequited schoolgirl crushes. When they reached Nardo, Daniella demurely kissed her cousin on both cheeks, then turned to Carla. "Carla, this is my cousin Leonardo, only you may call him Nardo since you are almost family."

"Yes, the *bella Americana,*" Nardo said, taking Carla's hand. "My little cousin talks so often of her friend Carla."

Carla stared into his heavily-lashed eyes. His dark-dark pupils made her a little dizzy. She forced herself to look away. Leonardo was as handsome as Daniella had promised, but he was not tall and dashing, as Carla had expected. Instead he was short, a little heavy, and very polite. His hypnotic eyes were bright and merry, and he laughed often, as though life were an endless comedy. While the three of them stood together, trying to talk to each other, they were constantly interrupted by men who shook Nardo's hand or, more often, embraced him and kissed both his cheeks, and by women who kissed him boldly on his lips. He was attentive to everyone who approached him.

When they were left alone for a moment, Nardo pulled Daniella and Carla through a doorway to the rear of the villa where his red Alfa Romeo was parked. The evening air was lavender, full of fragrance and mystery and a pledge of unbearably glorious adventures.

I'll always remember this moment, Carla thought as they drove through the Borghese Gardens with trees and statues suddenly looming up in the dusk on either side of the narrow road. Daniella and Carla shared the passenger seat and when the wind blew into the convertible it lifted their long dark hair into twin fluttering pennants behind their heads. Like most Italians, Nardo drove with a combination of maniacal recklessness and split-second precision.

He raced under the ancient arches of the Porta Pinciana, darted among the cars on the crowded Veneto, slammed through a tunnel and sped alongside the sluggish Tiber. When they parked on a narrow dark street the hundred-lira man—one of Italy's ubiquitous patron saints of parked cars—approached with hand outstretched.

"How are you tonight, *amico mio?*" Nardo asked as he handed the old man two hundred lira coins. "How is your cough?"

"*Meglio, meglio.*" The man bowed repeatedly.

"I'm glad you feel better," Nardo said, patting the attendant's shoulder.

Once more, Nardo took the girls' arms and guided them, this time down a flight of old stone stairs to a restaurant whose walls, like those of a library, were lined with shelves, but instead of books the shelves held thousands of wine bottles. Arched brickwork created intimate alcoves where men in dark suits and women in long gowns dined amid a festive babble of mirthful voices. Soft music was woven into the fabric of sound. Following the headwaiter to their table, they passed the musicians on a small stage, three elderly elves in red jackets who vigorously nodded their welcome to Nardo.

Carla was overwhelmed by the sensuality contained within these opulent walls and by the sight and aroma of the exotic foods which hurrying waiters carried by on platters: scarlet shellfish, steaming scampi, cheese-drenched cannelloni, Florentine steaks still glistening from the heat of the grill. They passed a long table laden with ornate antipasto and a pastry wagon whose intricately decorated delicacies formed a tapestry of brilliant color.

The waiters all knew Nardo and fought for the honor of serving him. The victor of this verbal battle brought them more food than they could consume in a week. Other patrons kept stopping at their table to joke with Nardo, or kiss or embrace him, and Nardo invited three elegant young men to join them.

Soon, Nardo took Carla's arm. "Excuse us," he said to Daniella and his three friends. He led Carla to the dance floor where they moved together slowly and intimately. He was only slightly taller than Carla so that his lips touched her cheek. She could feel the ripple of his muscles and his strong heartbeat against her breasts.

From her early teens, Carla had dreamed of being held like this, of being kissed the way Nardo now was kissing her as they danced: slowly, languorously, with the blood throbbing beneath their lips. She felt safe with Nardo. He was good, kind; didn't everybody love him? His husky body was strong and comforting. She wanted to drift with him forever.

When they returned to their table, Daniella threw Carla a troubled look. Carla was puzzled: was Daniella angry with her? Or disapproving? Or worried?

Much later, when Nardo brought them home, Daniella angrily said good night and rushed into the elevator. Nardo kissed Carla once more. "Tomorrow," he whispered, leaving her trembling and shaken.

In the morning, Daniella came down from her penthouse apartment to see Carla. Carla was sleepy, passionately happy, unprepared for the resentment on her friend's face.

"Carla," Daniella said at once, in the privacy of Carla's bedroom, "you behaved like a fool last night."

"I? How?"

Deeply concerned, Daniella searched for the right words. "Nardo is not a man for you to get romantically involved with."

"Daniella, you've been bragging about your cousin for six years. He's everything you ever said...even better. So why shouldn't I fall in love with him?"

Daniella made an impatient gesture. "You are so American!"

"But you said yourself, you want me to find an Italian husband!"

"Yes! But not Nardo!" Daniella said sharply.

"Give me one good reason."

Daniella started to say something, then abruptly changed her mind. "Carla, you are my friend. I do not want you to be hurt. Believe me, Nardo can never marry you."

"Why not? What's wrong with me?" Carla asked.

"What's wrong?" Daniella sighed. "Everything! You are the

wrong religion. You are from the wrong family. Your father is not rich enough, or important enough." She stopped, embarrassed.

"If Nardo is so calculating, how come everyone loves him?"

Daniella chose her words carefully. "He has all the right connections. Everyone thinks, this man is going to be important some day, maybe Prime Minister. So they all want to be his friend." She paused. "So you see, Carla, Nardo is ambitious. When he marries, his wife must be useful to him. Politically and socially." She paused, then added sadly, "Besides, when Nardo marries, he will continue to make love to half the women in Italy."

"You're jealous, Daniella!" Carla said angrily. "You want to keep your cousin safe in your family. You don't want to share him with outsiders. Is that why you don't want me to love him?"

"Love," Daniella scoffed. "What do you know about it?" She flicked her fingers in an Italian gesture with a dozen meanings, all of them derogatory. "You are so naive, Carla. You do not understand us Italians."

"I, naive?" Carla wailed, insulted.

"Yes, naive," Daniella sneered. "You Americans are so trusting. You do not understand! We Italians say only what you want to hear." There were tears in her eyes. "Carla, trust me. I am your best friend! When he calls you, please do not see him again. For the sake of your happiness."

Carla could see how distraught Daniella was. "All right," she lied, "I won't see him again."

"Promise?"

"Honestly, Daniella! I said I wouldn't!"

But when Nardo did phone a short time later, excitement leaped through Carla's body at the sound of his voice. "Yes," she agreed breathlessly. "Yes!" to whatever he suggested. He wanted to spend the day at the coast. "I'll meet you on the Ponte Milvio," she said, not wanting Daniella to see her get into Nardo's car in front of their building.

Nardo and Carla drove holding hands and exchanging stunned looks. Carla was oblivious to the scenery which ordinarily she visually devoured to the last umbrella pine.

He had keys to a friend's Moorish-style white stucco villa in Santa Severa. Once inside the heavy carved door they quickly kissed, a long dizzy merging of bodies that left both of them dazed. Despite Daniella's warning words, Carla was certain that Nardo was good and kind. Everyone loved him. And now she loved him…and he loved her! Again and again he murmured, *"Carla mia, ti amo! Ti amo!*

And to prove it, he respected her. He made no effort to seduce her. They took a long walk on the beach. They kissed, soulfully, until she was aglow with desire. Then they got back into his Alfa Romeo and returned to Rome, where he left her at the Ponte Milvio.

The next day and the next, they roamed the Alban Hills, holding hands, kissing, shivering with excitement, aching with longing. The following day, their fourth together, Carla decided that this man was for her. She was going to marry him and there was no reason to delay making love, even if she had to suggest it. All her fears—except one—were gone: her parents need not know, and she knew Nardo was too noble to scorn her for doing this beautiful act. The only remaining fear was the possibility of pregnancy.

She knew all about condoms and diaphragms. Her French school friend, Renee, who had married a Swiss diplomat the previous summer, delighted in sharing the details of her sex life with Daniella and Carla. They had listened eagerly to Renee's progression step by step from bashful bride to satisfied young matron. They had learned more from her than from their parents, their teachers, and all their biology textbooks combined.

Carla waited until her parents left for a holiday in Sicily, then she searched her father's dresser. Surely, she told herself, he must have some condoms. Or did her mother use a diaphragm? Or did they even make love any more? She grinned, trying to imagine her parents having sex—her tall, large-boned mother with her prissy manners and social affectations, and her tall, thin, tight-assed father with his stern clichés about right and wrong.

In the dresser's bottom drawer, beneath a stack of starched formal shirts, she found thirty-seven condoms in a box that once had held four dozen. Was forty-eight his annual ration? she wondered, giggling. She knew they were illegal in Italy. Did he replenish his supply on his annual business trips to his home office in New York? How did he allot them? Would he miss two?

That afternoon, when Nardo took her to a friend's vacant apartment in a 17th Century palazzo near the Piazza Argentina, their kisses were more ardent than ever. Slowly, still kissing, he unbuttoned her blouse and pushed down her skirt. She stood naked in front of him while he admired her body. At first she was shy, wanting to cover herself with her arms, but then the awkwardness passed and she proudly turned around, laughing, letting him see her from every angle.

Then he undressed himself while she watched, spellbound, for the first time seeing a living man without his clothes. She had looked at—and touched with curiosity when no one was watching—hundreds of nude male statues. Nardo's sturdy body reminded her of Bernini's powerful sculpture of Pluto lifting a frightened Persephone. But when Nardo reached for her, unlike Persephone, Carla was eager to be ravished.

"Nardo wait!" she said, breaking off a kiss. She got out of bed and took a condom from her purse.

He stared down at it. For the first time, she saw his handsome features disfigured by a frown. "I am surprised at you," he said, staring with revulsion at the condom. "How do you know about such things?"

"I heard…"

"They are illegal!"

"But…"

"I cannot use it, Carla mia. It is against the law, and against my religion!"

"But Nardo…"

"When was your last period?" he asked.

"A week ago."

"Then you are safe."

Carla put the condom on the bedside table. Nardo knew best. He was twenty-nine, with years of sexual experience. They kissed again and then he entered her unexpectedly. She lost all the passion that had built up in her for five days. She was aware only of pain and intrusion. With a long sigh, he abruptly withdrew.

She lay there, trembling with disappointment. She looked down at his thick penis, which he was wiping with reverence.

He smiled over at her. "Did you enjoy it?"

She hesitated, then shook her head.

"Ah, you American girls! All fire when you kiss, then nothing! Nothing when it is important."

Carla felt like a failure.

"It is the American movies," he explained . "You girls see all the romance, the kissing, the touching, and then, when the act is to be consummated, when the lovers are about to make beautiful love, what happens? They show you the waves in the ocean, or flames in a fireplace." He leaned over and kissed her lightly. "Next time, Carla mia, you will see. It will be wonderful. The first time is always difficult."

She looked down at her slender body. It was her enemy, she thought. How could it refuse to respond to Nardo's beautiful fat penis? Her eyes filled with tears: she was hopelessly frigid.

That night, on her absent mother's bookshelf, she found a sex manuel called IDEAL MARRIAGE, hidden behind some other books. Carla read it, staying up much of the night. When she finished, she realized that her friend Renee had not told her everything. Nor did Nardo seem to know all he should. Her new knowledge filled her with hope.

"Nardo," she whispered lovingly when they were in bed at his friend's palazzo the next afternoon, "if you would touch me here..."

Offended, Nardo wrenched his hand away from hers. "I am the man!" he said stiffly. "I *know* what to do!" He turned away from her and got out of bed. "See what you have done!" He stared down morosely at his penis, which had gone limp. But when he looked back at Carla and saw her fright and contrition, his face softened. He returned to bed and held her close. "You must never do that again, Carla."

Her grovelling abjection appeased him. He kissed her and fondled her gently, gradually intensifying his caresses until they both recaptured the urgent desire they had shared ever since meeting. But they were his caresses, not the ones she had asked him to do. Still, her body felt feverish and light. Joined to Nardo, she was throbbing and thrusting with sobbing joyful gasps.

It happened then: the headlong roar of blood and pulses, the trumpeting shout of victory, and afterwards the gradual reluctant return to reality with a triumphant Nardo whispering breathlessly, "Carla, my love, *mia amore*, you see? I promised you..."

She held him tightly. His semen was spread over her moist inner thighs and she could feel it, still hot, inside of her. She welcomed it, gloried in it, prayed it would impregnate her. A child...his child...they would marry soon anyway. She laughed at herself for her bungled attempt to have him use a condom.

And some day, she realized with a startled thrill, they would live in the magnificent villa which his parents presently occupied. But that was only frosting on the cake. She would be happy with Nardo anywhere, even in a primitive hovel.

That night, after he brought her back to the Ponte Milvio, they sat in his car and embraced, long and lovingly. She never had been so ecstatic. Nardo was her whole world.

"Carla mia," he murmured, "tomorrow I must go to Milano."

"I'll go with you!"

He clucked. "It is business, my love. I would have no time for you."

"Nights too?"

"Si, days, nights, work, work, work!" He smiled into her eyes. "It is just as well because now you will be in the dangerous time of your cycle."

"You mean, we'll always have to stop? In the middle of my cycle?"

"Do not worry about such things, Carla mia. After I return..."

"When?"

"In a few days." He kissed her brow. "Then we will be together...always."

Carla went up to Daniella's penthouse apartment the morning after Nardo left for Milano.

"Eh?" her maid gruffly answered her ring. "It is you." She gave Carla a strange look. "She is not here."

"Not here?"

"She has gone away. To meet her father in Paris."

Bewildered, Carla returned to her apartment. She couldn't believe that Daniella would leave Rome without telling her. She felt deserted. Her parents still were in Sicily. Even their two maids were on vacation, leaving the apartment curiously quiet. Caterina and Maria were sisters from Reggio Calabria. They never rested their vocal chords. As they cleaned and scrubbed and polished and ironed, they laughed and screamed and purred and joked, and when words failed them, they sang. Now, in the suddenly silent apartment, Carla felt fragile with self pity. She wandered through the luxurious rooms, running a restless hand over the cool marble walls. She phoned three friends, but nobody answered.

It was, she knew, the *Ferragosto,* the last half of August, when almost every Italian leaves Rome by vespa, by car, by plane or train, as though the marauding Visgoths were once again marching down the Via Flaminia. Alone in her apartment, Carla tried to console herself with the thought that Nardo would return in a few days.

But Nardo did not return in a few days, as he had promised. Since she did not know his telephone number, and since Daniella still was away, Carla took a taxi to his parents' villa.

"Nardo non e qui," a manservant said at the door, shaking his head.

"When is he expected?" she asked.

He gave her the Italian shrug, which could mean anything from ten minutes to the next millennium.

She asked to speak to Nardo's parents, but they also were away.

Every day, when she went up to Daniella's apartment to see if her friend had returned, the maid impatiently told her, "She is not here!" But after two weeks, her persistence was rewarded. When she rang Daniella's doorbell, her friend's father opened the door.

"Thank goodness!" Carla cried with relief. "Daniella's back!"

"No, Carla," he said, "she is in France."

"In France?" she echoed.

He nodded. "*Si.* In Nice. On her honeymoon."

Stupidly, she stared at him.

"She was married last week," he continued happily, "in Paris."

"No!" Carla protested. "She said she wouldn't marry for a year."

"All that was changed. Nardo wished to marry at once."

"Nardo?" Carla was puzzled. "Nardo who?"

"Her cousin Nardo. She told me you met him, at a party, at my uncle's house." He started to close the door, then remembered something. "Ah, Carla. *Uno momento.* Daniella sent you a gift." He went into his study and returned to the foyer with a beautifully wrapped small package.

Numbly, Carla took the gift, said goodbye, and got back into the elevator. With a shock she realized that Nardo's romance with her might have been his cruel way of telling Daniella: *when we marry, I will make love to anyone I wish, even your best friend, right under your nose.*

Daniella had warned her. Now Carla understood that when Daniella had begged her not to see Nardo, it had been for Carla's own good.

Listlessly, Carla sat down on the burgundy velvet couch in her living room and stared at Daniella's gift. Then she tugged off the satin ribbon and the gold-embossed paper, revealing a vellum journal. Why, she wondered, would Daniella send her a journal? Was she trying to tell her something?

Idly, as she looked for a clue on the blank pages, a letter fell out. Carla eagerly read:

"Dearest Carla, I have hidden this letter in the journal to be certain that no eyes but yours would read it. You must remember that I shall love you always. I know how hurt you must be. You think you are in love with Nardo, but Carla, try to cure yourself quickly, as though you had a terrible disease. It is dangerous to love him, for he does not know how to love back. Yes, everyone loves Nardo. All his life, everyone has loved him. He grew up expecting everyone to love him, and this twisted his soul.

"So why did I marry him, knowing he could not love me back? Ah Carla, you have lived among us for six years, but you do not understand how Italians think. You still have an American mind. You believe in romantic love, that when you fall in love you will get married and live happily ever after. In Italy, especially in my family, we marry for more important reasons than love. Yes, I am foolish enough to be in love with Nardo, knowing he does not love me. But my foolishness will pass, and then I will be a good wife. I am the correct religion, from a wealthy family whose connections will help Nardo's ambition to be Prime Minister some day. If we still had royalty, he would become King.

"Why did I do it? Because I was raised to be a Prime Minister's wife. I do not think it will be what you Americans call fun. But it will fulfill my family's dreams.

"I am not like you, Carla. I am not a rebel. I will do whatever is expected of me. But our six years together, both of us with parents too busy to spend time with us, it gave us such a gift of freedom! We spent our teen years with all the independence of street urchins. All adolescents should be set free as we were. And when it is over, when one reaches twenty, one is ready to settle down to life's serious business.

"I will never see you again, Carla. You would be too great a distraction from the demands of my new life. When I return to Rome, Nardo and I will live in a lovely little house near his parents' villa. But very soon his father will retire, and they will move to the family's penthouse in Monte Mario, and then I shall be the mistress of the grandest villa in Rome. You must understand that I go into my new life with my eyes wide open, Carla, and with my mind forever closed. Daniella."

Carla threw down the letter as though it might bite her. She knew she must leave Rome. At once. Forever. She couldn't bear to see Nardo or Daniella again. She quietly started to pack. She wouldn't wait for her parents to return; instead, she would fly to Washington tomorrow. She already had her plane ticket and flight set for later in the month. She phoned the airline and changed the reservation to the next morning. Her Aunt Lu wouldn't mind if she stayed with her for a while.

That afternoon, knowing it would be her last day in Rome, she took a bus to the city's center and made a pilgrimage to each of her beloved squares. She stood so close to the Esedra Fountain in the Piazza della Republica that its spray frizzed her hair. She bought a final bouquet of pink carnations from her favorite vendor on the Spanish Steps. She ran a loving hand in farewell over the flanks of Marcus Aurelius's bronze horse in the center of the Campodoglio. She stood on the Palatine Hill, above the Forum, and said a silent goodbye to Caesar's ghost and to all the Vestal Virgins. She haggled over six *biscotti* at a neighborhood *pasticciere* and flung the cookies to the feral cats living in the sunken ruins of Piazza Argentina.

She saved the Piazza Navona for last, where she sat on a stone curb and stared at Bernini's fountains. She felt as though every bone in her body had been broken. Accompanying the sound of gushing water, like a Greek chorus, the words kept screaming inside her head: I'M ALL ALONE.

She rose to leave but her skirt stuck to her legs. She pulled the cloth away from her body and felt wetness. Blood. She sat down and cried for the child that never was. She cried because she never again would experience Nardo's intoxicating lovemaking.

And most of all, she cried for Daniella.

The End

Printed in the United States
76530LV00002B/242